I0719892

Cover Design and Interior Format

Undone by a Lady

Elizabeth Rue

For all the real-life cinnamon roll heroes

CHAPTER ONE

London, England 1818

JAMES WRIGHT PUSHED OPEN THE soot-blackened door to yet another tavern, the sixth he had visited that evening. Each establishment was less respectable than the last, and each one held a greater chance that someone from his past might recognize him.

Inside, the smoky common room rumbled with conversation and reeked of beer and fish stew. James reached into his coat and pulled out a gilt-framed miniature. He ignored the curious stares of the patrons as the innkeeper approached him.

The man quickly assessed James's fine clothing and smiled. "Good evening—"

"Have you seen this woman?" James held out the miniature.

Frowning, the man leaned closer. His eyes widened slightly before he quickly hid his recognition. "No." He crossed his arms.

"Are you certain?" James asked. "Look again."

The man barely glanced at the picture. "I'm sure. Anything else you want?"

The innkeeper wasn't even looking for a bribe, James noted. She must have already paid him to remain silent if anyone asked about her. Despite her reckless actions, she wasn't entirely foolish.

While James spoke with the innkeeper, a patron sitting by the fire had risen and now approached the door. As the man paused to fasten his coat, he glanced at James several times. James was careful to avoid his gaze but managed a quick look, enough to decide that he didn't know the man. The hulking stranger had a shock of red hair and a boyish face, though he seemed near James's age. The man yanked open the door, pausing to eye James one more time before he stepped outside. A blast of cool air hit James as the door rattled shut.

His pulse sped up. Had he been recognized?

He had escaped these miserable streets a decade ago. At five and twenty, he looked little like that ragged boy anymore, and there was no better disguise than fine clothes. No, he wasn't likely in danger of being recognized—only robbed. The man had probably been sizing him up to steal his purse.

James thanked the innkeeper and quickly returned to his hired carriage. The red-haired man seemed to have vanished into the night. James instructed the driver to move down two streets and wait. Then James quietly backtracked, pausing in the shadows across from the inn.

The street around him was quiet, still with no sign of the man who had been eyeing him inside. Likely, the man had noted the driver and footman waiting at James's carriage and had decided against trying to rob him.

The breeze shifted and suddenly the brackish scent of the Thames was thick around him, threatening to engulf him in a wave of unpleasant memories.

Yet another reason he usually avoided London.

After a moment, two men, loud and likely foxed, stumbled out of the inn and strolled toward him. He could make out their Royal Navy uniforms as they neared. As always, the sight made his chest tighten and his stomach queasy. Even though the sailors couldn't see him in the shadows as they passed, he avoided looking at their faces. Their footsteps soon faded as they headed toward the wharves, and he let out a long breath.

He pushed away thoughts of sailors as he waited,

focusing instead on the miniature. Though it was too dark to see clearly, he knew the young woman's portrait well: golden hair, ivory skin, and a sweet-looking face that belied her troublesome nature.

Lady Cecelia Sinclair. Sister to a man to whom he owed his life. Despite his friendship with her brother Adrian Sinclair, Earl of Wareton, he had never met Lady Cecelia.

He had a feeling that was about to change.

Only a few moments later, his suspicions paid off. From behind the building, the creak of a door was followed by quick footfalls. In the shadowy alley next to the inn, two cloaked figures crept along, huddled together as they headed in the direction of the docks. When they passed beneath a lit window, the candlelight revealed two well-dressed ladies.

The taller one with a fancier hat was likely Lady Cecelia, and the other seemed young enough to be her lady's maid. The inn was on the edge of a somewhat respectable neighborhood, but now they were headed toward more dangerous streets. The innkeeper must have alerted Lady Cecelia that someone was looking for her. But why were they alone? Wareton's message had said Lady Cecelia was with her lady's maid but also two others—an older woman companion as a chaperone and a male servant.

The fact that the women were alone now probably meant Lady Cecelia was still waiting for the man with whom she planned to elope. That would make it far easier for James to recover her.

He shoved the miniature deep into his pocket and strode toward them.

"Lady Cecelia!" he called out.

The two women abruptly stopped and turned. The shorter woman—definitely the maid he decided— looked to the other. The woman he assumed to be Lady Cecelia hesitated only an instant, then grabbed her maid by the arm and spun away. They began to run.

James hurried after them, past a warehouse and onto a narrow street that ran close to the waterfront. When he had last walked here a decade ago, the dirt lane had been one of the more dangerous streets in London. He doubted much had changed. The jumble of buildings still offered numerous shadowy hiding places, and the lane still reeked of garbage and filth.

As he closed in, the women slowed before a dark alleyway. Lady Cecelia glanced back at him, as if deciding which option was worse, him or the alleyway. Then she abruptly stepped back, as if startled, and reached out for her maid.

He thought at first that his own footfalls had frightened her. Then only a few paces from the women, a man stepped out of the shadows. The man lunged at the maid, trying to tear the bag from her grasp, but the woman resisted. Lady Cecelia swung her own heavy satchel at the man, slamming it against his back.

The man groaned but held on to the bag. Lady Cecelia walloped him again, even harder.

"Let go!" she cried, her voice clear and strong.

As she prepared to swing her bag again, the man gave a fierce yank. He pulled the bag from the maid and sent her sprawling to the ground.

Still a street away, James rushed forward as the thief turned and ran with the bag. The man disappeared into the blackness of a nearby alley, his footfalls quickly fading.

James slowed as he approached the women, hoping not to frighten them. He watched as Lady Cecelia dropped her bag and rushed to the other woman. She kneeled and slid one arm around the woman, helping her to sit up.

"Are you all right, Reed?" Lady Cecelia said.

"He…he took my bag—"

"Are you hurt?"

Reed raised one gloved hand to her head. "I…I hit my head when I fell."

"Let me see," Lady Cecelia said.

"I am fine, milady," Reed said. "We should—"

"You should come with me," James said, stopping in front of them. "Now, before something worse happens."

Lady Cecelia rose and turned to face him. Her bonnet cast her face in shadow.

"Who are you?" she asked, a slight tremor in her voice now, unlike when she'd confronted the thief.

"A friend of your brother."

"What friend?" She took a step backward.

"James Wright."

She tilted her head to one side, staring at him in silence.

"Surely he has mentioned me before?" he asked.

"He has." She did not move.

He held out his hand. "Come with me."

"No." She promptly turned her back to him.

Foolish woman. He dropped his hand. Lady Cecelia helped Reed to her feet, retrieved her own bag, and turned back to him. As she gazed up at him, she shifted the bag in her hand, gripping it more firmly.

The insane idea that she might actually hit him with the bag and try to continue her escape flashed through his mind.

Ludicrous, surely.

Then again, how much did he really know about her? Only what he had learned from her brother, Lord Wareton. The image James had formed of Lady Cecelia was of a sheltered, pampered young woman. He would have expected her to scream and cower in the face of a thief, not pummel him with her bag.

"My carriage is nearby," he said. "I will take you both to safety."

"No," Lady Cecelia replied. "We are fine on our own." She turned away again and stepped toward Reed.

Even after being robbed, she wanted to continue alone

through the London streets? Wareton had told him that his sister was difficult. Willful, even. But not insane.

He strode forward and took her by the arm—the arm that held the bag so she could not swing it at him.

She tried to pull away from him. "Let go of me!"

He fought the instinct to release her. He was accustomed to being gentle with women, but most women he knew had far more sense.

"After all the worry you have put your brother through," he growled, "after all I have risked to find you, and now, even after your maid has been robbed, you would still continue with this folly?"

She stopped struggling. "It is not folly," she said. But she had stiffened at the mention of her brother, and she had flinched when he mentioned her maid. Clearly, she felt some guilt. He must use that to convince her to return with him.

"Come back with me," he said gently. "At least speak with your brother again before—"

"Do you not think I've tried?" She shook her head. "It is hopeless." The ragged despair in her voice surprised him. "It is not folly. It is also not your concern."

"Your brother has made it my concern," he said. "And this is one of the worst parts of the city. You put us all in danger."

She inhaled sharply at his accusation. She tried to pull away from him again, and this time, he let her go.

"Milady," Reed said quietly.

He turned to look at her maid. Reed had pushed back her bonnet and touched her head. She lifted her hand away, holding it out to them.

Blood stained her glove.

Lady Cecelia gasped and stepped toward her. "You are hurt! Let me see."

"I…I don't think it's bad," the maid said.

Lady Cecelia slid an arm around Reed. Reed seemed

dazed, though it may well have been from the shock of the attack rather than from her injury.

Then the quiet was broken. From the direction the man had gone, footfalls sounded, growing louder—fast, heavy steps of two or possibly even three men.

The thief could be returning with reinforcements.

James might be able to best two men, but three was less likely.

"Come with me," he whispered. He grabbed Lady Cecelia's bag and took her by her free arm. Now she came willingly.

He rushed the women down the street in the opposite direction of the approaching men. Thankfully, despite her injury, Reed was able to move quickly.

Years ago, the jutting corner of an old warehouse had concealed a narrow alley, a route that had saved him from trouble before. With any luck, it would still be passable.

As he led the women toward what looked like nothing but a dark corner, Lady Cecelia slowed.

"Where are you taking us?" she whispered.

"Trust me." He pulled her closer. She smelled faintly of what was likely expensive lavender soap. He breathed in the scent more deeply—purely to mask the stench of the city.

The alley was still there and appeared passable but too narrow for more than two at a time. He gently pushed Lady Cecelia and Reed ahead of him.

"Go!" he whispered.

They hurried down the passage, their boots splashing through foul-smelling puddles, and he stayed close behind them.

"Wait," he whispered. "Go left!"

Another narrow alley twisted left, and then left again. Soon they were in the open once more. He could see his carriage two streets away, and he heard no sounds of pursuit.

Taking Lady Cecelia by the arm once again, he rushed her and Reed down the street. He kept a careful watch behind them until they reached the carriage, but no one seemed to follow them. The footman heard them approaching and quickly opened the carriage door. After the women stepped into the coach, James tossed Lady Cecelia's bag inside and instructed his driver to leave quickly.

A small hanging lantern cast dim light inside the carriage. James fell onto the seat across from Lady Cecelia and her maid, who were looking in surprise at the woman seated beside him.

"May I introduce my grandmother, Mrs. Stewart," he said quickly. "This is Lady Cecelia Sinclair. And Reed."

Lady Cecelia acknowledged his grandmother with a nod. His grandmother remained silent, her eyes narrowed and her mouth set in a thin line. She'd looked the same ever since he'd first requested her company as chaperone and throughout the entire journey to London. Quite understandably.

As he adjusted the lantern to cast more light on Lady Cecelia and her lady's maid, he got his first good look at Reed's injury. Lady Cecelia had already removed the young woman's bonnet and was examining the wound. Though some blood caked the woman's dark hair just above her brow, the gash was small, not more than an inch. The bleeding had slowed considerably.

As Reed leaned back against the seat, Lady Cecelia pulled a handkerchief from her bag. With trembling fingers, she pressed it gently against her maid's forehead.

Then Lady Cecelia finally turned and looked at him. When she met his gaze, her blue eyes widened.

He tried to hide his own surprise.

Pretty though the miniature of her was, in person she was even more striking. In fact, she was one of the most beautiful women he had ever set eyes on.

She was clearly startled to see him in the light as well. But for good or ill? He scowled. He shouldn't care. Really, he did not.

Beside him, his grandmother cleared her throat softly, and he dragged his gaze from Lady Cecelia.

The carriage shook as it hit a large bump, and Reed raised her head. After a moment, Lady Cecelia allowed Reed to take over holding the handkerchief.

"Mr. Wright," Reed said, "thank you for coming to my aid."

"Of course. It is fortunate you were not more badly hurt," he added, looking at Lady Cecelia. "You should have never been in such a dangerous area."

Anger, and perhaps a touch of guilt, flashed in Lady Cecelia's eyes. She clutched her gloved hands tightly together in her lap.

"Please do not blame Lady Cecelia," Reed said in a rush. "I insisted on going with her. And…" She glanced between him and Lady Cecelia. "And I'd gladly suffer worse for her."

"I do not wish anyone to suffer on my account," Lady Cecelia said gently, smiling at Reed.

"Your actions suggest otherwise," his grandmother snapped.

James could hardly blame her. His grandmother was not usually so blunt, but she was not usually asked to do what this night had demanded of her.

Lady Cecelia's smile vanished, but she said nothing.

"Where is your companion and your manservant?" he asked. "Your brother's message said you were likely with them as well."

Lady Cecelia's expression darkened. "They both ran off soon after we arrived at the inn."

He raised an eyebrow. "Together?"

"I believe so." Lady Cecelia sighed. "Thank goodness for Reed," she added, looking to her maid again.

Reed lowered the handkerchief from her forehead. The bleeding had stopped. Reed quietly insisted to Lady Cecelia that she was fine and she only needed to rest.

At least Lady Cecelia had the sense to show concern for her maid's injury. However, because of her recklessness, they could have all been hurt, or worse.

And he might have been recognized.

The image of the red-haired man flashed in his mind, but he quickly dismissed the idea. Surely he looked too different now to be identified.

He let out a deep breath. Though he had taken a big risk, the gamble had paid off. Wareton would be profoundly relieved that James had recovered his sister. He'd no doubt been sick with worry over her.

He stole another glance at Lady Cecelia. She might be remarkably beautiful, but she was also reckless. And foolish. Wareton hadn't been exaggerating when he'd said his sister was trouble.

The whole incident reminded James that in some ways he was fortunate to have no family other than his grandmother. Such ties only meant more people to worry about, and he had learned too well the danger that could bring. Even now, his affection for his friend—one of his few friends—meant he had put himself at risk.

The fewer such attachments he had, the better off he was. And the less time he spent in London, the better.

Now, he must give the foolish Lady Cecelia the letter from her brother and learn her response. Then he must leave this city and its troubles behind, and return with his grandmother to the safety and peace of the country.

He only hoped the troublesome Lady Cecelia would refuse to go with him.

CHAPTER TWO

CECELIA PEERED OUT THE CARRIAGE window, watching with increasing heartache as the streets grew brighter and the buildings grander. She clutched her hands together, willing her fingers to stop shaking. When they entered Mayfair, the familiar mansions and town houses seemed to rise up around her like prison walls, blocking out the night sky.

The dashing Mr. Wright believed he was rescuing her. But he was merely returning her to her gilded cage—a cage that soon would snap shut again and, thanks to her failure this evening, would lock even more tightly than before. In only six weeks, her aunt, who had raised her and usually controlled her nearly every move, would return from her travels. Then Cecelia's chance to marry William Trent would likely be gone forever.

Tonight had been her best chance to escape, one she'd planned carefully for the past few weeks. It had been bad enough when, after settling into the inn, Mrs. Clarke, her aunt's companion, had vanished along with the manservant whom Mrs. Clarke had recommended to accompany them in London. Now Cecelia understood why her aunt's companion had been so agreeable to helping her elope. Mrs. Clarke apparently also saw her aunt's absence as an opportunity to change her life for the better. She could not truly blame the woman for that, although the deception still stung. But even after that abandonment, she and Reed would have been fine waiting at the inn for William. Except Mr. Wright's interference was a complication she had not anticipated.

Much as she was grateful for his assistance after Reed was injured, if he had not come looking for her in the first place, none of the trouble would have occurred. She wouldn't have had any cause to flee the inn, so she and Reed never would have been alone on the streets. Instead, soon enough William would have arrived at the inn, and he and his valet would have escorted them safely to the ship. Then before they sailed, she would have sent a message to her brother Adrian, informing him of her plans so he would not search for her.

Perhaps her decision to elope was selfish, but she was not as wholly without consideration for others as Mr. Wright seemed to believe.

Still, his words stung. *You put us all in danger.* His grandmother's comments about her causing others to suffer had also made her feel a twinge of shame. She could not deny that if not for her, none of them would have been in London.

Of course, if William had appeared on time, this misfortune might have also been avoided. When Mr. Wright had arrived at the inn, she'd already waited for William several hours beyond the agreed upon time. Even so, she forced away her annoyance with him. Likely he had a good reason for the delay, and merely bad luck had brought Mr. Wright to the inn first.

And William would surely reach the inn at any moment now—if he hadn't already. After being warned that someone had just inquired after her, she had quickly gathered her things. She'd left a message with the innkeeper to let William know that she feared her brother was trying to stop them, and that she was going to another inn and would send word where soon. Now, thanks to Mr. Wright's interference, she must let William know that her plans had changed once more.

"Are you taking us to my brother's town house?" she asked Mr. Wright. Adrian's London residence was only a short distance away. Although the servants would not be expecting anyone, it was the logical place to take her. From there, she could easily send a message to William.

"That is your decision," Mr. Wright said. Once again, the deepness of his voice startled her. Indeed, when he had first called out to her in the street, she had immediately believed his claim that he was her brother's friend. Such a commanding voice was hard to doubt.

"However," he added, "your brother hopes to avoid scandal by keeping your...*adventure* quiet." Disdain was clear in his voice.

"Where is Lord Wareton now?" she asked. The shaking in her hands had finally subsided, and she folded them in her lap.

"Somewhere north. He believed that you were most likely on your way to Gretna Green, but that there was a chance it could be London." He paused. "If I found you, he asked me to give you this." He reached into his coat, drew out a folded paper, and handed it to her. The paper held a faint scent, unfamiliar but pleasant, perhaps from being in Mr. Wright's pocket.

She unfolded the message, tilting it toward the lantern to cast more light upon the page. Adrian's handwriting was messier than usual, no doubt because he had written it in haste. Stifling a pang of guilt at having distressed him, she began to read:

Dear Cecelia,

If you are reading this, Wright has succeeded in finding you. I am deeply sorry that you felt compelled to resort to such drastic measures. Perhaps I am mistaken in not supporting your wishes. However, I must know that you are not making such an important decision impulsively. If you will delay but a month, I promise that I shall reconsider giving the match my blessing.

If you agree, Wright will take you to his estate in Westbury where a visit with his grandmother will provide a suitable explanation for your travels. I will join you in a month and will accompany you back to Wareton, where I hope we might reach a resolution that ensures your happiness.

Please consider my request knowing that I only have your best interest at heart.

Your loving brother,

Adrian

Cecelia sat in stunned silence, staring at the paper.

Adrian wanted her to stay with Mr. Wright and his grandmother for an entire month? True, she had mentioned many times that she wished to see that part of the country—someday. So perhaps the visit would hide the truth of her abrupt departure. Still, the plans would be unexpected to the servants, which might start tongues wagging. She'd also not brought enough belongings for a month's stay.

To suggest such a long visit, Adrian must want her away from home and the likelihood of seeing William. No doubt Adrian hoped that the time would allow her to think more prudently and to change her mind about the match.

She looked up at Mr. Wright's grandmother, who sat stiffly with her arms crossed. Mrs. Stewart was petite, perhaps no more than five feet tall. Gray ringlets curled out from her bonnet, which was tied tightly on one side, the ribbon so taut beneath her chin it was a wonder it didn't choke her. Mrs. Stewart met her gaze only briefly before looking out the window again, still frowning just as she had ever since Cecelia had stepped into the carriage.

Cecelia returned her attention to Mr. Wright, who stared back at her, his expression inscrutable. However, the way he tapped one long finger against his muscular thigh gave away his impatience for her response.

He likely wanted nothing to do with her. Perhaps he even hoped that she would refuse to go with him.

"You have both agreed to this?" she asked, looking between him and his grandmother.

He sighed and gave a curt nod. "I would not deny your brother any request."

His grandmother finally met her gaze but did not answer at first, allowing the silence to grow uncomfortably long before she finally spoke.

"I could not refuse James when he requested my help," Mrs. Stewart said, "which was wise since as it turns out, you very much need a chaperone."

Cecelia would not argue with that, nor could she blame Mrs. Stewart for feeling put out by the whole situation.

Cecelia looked back at the letter. Should she delay her plans a month and travel to Westbury? She could refuse, and then it seemed that Mr. Wright—likely relieved— would take her to Adrian's town house. There, she could make new plans to elope with William.

But then her brother's blessing would undoubtedly be lost to her forever.

She knew that when Adrian had made his disapproval of William's suit clear, her brother only wanted to keep her from making what he believed was a terrible mistake. But well-intentioned as he was, he was wrong about William, and about her ability to wisely choose her own husband.

The fact that Adrian had admitted he might be mistaken, and that he would reconsider a decision, was a rare event. He would not say that he might give his blessing unless he truly meant it. Chances were high he might change his mind—if she agreed to his timeline.

And if Adrian decided to approve the match, even their fearsome aunt would be forced to concede defeat.

She had no great interest in going to Mr. Wright's estate, but if it meant receiving her brother's blessing, it would be well worth the delay. She knew William very much wished for her brother's approval too.

"Very well," she said, looking up at Mr. Wright. "I shall go to Westbury."

His frown deepened, but he nodded. Beside him, his grandmother stiffened.

"However," Cecelia added, "I do ask that we stop as soon as possible. I must tend to Reed's injury, and I would like to have a message sent before we leave the city."

His expression softened. "Of course."

"I am fine, milady," Reed said. "There is no need to stop soon on my account."

"Then we shall have it properly attended to when we next stop to rest," Mr. Wright said. He looked toward Cecelia. "However, first I must send a message to your brother that I've found you. I will send one for you as well if you wish."

A few moments later, they stopped at an inn and Mr. Wright went inside to arrange to have two messages sent.

Mrs. Stewart remained in the carriage. From a bag beside her, she drew out needles, blood red yarn, and a partially finished item that looked destined to become a scarf. She began knitting without a word, clacking the needles together far more loudly than seemed necessary.

Cecelia could hardly blame the woman for her disapproval. However, if she was to be a guest in Mrs. Stewart's home for a month, she must make an effort to improve matters.

"Thank you," she ventured, "for your help. I sincerely appreciate it."

Without pausing her knitting and without looking up, Mrs. Stewart replied, "I will not pretend I am pleased about this situation. I believe in doing things properly, and I do not condone such…unconventional behavior." She took a deep breath. "However," she added in a slightly softer tone, "since this is what my grandson wishes, I am prepared to make the best of the situation."

"I am grateful," Cecelia said gently.

Mrs. Stewart gave a stiff nod but said nothing else.

Cecelia checked on Reed's injury once more, and then they sat silently.

Mr. Wright returned after only a few moments and assured Cecelia that the messages for Adrian and William would be relayed quickly. So hopefully her brother would soon no longer worry about her. And when William reached the inn, he would not have long to wonder what had happened to her.

Though Mr. Wright still looked grim, he had stopped scowling at her. Perhaps he had no wish to take her to his estate, but he seemed resolved to assist her brother, and she could not fault him for being a loyal friend. Indeed, he must have responded quickly to Adrian's request to search for her.

"Lord Wareton sent a message asking for your help?" she asked him.

He nodded. "As you may know, I live closer to town, and he trusts my discretion."

"He told me that you never go to London."

"Not often. But I could not refuse him." Mr. Wright's tone suggested he wanted very much to refuse him.

Despite his somber expression, she was struck again by how attractive Mr. Wright was. Once she'd seen him in the light, the handsomeness of his face had surprised her. She recalled quite clearly that when she had once asked Adrian what Mr. Wright looked like, her brother had shrugged and said he was tall but otherwise quite ordinary.

Adrian had never been so far off the mark.

There was nothing ordinary about the broad-shouldered young man who sat so close to her now, with his intense dark eyes and startlingly deep voice.

Mr. Wright had apparently befriended her brother when they had served together in the army, before Adrian had unexpectedly become Earl of Wareton. According to Adrian, Mr. Wright had saved his life while fighting the French, and the lives of many other soldiers. Over the past several years since leaving the army, Adrian had invited Mr. Wright to join him in London and at his country estate on several different occasions, but each time Mr. Wright had declined. Adrian said that his friend preferred the quiet of the country and had little interest in leaving his estate. Mr. Wright apparently lived with only his grandmother for company, and he detested London.

However, for someone who supposedly loathed London, he seemed to know the streets remarkably well.

"How did you know about that alley?" Cecelia asked.

Reed shifted beside her, clearly interested in the answer as well.

Mrs. Stewart began to knit more slowly.

Mr. Wright leaned back and crossed his arms. "Many years ago," he said, "I spent time in town, and sometimes I walked down to look at the ships. I learned shortcuts."

"You said yourself how dangerous those streets are," Cecelia said. "Why would you choose to walk there?"

He shrugged. "I was reckless when I was younger." He was obviously trying to evade the question, and she should simply let the matter drop. But from the way he was now avoiding her gaze, she suspected he had an interesting reason.

"Truly," she said, "why would you walk there?"

For a few seconds, he sat in silence. "A more important question," he finally said, "is why would Mr. Trent have you meet him so near to such a dangerous part of the city?"

His grandmother's knitting grew faster again.

"That inn was respectable," Cecelia said quickly.

"Barely," he said.

"And it is near the docks, so we would be difficult to find."

"He put you at risk," he said. "And you wonder why your brother would not approve the match?"

He *put you at risk*. As if William must have planned everything and she was simply foolish enough to go along with him.

Well, so what if Mr. Wright believed that? But as she met his gaze, her mouth opened seemingly of its own accord.

"It was my idea to sail from London," she said, "and to meet at that inn."

"Indeed." He did not look surprised. "How incredibly foolish."

"Is it?" she said. "Riding north to Gretna Green is what most people would expect. Too predictable."

The corner of his mouth quirked, as if he were trying not to smile. "Even having just met you," he said, "I can say with certainty that you are anything but predictable."

"What do you mean?" She wasn't sure from his tone whether he meant it as a compliment or an insult.

"Oh, perhaps the fact that you foolishly walked at night with only a lady's maid for company in one of the most dangerous parts of London." He sounded half-amused, half-irritated.

Without looking up, his grandmother seemed to knit even faster, her frown deepening.

"Then," he continued, "when you were attacked, you screamed like an army officer and defended yourself and your maid with amazing skill, wielding your luggage as if you fight off robbers with it every day."

From beside Cecelia, Reed made a choking noise. Cecelia snapped her head around to look at her maid.

Reed was biting her lip as she did whenever she was trying not to laugh. "You *were* very brave, milady," Reed murmured.

Brave? Now that the shock of the evening's excitement was wearing off, realization sank in. Her fingers trembled again, and she clutched her hands together. Heavens, she *had* hit the thief with her bag. Repeatedly. She never imagined doing such a thing, but she had never been in such a situation before. There had been no gentleman there to defend them. And while she had been frightened, she had been even more angry at the thief.

But brave?

Shame filled her because it was so far from the truth. She was unquestionably a coward. If not for her failure to stand up to her family, none of them would be in this carriage right now.

CHAPTER THREE

Two weeks earlier

CECELIA TRIED TO APPEAR CALM as she stood in the sunlit meadow, pretending to admire the view of the verdant hillside and sparkling river below.

She must seem happy but not *too* happy. Too much happiness could ruin everything.

To distract herself, she slipped the raspberry tart from her pocket, unwrapped it from the kerchief she'd hidden it in, and quietly devoured the pastry, savoring only the final sweet bite.

Scrumptious as the confection was, it was still nowhere near as delicious as her secret.

"The breeze is picking up, wouldn't you say?" Cecelia's brother Edmund asked as he stopped beside her. Edmund held on to his hat until a wind gust subsided.

Cecelia smiled at him as she tucked the kerchief back into her pocket. "Are you joining me for a walk?" She brushed the last of the tart crumbs from her fingers and they were swiftly carried away by another gust of wind.

"That's what I told everyone." Edmund glanced back toward the other guests, about two dozen family and friends scattered around the picnic area a short distance away, most still sitting on blankets and eating. "However, my true motive is to find out what you are trying so hard to not look ridiculously pleased about."

She had apparently not hidden her excitement as well as she'd hoped. Then again, Edmund noticed her moods far better than anyone else.

"Is being free of our aunt not enough reason for unbridled joy?" Cecelia whispered. They were well out of earshot of the others, but she was taking no chances.

Edmund's blue eyes narrowed as he gazed down at her. "Of course, but why do I sense there's more to it?" He checked that no one else had moved nearer, leaned closer, and added quietly, "Tell me."

"Well…" Of her two brothers, Edmund was the one who would most understand. He was one of the kindest and most sympathetic souls she knew. Yet she wasn't sure that even he would be pleased. "No. Not yet."

She began strolling along the top of the slope, and Edmund kept close beside her.

"So you do have a secret," he said. "I knew it." He glanced back toward the others. "Whatever it is, you best not let our aunt see how happy you are."

Cecelia followed his gaze to where their aunt Lady Carlton sat in the shade of a fluttering white canopy. She was perched upon not one, not two, but three layers of blankets she'd demanded to protect her muslin walking gown. A fortification of pillows surrounded her as well.

To her aunt's left and a few feet back, half-hidden by the wall of pillows, was Mrs. Clarke, her aunt's companion of the past year, appearing less miserable than usual. Perhaps Mrs. Clarke was also looking forward to a break from Lady Carlton.

To her aunt's right was Viscount Moreland, Lady Carlton's weary-looking betrothed. Soon to become a bride for the fourth time at age fifty, her aunt relished discussing every detail of the upcoming wedding. For some time now, Lady Carlton had kept her back to Lord Moreland while she talked to—or rather at—the other guests. The gray-haired viscount had fallen silent and seemed to have lost his usually robust appetite, as his roast chicken remained almost untouched beside him. Cecelia could see the regret taking root in his eyes.

"Poor man," Cecelia said. Their aunt still drew men's admiration with her silver-blond hair, striking gray eyes, and fashionable clothes. Her considerable fortune from three previous husbands helped as well. For the past few months, when in Viscount Moreland's company, her aunt had been charming and restrained—utterly unlike her real self. But now that their betrothal had been announced, that façade was beginning to crack.

"He was warned," Edmund said quietly, shaking his head. "But like so many, the fool was blinded by beauty and fortune."

Cecelia did pity the viscount, truly, but his misfortune was her blessing. For the past nineteen years, ever since Cecelia was orphaned at the age of two, her aunt had dictated Cecelia's nearly every move. However, tomorrow Lady Carlton would leave for a long visit to see her betrothed's properties in northern England. She would be traveling with the viscount's sister, and Cecelia would remain behind. For a few precious weeks, Cecelia would finally be free of her aunt's stifling control.

Cecelia could barely contain her excitement. She felt like running down the hillside, singing with joy. Yet she must restrain herself for just a bit longer.

"Are you ready for your own journey?" she asked, glancing at Edmund.

"Yes," he said, his expression brightening. Edmund was about to embark on a long-awaited trip to visit friends in Manchester and Liverpool, after which he would sail to Dublin.

Ireland in particular sounded so lovely and interesting. Cecelia's heart ached with envy.

"I've agreed to travel with our aunt on the first part of her journey," Edmund said, "since it overlaps with my plans, but then, thankfully, we will part ways."

Cecelia sighed and stopped walking. "How I wish I could go with you."

"I wish so too," Edmund said. "But alas, as much as I enjoy upending convention…" He paused as he glanced at their brother, Adrian, who was now strolling toward them. "There are some things even too reckless for me."

"Did I overhear that correctly?" Adrian said, stopping before them. "What on earth could be too reckless for you?" Despite his words, his tone was warm.

For many years, whenever he teased Edmund, Adrian's manner had been harsh, and hearing the two of them clash had made Cecelia heartsick. But two years ago, not long after the death of their cousin meant Adrian became the Earl of Wareton, the brothers had at last made peace. Though their teasing continued, these days it was driven far more by affection than anger. Cecelia now usually found their banter comforting—except when they occasionally still argued about her.

"Taking Cecelia with me on my travels," Edmund said, straightening until he stood nearly as tall as his older brother.

The good humor vanished from Adrian's face. "I'll not be dragged into discussing that again." He added in a softer tone, "Let's not ruin this happy occasion, when we have the impending absence of our dear aunt to celebrate." He sighed. "Which is why I've come after you. The poor viscount could use some cheering up. Come help me."

"There's no help for him now," Edmund said, shaking his head. "Dying of melancholy would be an infinitely better fate than marriage to our aunt."

Adrian sighed again. "I fear you're correct."

Shouts erupted from the other picnic guests. Two of the footmen who had been waiting near the carriages had apparently been summoned to take hold of the wildly flapping canopy, which was now in danger of blowing away.

Cecelia watched as her aunt motioned for them to secure the shade. Only a few sharp words were audible between the wind gusts, but her aunt was clearly berating the servants for moving too slowly.

Cecelia knew that scathing tone all too well.

Only a few more hours, and her hateful aunt would be gone. And her life would change for the better. Finally.

Then her aunt turned and caught her gaze. It was one of those all too frequent instants when her aunt seemed to read her mind. A moment later, Lady Carlton was striding across the field, the shock of ridiculously long purple feathers on her hat trembling in her wake. Her icy glare was focused on Cecelia.

"Well, what is it?" Lady Carlton said as she stopped before her. "All afternoon you have looked far too pleased."

"I am just so happy for you, aunt," Cecelia said, forcing a smile. She clutched her hands together to hide her now shaking fingers.

"Nonsense." Lady Carlton's gray eyes narrowed. "More likely, you're planning some mischief for while I am away."

Yes. Precisely. "Of course not," Cecelia said sweetly.

"And don't think I didn't notice your vulgar behavior with that raspberry tart," Lady Carlton said. "I simply didn't wish to mention it in front of the viscount. I can only imagine how your manners will suffer without my guidance these next weeks."

"Vulgar behavior with a tart?" Edmund said. "Were you addressing me?"

Lady Carlton barely spared Edmund a glance. Her scowl deepened as she continued to glare at Cecelia. "I should not even *have* to worry about you. It is simply ridiculous that I am marrying again, while you remain unwed at twenty-one."

"I must agree, aunt," Edmund said amiably. "It is ridiculous."

Adrian grimaced.

This time, Lady Carlton's gaze snapped to Edmund. She eyed him suspiciously, apparently aware he was insulting her. "*You* should be married as well," she said. "However, I gave up on you long ago." Dismissing Edmund with a sniff, Lady Carlton once again fixed her stare on Cecelia.

Lady Carlton's life was hardly an argument in support of marriage; Cecelia strongly suspected that her aunt had driven at least two previous husbands to an early grave with her overbearing personality.

Cecelia would rather never marry than be trapped with a horrible spouse like her aunt. However, in spite of her aunt's dismal examples of matrimony, Cecelia still wished to marry—but only in a way that would both benefit her family *and* please herself.

While she had attracted many suitors whom her aunt viewed as acceptable, until recently Cecelia had found them all lacking. They were either too old, too stuffy, too dull, too greedy, too deceitful, too unkind, or too irritating. Or, worst of all, too controlling.

She'd had quite enough of *that* for one lifetime.

The few gentlemen whom Cecelia had found at all promising had all proved unacceptable to her aunt, and her aunt had found a way to frighten them off.

But even her fearsome aunt could not drive off a suitor while far away in York.

"And do not even think of encouraging anyone unsuitable while I am gone," her aunt added. "Such as Mr. Trent."

Cecelia opened her mouth to protest.

"No," her aunt said, "do not waste your breath arguing his merits again. Or bother trying to convince Adrian while I am away. I have already discussed the matter with him, and he agrees with me."

"Does he?" Cecelia said, her face warming. How did her aunt always know what she was planning? But surely, about Adrian and William, this time her aunt was wrong.

"Tell her," Lady Carlton said to Adrian. "Tell her that Mr. Trent is not acceptable. We must put an end to this ridiculous idea before I leave."

Adrian was slow to meet Cecelia's gaze. When he finally did, his hazel eyes were full of regret.

"Much as it pains me, I do agree with our aunt," Adrian said softly. "I am sorry."

Cecelia felt as if she'd been struck. All the happy anticipation of the past few days dissolved in an instant.

Looking insufferably pleased, Lady Carlton lifted her chin even higher so she could look down her nose at Cecelia. "See? The matter is settled."

Cecelia looked to her brothers, but they both seemed unwilling to meet her gaze.

Her aunt grasped her arm. "And when I return, there will be no more foolish delaying. You will choose a *suitable* husband."

Cecelia's pulse raced. She curled her hands into fists. *Stand up to her. You are no longer a child, so you must demand that she no longer treat you as one.* A rush of furious determination filled her. *Tell her you are getting married to a gentleman whom she would not approve of, and she cannot stop you.*

Cecelia opened her mouth. But as she met her aunt's steely gaze, her stomach churned, and the words of defiance died on her lips. As they always did.

She felt as if she were six years old again, facing a barrage of scornful words from her aunt after she'd tripped and spilled tea on the shoes of one of her aunt's suitors. Or when she was ten and her aunt had scolded her for crying after her brothers left from one of their all too rare visits. Or when she was nineteen, and her aunt had berated her in front of her relations for refusing the suit of some horrid gentleman.

As always when her aunt bullied her, Cecelia's heart

raced, her fingers trembled, and her mouth felt frozen shut.

No matter how many times she imagined standing up to her aunt directly, icy fear stopped her. Every time.

Her aunt smiled coldly, clearly satisfied, and she released Cecelia's arm. Lady Carlton turned to look back at Lord Moreland, who caught his intended's gaze and forced a weak smile.

With a sigh, Lady Carlton again faced Cecelia, Adrian, and Edmund. "The viscount simply cannot bear to be away from me for long," she said. "I must return to him."

Cecelia thought the viscount looked as if he wished to bolt from the meadow, but she wisely kept silent.

Her aunt fixed her with another piercing stare, as if she knew what Cecelia was thinking. "And although I'll be leaving tomorrow," Lady Carlton said, "I'll be returning in several weeks. Perhaps sooner, if I hear of anything that requires my attention." With that final threat, she spun around and marched back to her intended.

As she watched her aunt return to the viscount's side, Cecelia's fear was swiftly replaced by shame over her cowardice.

"I should have…" She hadn't meant to speak aloud. A gentle hand touched her arm, and she looked up to see Edmund, smiling sadly.

"Do not be hard on yourself," he said. "You suffer enough of that from her."

The love—and was it pity? —in her brother's expression only made everything worse. Tears threatened, but she forced them back.

She began to walk again, much faster this time. Edmund quickly caught up with her, but Adrian was slower to follow.

"She is one of the most frightening women in England," Edmund said. "I'd prefer to battle a field of French cavalry or a horde of bandits any day. In fact, I'd choose both at once over her."

Cecelia barely heard Edmund's words as she glanced, frowning, at Adrian. Her eldest brother was nothing like her aunt, but Cecelia nonetheless found it almost as difficult to challenge him, even if for far different reasons.

But suddenly, she was so angry it was as if someone else controlled her. Someone who was less of a coward. She stopped walking and spun to face Adrian.

"Why?" she said, even managing to meet his gaze. "Is…is it because of…what our aunt says about Trent's family?" She hated the tremor in her voice, but at least she'd managed to get the words out.

Adrian shook his head. "My objections are different."

"Wh-What are your objections, then?" she stammered, her heart pounding only slightly less than when she faced her aunt.

Even now at twenty-one, whenever she thought of directly standing up to her oldest brother, anxiety flooded her. As a child, she'd idolized him. She'd been so desperate for his rare visits that she'd been afraid to show him any negative emotion, any hint of anger that might risk driving him away. The past two years of sharing a home with him had tempered her view of him, allowing her the chance to finally get to know him well, flaws included. Though she had become much more comfortable around him, direct defiance still seemed out of the question.

Adrian shifted on his feet and crossed his arms. "William Trent…is not worthy of you."

He was her oldest brother, only trying to protect her. But he was wrong. Why should anyone else, even Adrian, decide who was worthy to be her husband?

Her heart raced faster, and she imagined opening her mouth and saying what she truly thought. But, of course, her mouth remained closed.

Adrian exchanged a frown with Edmund and then looked back at her. "You don't know Trent well," he said softly.

From the uncomfortable expression on Edmund's face, he clearly agreed with Adrian.

Her brothers assumed she was foolish, as if she believed fairy tale happiness was all that would follow. Perhaps when she was younger she might have been so naïve, but over the past several years she had grown far more practical. Yet her brothers still viewed her as a child incapable of making a wise decision. And they likely would continue to do so until she convinced them otherwise.

"I simply cannot believe that you will be happy," Adrian said quietly. "And your interest in him is so sudden."

You mean he will not make you *happy*, she imagined herself saying. Fear knotted her stomach and constricted her throat. *I have considered the matter carefully, and I am certain that the advantages of the match far outweigh any shortcomings. The alliance will not only benefit our family, but it will also bring me great happiness.*

The words sounded so resolute and confident—in her mind.

Frowning, Adrian murmured, "Has he truly captured your affection?"

For the past two years, ever since Adrian had been so fortunate as to have made a love match for himself, he had made it clear that he wanted Cecelia to marry for love as well.

She knew what he wanted to hear, but still, she would not lie to him. Not about this. "I…am very fond of Mr. Trent," she said, at last finding her voice, "and I am certain I shall only grow even more fond of him."

Adrian's frown deepened. "Fond?"

Her heart still racing, she took a deep breath. "You may not wish to see it, but I…I am a grown woman now, wise enough to choose my own husband."

Adrian's eyes widened. Edmund's mouth had fallen open. A silence followed that felt like an eternity.

What had she done? She had never spoken to Adrian in such a tone before.

But rather than angry, he looked only startled. Or could he even be…uncertain? Her nausea was abruptly gone. Warmth rushed through her. Was…was he at last seeing her as the adult she was now?

Then he scowled. "No, I cannot in good conscience give the match my blessing," he said, sounding, as always, unshakably certain of his own opinion. "Now is not the time to discuss it, anyway."

Silence followed, in which any remnant of courage fled her.

"V-Very well," she said. Of course, as always, she acquiesced quickly. But what was the point of arguing with him, even if she were brave enough? There would never be a good time to discuss the matter. Once he'd decided something, her oldest brother almost never changed his mind.

He would not allow her to travel, and now he would not support her choice of husband. And she was too cowardly to insist he do otherwise.

Adrian sighed and looked back at the others. "I should return to our guests." His gaze, however, was clearly focused on a single person: his wife, Anna, sitting with one hand resting on her very round midsection.

Impending fatherhood had seemed to make Adrian even more protective of his family, which might be well and good, except that it included his now grown younger sister.

"We will speak more later," Adrian added, looking back at Cecelia. "Yes?"

She forced herself to nod. Speak later? For all the good it would do. He would speak, telling her what he believed was best for her, and she would listen, only imagining what she truly wished to say.

With a stiff nod, Adrian turned and strode away.

"He will never change his mind," she murmured.

"Indeed," Edmund said, "we both know too well how hopelessly stubborn he is."

She looked up at Edmund. "But this time, you agree with him," she managed.

"I want the best for you," Edmund said gently. "I hope to see you married to a man who is worthy of you."

With that, her last hope for an ally died. Resignation crept over her. Even the temptation to cry faded.

She had years of practice pretending to be content, no matter how she truly felt inside. Sometimes she could fool her brothers, even Edmund. This must be one of those times. At least dear Edmund would forgive her quickly, of that she was certain.

Edmund was staring at her, his brow furrowed. "Oh no. I know that look," he said with a sigh. "Please, promise me that you will not do anything foolish." He paused. "Do not do anything that I would do."

She took a deep breath, avoiding his gaze. "You heard our wise older brother. He says the matter is settled."

"Yes, but is it settled?"

"Quite settled," she said truthfully, adding silently, *just not in the way Adrian believes.*

She might lack the courage to stand up to her aunt directly or defy Adrian openly, but she'd had enough of anyone else dictating her future. It was time to take matters into her own hands.

CHAPTER FOUR

THOUGH IT WAS THE MIDDLE of the night, James was too angry to fall asleep. Dimming the lantern had not helped. Despite looking exhausted, Lady Cecelia also remained awake across from him, repeatedly fidgeting with her gloves and reticule. Beside her, Reed slumped against the window, snoring softly. His grandmother was likewise asleep next to him, her half-finished scarf still in her lap. He carefully eased the needles from her hands and tucked them back into her bag without waking her.

He should be sleeping soundly in his own home after a peaceful day spent on his estate, not stuffed in a cramped carriage uncomfortably close to Lady Cecelia Sinclair.

He generally made a point to avoid the company of eligible young ladies, especially attractive ones. Now he was faced with having a young lady—a particularly beautiful and troublesome one—as a guest in his home. For an entire month.

Just as she had for the past few hours, Lady Cecelia glanced in his direction, but then avoided his gaze. She brushed imaginary lint off her gown yet again.

Wareton was a good man, but he had made mistakes with his sister. While in the army, Wareton—then Captain Sinclair—had spoken of her often, making it clear that he regretted allowing their harridan of an aunt to have the sole charge of her for so long. Feeling guilty, Wareton had indulged his sister, which also had not improved the young woman's character. In James's opinion, she was spoiled, selfish, and headstrong—the latter one quality she shared with her brother.

However, she was not the fragile damsel in distress that James had imagined. Frightened as she'd clearly been by the events of the evening, she had shown remarkable courage. Which made her far more interesting and, therefore, far more irritating.

"How much longer until we stop?" Lady Cecelia whispered, breaking the long silence. She stretched and rubbed one shoulder.

"We should arrive at a suitable inn soon after daylight," he said quietly.

"How long will we stop? I could use a rest from the carriage." She shifted, leaning toward the window, and he tried not to think about her backside pressing against the seat. Over the past few hours, he'd become increasingly aware of each time she stretched, shifted, or moved her legs beneath her gown.

Such distractions only made him more annoyed at the entire situation.

"*You* could use a rest?" He straightened. "I'd prefer to be resting at home, having never left for London." He paused and added, "This is all your doing."

She flinched and scowled at him. Clearly, she was unaccustomed to being spoken to so bluntly.

She shifted forward and took a deep breath. "If…if my brother had allowed Mr. Trent to court me properly—"

"He was correct to discourage his suit."

Her eyes widened. No doubt she believed him ill-mannered for his outspokenness, but he was too annoyed to care. Just for good measure, he added, "You should thank him."

Her eyes widened even further. Then, to his inexplicable delight, they narrowed.

"Th-Thank him?" she blurted. "For trying to keep me away from the gentleman I wish to marry?" She shook her head. "I know my brother means well," she added, her tone pleasingly candid, "and he thinks I am being foolish and in need of rescuing. But he is wrong."

Was she in love with William Trent? Was she merely being rebellious? James knew little of her history with Trent except that her interest in him had apparently developed quickly, within the past few months, and that Wareton had discouraged Trent's suit.

William Trent was a reputed scoundrel whose family had grown tremendously wealthy through their shipping company, rising in influence over the past two decades. However, despite their wealth, the Trent family had not yet wed into the nobility. William marrying the sister of the Earl of Wareton would be a considerable step toward greater respectability.

Perhaps if Trent were a man of better character, the situation would be different. Trent did have some redeeming qualities. He was charming, certainly. If the rumors were true, he had charmed his way into plenty of beds. He had charmingly lost heaps of money at cards as well.

She must be in love with the undeserving scoundrel. Why else would she choose him over the many far more suitable gentlemen who were no doubt eager to marry her?

"Why do you admire William Trent?" he asked quietly.

She was silent for a moment, clearly surprised by his blunt question. Would she even answer him? Not that he truly cared, but it was a long ride to Westbury.

"I…I enjoy his company," she said at last. "He is charming, and he makes me laugh. He is not overly serious or critical, like…some gentlemen." She held his gaze.

Overly serious and critical? Did she think him so? Not that her opinion mattered.

"He is intelligent," she said softly. "And like me, he

wishes to—" Whatever she'd been about to say, she clearly thought better of it. "He suits me," she said instead, a disappointing reserve returning to her voice.

Even far outside of London, Trent was a regular subject of gossip and infamous for a string of short-lived affairs. The man clearly loved novelty, and his feelings toward his wife would likely be no different from his affection for other women—intense but fleeting. I f s he c raved excitement, Trent would certainly deliver, although not in the way she'd probably wish.

"Are you acquainted with Mr. Trent?" she asked.

"I have never met him."

"Then you have formed your opinion of him solely from my brother?"

"A small amount, perhaps," he said, "but mostly I have heard about him because talk of him has reached us even far out in the country."

She frowned. "What sort of talk?"

"That he loves novelty in his pursuits." As outspoken as James generally was, this was one area in which even he would keep the rules of decorum.

She straightened. "Such as?"

"Supposedly, one month he's obsessed with carriage racing, the next month gaming, and the next, something different." He wasn't lying. Seemingly it was true of all Trent's pursuits, romantic and otherwise. He paused and added, "Apparently, he spends a fortune on each new interest, so naturally, people talk."

Her frown disappeared. "He enjoys life and enjoys trying new things. He's exciting, adventurous." She sounded as if she was trying to convince herself as much as him.

He might even feel sorry for her, for falling for a scoundrel like Trent, if she wasn't disrupting his life so much at the moment.

And she was a far too attractive disruption. Sitting so

close to her in the carriage made that fact impossible to ignore. Even after the night's adventure, she didn't smell like the smoke and grime of London, but still of fine soap. And it mattered little that the carriage was dimly lit now, because what he'd seen of her earlier—smooth skin, lovely mouth, and pleasing curves—was still fresh in his mind.

He had expected her to be pretty, but not this beautiful. And the fact that he was increasingly aware of her beauty made him horribly uncomfortable.

He should not think of her in that way for so many reasons.

First, she was his friend's sister.

Second, she was clearly trouble. Enormous trouble.

Third, he was too far beneath her in status to be considered a suitable match.

And fourth, any respectable woman was off limits to him anyway. He could never marry, not without deceit involved, which he refused to do.

Lady Cecelia did not recognize how fortunate she was. She could marry, and she could have her choice of wealthy and honorable gentlemen. Yet she would throw all that away for a scoundrel like William Trent.

But even such an unsuitable marriage was more than James would ever know.

His chest tightened with a familiar ache. He would never have a wife or children. Joys that many men took for granted were impossible for him. As always, he pushed away the sadness, refusing to wallow in self-pity. He had made his choice long ago, and torturing himself over what could not be changed was pointless.

He reminded himself that he was better off without a family. No wife or children to worry about should something befall him. No one else who might be harmed because of his past.

Besides, even without a family, he already had so much:

freedom and a life of comfort. Indeed, in that sense he already had far more than most souls, and far more than he likely deserved.

He glanced at Lady Cecelia and then forced his gaze to the window beside him.

While her beauty might be distracting, it was fortunate that he—mostly—disliked her. For even if she weren't so troublesome, there was no place in his life for a woman like Lady Cecelia Sinclair.

Cecelia paced slowly alongside the carriage, stretching her legs while she waited for the others. Just after sunrise, they had stopped at an inn, and the innkeeper's wife had tended to Reed's injury. Then they had all enjoyed a breakfast of ham, bread, and fruit. Now Mrs. Stewart was visiting a nearby shop, along with Reed, who needed to buy a few things to replace her stolen items.

As Cecelia paced, she pretended not to watch Mr. Wright, who stood outside the inn speaking with a man, apparently arranging to send a message. Earlier he had mentioned to his grandmother that he would send word ahead to allow his staff more time to prepare for their houseguest.

Uneven as his manners had been to her, he certainly seemed to be a considerate gentleman in many ways.

More so than William. The thought came in a rush, followed by a pinch of anger yet again at William for being late to meet her in London. But perhaps she should be grateful instead. Now she—they—had a chance to gain Adrian's blessing. And surely by now William had learned what had happened to her. Despite the disruption to their plans, she had little doubt that William would be pleased at the chance for Adrian's approval.

Mr. Wright finished speaking with the man and strode

toward her, his face somber under his dark hat. He should be called Mr. Grim—she had yet to see him truly smile. At five and twenty, he was only four years older than she was, yet there was a seriousness in his manner that seemed suited to a much older man.

At least some of his disagreeableness was likely due to the situation. She could hardly blame him for being irritated with her under the circumstances, and therefore she should forgive his bluntness in the carriage.

And after her initial shock had subsided, she had in fact found his candor oddly appealing. Perhaps it was that honesty, the unusual situation, and the darkness of the carriage that had enabled her to speak so openly herself. Or perhaps it was simply exhaustion.

It was of course possible that he was always so ill-mannered. She supposed she would learn soon enough.

Even when ill-tempered, he was still quite handsome, and even more so in the daylight. She wished to find flaws, something that would make him less attractive. But even the stubble along his jaw only drew more attention to the strength and evenness of his features. His clothing was plain, clearly not chosen to draw attention, but the garments were all of good quality and flattered him. Likely any clothing would look good on his tall, muscular frame.

As he stopped before her, she glanced at his impressive legs and then up at his somber face again. He must have a softer side, even if he hid it well. Did he have a lover? A mistress?

He met her gaze, and she hoped her expression didn't give away her improper thoughts.

"I thought I'd take a stroll while we wait," she said quickly.

"May I accompany you?" His tone now was cordial enough, although he still didn't smile.

"Of course," she said. She wasn't certain if he was merely being polite or truly wished to walk with her, but she was grateful for his company.

They began strolling along the quiet road, past the few dozen stone two-story buildings that made up the heart of the village. He didn't offer her his arm, and he kept several paces distance from her as they walked.

"A better breakfast than I expected," she said after a moment, to break the silence.

"Really?" He glanced at her with a furrowed brow. "No complaints?"

"None. Why do you seem surprised?"

He shrugged. "Your letters to your brother were full of complaints."

"My letters?" She hadn't considered that Mr. Wright might be familiar with her letters to Adrian while he was in the army. But she supposed Adrian likely had shared news from home.

She frowned. What had she written that had been so terrible? Furthermore, who was Mr. Wright to judge her? As they passed more widely spaced buildings, she quickened her pace. He easily matched her stride.

"I am flattered that you remember so well what I wrote," she said.

"Don't be." His deep voice held a hint of amusement.

"My letters were for my brother," she said. "I know he appreciated them."

"True. Any correspondence is a treasure in such situations. Even complaints."

To avoid a stretch of mud, she was forced to walk closer to him. He seemed about to offer her his arm, but then apparently changed his mind. As soon as she could, she shifted a comfortable distance away again.

It seemed he was not always considerate.

"I do not think my letters were full of complaints," she said. "I told Adrian—Lord Wareton, that is—what was happening back home." Why was she even justifying herself to him?

He said nothing, only glanced at her with one eyebrow raised in the annoying, smug way that he had. As if he were holding back from saying more because it simply wasn't worth his effort.

She abruptly stopped walking. She knew she should not ask, but her mouth opened anyway. "And what exactly did I write that bothered you?"

He stopped as well, turned toward her, and drew a deep breath. "How the weather ruined your picnics. How you were forced to ride a temperamental horse. How your French tutor smelled of onions." He sighed. "How your aunt wouldn't let you choose your own clothes, parasol, breakfast—anything." He looked down at her with shrewd dark eyes, as if she were a spoiled child. "And the fact that I recall all this is a testament to how little there was to occupy us at times."

Her face suddenly felt warm. Those did all sound like things she had written. But had her letters truly seemed as frivolous as he described? Even if they had, who was he to criticize them?

She spun away and began walking again. He kept beside her, striding closer to her now. They trod in silence as the houses gave way to hedgerows and fields.

She wanted to tell him that he was pompous and ill-mannered.

"And what should I have written to my brother?" she finally said instead. "Should I have asked about the war?"

She glanced at him long enough to see him frown.

"Or perhaps about how I was worried about him?" she added. "About how I feared it might be the last letter he would read from me?" She hated how shrill her voice sounded, but she couldn't stop. "Or that he might never read my letter at all?"

He met her gaze for a second. Then he quickly looked away, focusing on the road in front of him.

"Of course not," he said, his voice rough. At least he had the decency to appear embarrassed.

Their pace gradually slowed. They walked on in silence.

The truth was that she hadn't known what to write to Adrian when he was in the army. She had tried not to imagine what might be happening to him, and she had pushed away horrible, frightening thoughts each time she took pen to paper. So she'd filled the pages with the mundane—the small, ordinary things that were as far from what he was experiencing as she could imagine, including the complaints of regular life. Petty, perhaps, but she'd hoped they were still a distraction he needed.

Adrian had never taken her to task for anything she had written. And friend of Adrian's or not, what business was it of Mr. Wright's, anyway? He was stuffy and judgmental.

Perhaps her words had hit their mark, however, for he was glancing at her with no arrogance now. Still, he made no move to apologize.

"And I suppose all the letters you received in the army were only of the most serious matters," she said. "Nothing ordinary that might take your mind off the war for a few moments?"

Something flashed across his face. Sadness?

"I received no letters," he said.

"None?" she blurted. "Not a single letter?" The possibility had never occurred to her.

"Not one," he said quietly.

"But surely…surely at least your grandmother wrote to you?"

"No. Until recently, we had not been in contact for many years."

She walked on in stunned silence. Adrian had told her that Mr. Wright had no other immediate living family outside of his grandmother. But she had assumed that he would have someone—other more distant relatives or friends—with whom to correspond.

"You have no other family at all?" she asked.

He clasped his hands behind his back and shook his head.

What must that be like? She might not remember her parents, who had died when she was only two, but she had her older brothers. Adrian and Edmund had been raised by their grandfather's brother, while she'd been put in the care of her horrid aunt. Painful as it had been to be separated from her brothers, she had at least seen them several times a year, and she always knew they loved her. Indeed, their visits had been her greatest joy growing up, and had made the many miserable days with her aunt bearable.

And after Adrian became an earl, she and her aunt had gone to live with him at Wareton, and her family had grown even more. She had then shared her home with her cousin Madeline, who had become like a sister to her, and with Madeline's stepsister, Anna, whom Adrian had fallen in love with and married, making her Cecelia's dear sister-in-law. Madeline had recently married and moved far away, and Cecelia missed her dearly.

She couldn't imagine having no one to call family for so many years. How lonely Mr. Wright must have been and might still be. Was that why he was so grim?

She wished to ask him about his past and why he had been out of contact with his grandmother. His stern expression suggested that he would not wish to speak of anything that might invite pity, but she had to say something.

"It must have been difficult to receive no letters," she said gently.

He shrugged. "I have often felt my lack of family to be a blessing."

"A blessing?"

His mouth curved into a hint of a smile. "No troublesome siblings to rescue from foolish behavior."

She bit back a retort, remaining silent as they walked on. Feeling sorry for his lack of family did not change the fact that he was rude. It seemed he was trying to annoy her, but she would not give him the satisfaction…

Her steps slowed. Or was he once again deliberately trying to vex her to deflect the conversation from himself? She glanced at him intently, trying to read through his annoyingly inscrutable expression.

Despite being somewhat disagreeable, she understood why Adrian spoke so highly of him. He was clearly trustworthy, or Adrian would never have asked so much of him. And reluctant as Mr. Wright obviously was to be involved in their affairs, he was nonetheless conveying her to Westbury and welcoming her into his home. Furthermore, the concern he had shown for her safety—and for Reed—was unquestionably genuine. And she could not help but notice his consideration for his grandmother, including the gentle way he'd tried not to wake her in the carriage.

She also had to admit that she liked the way he spoke. Clearly he was an educated gentleman, but there was a lack of pretense, a directness about him that was refreshingly different from the gentlemen she was accustomed to. His unusually deep voice was also nice to listen to—when he wasn't being disagreeable.

Most important of all, and what she must always remember, was that in the army he had saved her brother's life. Therefore, no matter how rude Mr. Wright was, she would always—always—be deeply grateful to him for that.

He was also an enigma. Rather than the quiet recluse she had expected from her brother's description, Mr. Wright was shockingly direct, evidently quite clever, and simply not the sort of man she would expect to be content holed up on a quiet country estate with only an elderly relative for company.

And even if he were a country recluse, it was still surprising that such an appealing gentleman would remain a bachelor. In London, he would be pursued by many young women. It was quite intriguing that some country lady had not yet brought him up to scratch. But if he always avoided questions about himself, learning more about him could prove challenging.

If she wanted to get to know him better, she simply must not be easily put off. She would continue to speak with him, and she would not just talk about trifling matters. Perhaps to coax him into revealing more about himself, she must tell him something…personal.

They had reached a large pasture at the edge of the village. An old chestnut horse grazed close to the stone wall beside them and lifted its head as they approached. The animal gave a soft snort and moved closer, poking its nose over the wall.

Mr. Wright stopped to pet it and Cecelia paused too. As he gently stroked its neck, he seemed about to speak to the horse. Then he glanced at her and closed his mouth.

Mr. Grim was less grim around horses, it seemed. She hid a smile.

A carriage clattered toward them along the road, and the horse snuffled and backed away.

"Shall we turn around now?" she asked once the coach had passed.

He inclined his head. "As you wish."

They began strolling back toward the inn.

"Earlier you asked why I admire William Trent," she said. "Well, there is one additional, very important reason that I did not share."

His eyes widened. He looked away, pretending not to be especially interested, but with his next steps he angled nearer to her.

She let a long, quiet moment pass.

Finally, he sighed and gave her a lingering glance. "Well, what is it?" he said.

She hid a smile, keeping her gaze on the road.

"Like myself," she said, "Mr. Trent wishes to…travel." She couldn't resist glancing at him to see his reaction.

A wrinkle appeared in his brow. "Travel? Where?"

"Wherever we like. Anywhere, really, besides England."

"Why are you so eager to leave England?" He moved even closer.

"I wish to see more of the world," she said. "Cities beyond London and Bath and the few fashionable places considered acceptable for me."

"You long for adventure?"

"Yes." It felt surprisingly good to tell someone else besides William and Reed. And strange as it should feel to speak so freely with a new acquaintance, somehow with Mr. Wright it felt…natural. Paradoxically comfortable and unnerving at the same time.

He shook his head. "You do not realize how fortunate you are."

It had felt good for a moment, anyway.

He was once again being critical and making assumptions about her, and she need not explain herself to him. Still, she couldn't help responding.

"I am well aware," she said, her steps growing faster, "that I enjoy a privileged existence."

"And yet you seem to value it little," he said quickly.

"You are quite wrong."

He raised an eyebrow. Likely he was unaccustomed to being told he was wrong. Yet he didn't look annoyed; if anything, he seemed even more interested.

"I know how fortunate I am," she continued. "I also know that it is my duty to marry well, and I have thought carefully about how best to fulfill my obligations to my family."

Again, he raised one eyebrow. "And eloping with an unsuitable gentleman of whom your brother disapproves is how to best fulfill your obligations?"

"My brother is mistaken. William Trent is not unsuitable. While the Trent family might still be looked down upon by some, their power and influence are growing. I believe that a marriage to Mr. Trent will be highly advantageous to our family."

He said nothing, only stared straight ahead, his mouth set in a thin line. He obviously disapproved of her, and he agreed with Adrian that she was being reckless. And so what if he did? She did not care what he thought of her.

Even so, the urge to explain herself got the better of her.

"Gentlemen of means have a choice," she said. "They can easily travel without anyone's approval. And no one questions them for desiring to see more of the world."

As he listened, his frown slowly vanished. "I suppose that is true."

She felt a spark of pleasure at his acknowledgment. "So why should I not choose a marriage that will enable me to travel if I wish?"

"But you are also choosing a gentleman who has a questionable reputation," he said. "A man whom your brother fears will not make you happy."

The small satisfaction she had felt from him listening to her vanished. Like her brothers, he apparently assumed that she had not thought deeply about what she was doing.

Adrian believed she was foolish, still seeing her as a child in need of her older brother's guidance. But the fact that Edmund seemed to agree with Adrian…was far more unsettling. Edmund often found being disapproved of by their oldest brother and aunt something to aspire to, and usually supported Cecelia's wishes. So, the fact that he, too, was not in favor of William was—

No. When it came to the matter of whom she should marry, both her brothers were simply wrong. William Trent was a good choice.

She knew that William had many faults, of course, including what Mr. Wright had—in one of his few demonstrations of tactful, restrained speech—refrained from saying about him earlier.

She again pushed aside a twinge of annoyance that William had been late to meet her in London. No doubt he had a good excuse, not to mention that punctuality was hardly the most important quality in a husband.

She could easily tolerate such failings given William's many positive qualities, and especially their shared desire to travel. Furthermore, though it was true that she had not known him long, she trusted William because he was remarkably honest. While he seemed to have genuine regard for her, he had also admitted from the start that he was under intense pressure from his family to marry well, and for connections in particular.

As the sister of an earl, she had status and connections that would please William's family and would end the pressure for him to marry. In turn, he had promised her the freedom to travel and a charming husband as a companion on her adventures. William seemed as eager to leave England—at least for a time—as she was.

No, she was not being reckless but, in fact, highly practical.

Mr. Wright was still glancing at her as if he believed her foolish.

"I am aware of Mr. Trent's reputation," she said. "He may not be the gentleman my brother or my aunt would choose for me, but it is *my* decision to make."

Mr. Wright raised an eyebrow once again. However, even if he still disapproved of her, the disdain had left his expression. Now he seemed to be looking at her with genuine curiosity. Though she should not care, his interest pleased her.

"Gentlemen not only have the freedom to travel," she continued, "but they have more time as well. Even if they have a duty to marry, they can usually wait longer to do so."

"Not always," he said, frowning again. But she could tell he was truly listening to her and contemplating her words.

"You have traveled and had adventures," she said. "You did not need the help of anyone to do so. And unlike ladies who must marry as soon as possible, you can choose to marry whenever you like. Now, or ten years from now."

"Or never," he said. He half-smiled, but there was an edge to his voice.

"You plan to remain a bachelor, then?" she asked. If he could be outspoken, well, so could she.

For an instant, sorrow darkened his face, swiftly replaced with anger. But then he was once again composed, his expression so serene she almost thought she'd imagined the intense flashes of emotion.

"It suits me," he said curtly. "My life is my own."

"Ah."

He would certainly not be the first gentleman to prefer to remain a bachelor. But that hint of darker emotions suggested there was more to it. Had someone broken his heart? She wished to ask him, but his countenance was too serious now, and she had stretched the bounds of propriety enough with their discussion. She longed to regain the open, relaxed conversation they'd shared before.

"Shall I tell you about when I realized that I wished to travel?" she said.

He glanced at her, the tension easing from his face.

Again, it seemed that he tried not to look too interested, but he nodded.

"Last year," she said, "I accompanied my brother Edmund on a journey to Cardiff. By ship. I had never been at sea before." Her pulse sped up a bit even from the memory. "I did not expect to, but I absolutely loved it."

He glanced at her openly now, no longer trying to hide his interest. "What did you love about it?" he asked. His deep voice was startlingly gentle.

"Everything," she said, smiling. "The smell of the ocean, the sounds of the birds and the waves against the ship. The seeming endlessness of the water on the horizon. I felt so…free."

A hint of a smile softened his face. Even that small glimpse of happiness had a disturbing effect on her. She wanted to share more. Wanted to see him smile more.

"And," she continued, "we even saw dolphins. Scores of them. Jumping from the water, over and over again. I could have watched them all day, they were so beautiful."

He nodded. "Indeed, they are." His eyes shone as if he knew exactly what she had seen.

"And then," she went on, not bothering to temper her excitement, "when we went ashore, I absolutely loved being someplace new, seeing a town and landscapes and people and food and, well, everything, all different than what I am accustomed to. Edmund allowed me to choose most of what we did and where we went." She sighed. "I felt more alive than I ever had before. I felt, for once, as if I controlled my own destiny."

She had not meant to speak that last part out loud. But he was not looking at her as if she was foolish. Quite the contrary.

"I understand." His expression was delightfully unguarded, his voice gentle. "Once I felt the same."

Warmth crept through her. She could not resist telling him more.

"On the journey home," she said, "I made the acquaintance of a remarkable lady who was traveling simply for adventure. She carried a beautiful walking stick with a lioness on the handle."

"A lioness?" he said. "How unusual."

"Yes. She told me of the many fascinating places she had been. She told me of how she had chosen a husband who shared her love of travel, and who gave her the freedom to choose where they went and how they should live."

"Ah." His expression had become somber.

"After I returned home," she said quickly, "all I could think about was the journey and how I wanted to travel again." She sighed. "But Adrian did not want me to."

"Why not?" From the way he frowned, it seemed Adrian had not told him about what happened.

"As we left to return home," she said, "our ship hit some rocks. We were never in danger, truly—we were close to shore and quickly put into a smaller boat and rescued—but when Adrian learned of it, he was so upset."

Adrian had only reluctantly given his blessing for her to make the journey in the first place, and the incident had apparently confirmed his fear that allowing his sister to travel so far away had been a terrible mistake. Now he refused to permit her to once again sail off into what he viewed as the wild, murderous ocean that had claimed their parents so many years ago, and in his view nearly killed her and Edmund as well.

"Because of what happened to our parents," she added, "he would hear no more talk of me traveling."

"No," Mr. Wright said gently, "I imagine he wouldn't." He fell silent.

She wanted to tell him more. She wanted to share how afterward, having tasted the freedom of traveling, returning to her aunt's stifling control and to her scripted life had become increasingly unbearable. Soon, she grew determined to find a way to escape the rigid rules dictating her existence and the expectation that her life was not her own. To find a way to gain some freedom and self-determination without completely abandoning her duty to her family.

To marry wisely and practically, but also in a way that suited her own dreams, like the remarkable lady on the ship.

Mr. Wright kept glancing at her intently. She felt oddly flushed and a touch breathless, almost as if she'd been running rather than walking. She had been looking at him too often. And speaking too long, revealing too much. Although he seemed genuinely interested, sharing so much with a man she hardly knew—even if he was her brother's friend—was awkward. Yet somehow…not as awkward as it should be.

It was time to learn more about him.

"Do you not wish to travel?" she asked.

He shook his head. "I've had enough adventure for a lifetime."

He must mean the war. She could imagine how that might make a man crave the serenity of the country. Still, she felt quite disappointed at his answer.

"Had you traveled much before the army?" she asked.

"Some. Enough to know that I want to be at Westbury Park and would be content to never leave England again. Or the countryside, for that matter." He frowned, as if he regretted speaking so candidly.

After the war, perhaps it was little wonder he had no taste for travel. Even so, he was young to have given up on seeing more of the world, or even visiting London. Was a life spent almost entirely in the country truly enough for him?

His gait slowed. They were only steps from the carriage. She hadn't even noticed they had walked all the way back.

"Thank you for walking with me," she said. Surprisingly, she truly meant it. Awkward as it had begun, his conversation had been the best she'd enjoyed for, well, a long time. She felt at ease speaking with him in a way she'd rarely known.

"It was my pleasure," he murmured, his tone reserved, polite. But then he met her gaze and smiled at her—a full, genuine smile. A smile that, impossibly, made him even more handsome. A smile that made her breath hitch.

I could gaze at his face and his smile forever.

She quickly looked away, dismissing the peculiar and unsettling thought.

How silly. It must be the lack of sleep, surely.

The creak of a door opening broke into her thoughts. She turned to see Mrs. Stewart and Reed step outside the shop.

Mr. Wright abruptly took several steps away from her. He was suddenly absorbed in adjusting his hat.

As Mrs. Stewart approached, she glanced between them and frowned.

"We went for a stroll," Cecelia said. Why had she blurted that out? And why was Mrs. Stewart looking at them so disapprovingly?

An awkward silence followed.

Once they were all inside the carriage, Mr. Wright crossed his arms and fixed his gaze out the window.

Cecelia felt an oddly strong sense of loss. But perhaps it was best that their private conversation was over. Curious as she was about him, when she had raised the subject of marriage, his expression had turned so dark. She certainly had no wish to cause him pain, but she could not deny she was quite interested in him and his apparent secrets.

However, she would be in his company for a month. Surely soon enough, she would unravel the mystery of Mr. Wright.

CHAPTER FIVE

SEVERAL HOURS LATER, CECELIA PEERED out the window as the carriage turned onto the road to Mr. Wright's estate. The narrow lane curved between meadows dotted with sheep and then continued up a long, gradual hill.

They had finally reached Westbury Park. She could hardly wait to be free of the carriage and of being so close to Mr. Wright. He had barely spoken since they had resumed their journey, but she nonetheless had difficulty keeping her thoughts from him. She was also strangely aware of his every small movement. Surely it was simply the close quarters of the carriage and the lack of other diversions.

Next to her, Reed looked out the opposite window, while across the carriage, Mrs. Stewart remained silent. She had traded her knitting for what appeared to be a well-worn copy of Dante's *Inferno*.

Since they'd left the inn, Mr. Wright had appeared somber and deep in thought, and he avoided Cecelia's gaze. The connection they'd shared while walking now seemed almost imagined.

He was…an unusual gentleman. Less polished in manners at times than most gentlemen she knew, and perhaps less particular about his appearance as well.

After all their travels, his coat was quite wrinkled, his cravat was scandalously loose, and he'd even undone the top button of his shirt, revealing several inches of his very masculine neck.

She imagined what her aunt would say about his lack of concern for his neckcloth. *Ungentlemanly. Common.* Likely it was the novel impropriety of it, but Cecelia rather liked seeing a part of him usually concealed. Not that she was staring. Much.

He shifted, and his long, muscular legs once again stretched out close to hers.

He seemed to catch her staring at his legs and he finally looked her in the eye. After perhaps one second too long of meeting his dark stare, she shifted her gaze out the carriage window. She took a few deep breaths. She should be thinking of William. He was handsome too, almost as handsome as Mr. Wright. And a more modish dresser by far. William's hair was also always carefully styled, whereas Mr. Wright's seemed to be in a constant state of moderate dishevelment. Though it did have the strange effect of making her want to smooth his thick sandy brown hair.

She had also noted that when Mr. Wright moved closer, he smelled pleasant. Like what exactly she couldn't say— his soap, perhaps—but it was unquestionably pleasing. William sometimes smelled pleasant too, although occasionally he applied a touch too much cologne. And perhaps more than occasionally, he smelled faintly of stale cheroots.

She frowned. Why was she even comparing them like this? And yet, one aspect in which William was unquestionably superior was his demeanor. William was unfailingly pleasant and agreeable to everyone. Certainly not grim and judgmental like Mr. Wright seemed to be, at least much of the time.

Though if Mr. Wright was suffering from heartbreak, as implied by his expression when he'd said he did not plan to marry, perhaps that was the cause of his grave demeanor.

When Adrian had first told her about Mr. Wright a

few years ago, she had naturally tried to establish any social connections they might have in common. She'd even written to her cousin in Portsmouth, where Mr. Wright was from, to ask what she knew about him or his family. Her cousin, who knew nearly everyone who had resided in Portsmouth for the past forty years, had never even heard of the Wright family.

When she'd mentioned it to Adrian, he had seemed unconcerned, but she had found it odd. Perhaps now she might learn more.

"Mr. Wright," she said, "when you were young, you lived in Portsmouth?"

"Yes," he said. Beside him, his grandmother turned a page rather forcefully.

"My cousin, Lady Anne Lawton," Cecelia said, "lives there. Her home is near the cathedral. Where did you live?"

"Closer to the river." He gazed down at his gloves, flexing his fingers while examining the stitching closely.

"What street?" she asked.

"It was so long ago." He dropped his hands, but still did not look at her. "I do not recall."

Did he truly not remember, or did he just not wish to discuss it for some other reason?

They fell into silence again. The carriage tilted and the wheels rattled loudly as the road grew steeper, climbing toward a modest stone manor house with adjacent stables and a small carriage house. Cecelia expected to pass the home and continue down the road, but the carriage slowed and turned onto the drive.

Surely this wasn't his home? She glanced at him.

He nodded. "Westbury Park. Not as grand as you'd imagined, Lady Cecelia?" he added dryly.

"It's lovely," she said quickly, turning back to the window. She should have hidden her surprise. She didn't want to appear haughty, as her aunt no doubt would if she were here.

"The entire estate is a little over two hundred acres," he said, "with a dozen farms, all quite productive."

Modest as the estate might be compared to many that she was familiar with, Mr. Wright sounded quite proud of his home. As he should be.

"This is the largest house on the estate," he added.

"Will you change that?" she asked. Perhaps he planned to build a bigger home, one that could host large house parties or balls.

He shrugged. "I like this house well enough. I've no need for anything grander."

She was about to say that if he married, his wife might feel differently, but then she recalled what he'd said earlier about marrying. *Or not at all.*

He had implied that he had no plans to wed, and he had made clear he did not wish to discuss the matter further. If she'd not seen that flash of dark emotion on his face, she might believe it was as simple as preferring to be alone.

From her side of the carriage, she could now see fields beyond the hill, as well as a small wood, a scattering of ponds, and a narrow river. Westbury Park was a smaller estate than she'd expected, true, but it was lovely. A riot of flowers bloomed along the end of the drive and in front of the house. She spied what looked like a surprisingly large and well-tended garden behind the home.

As the carriage stopped before the entrance, only four servants—two men and two women—hurried out to greet them, leaving the door to the house open behind them.

One servant, a tall young man in ordinary clothes rather than livery, opened the carriage door. After Cecelia, Mrs. Stewart, and Reed stepped down, Mr. Wright quickly followed, and they all turned to greet the servants.

"Lady Cecelia," Mr. Wright said, "this is Long, the butler."

Long was stocky, several inches shorter than Mr. Wright, and smelled faintly of…fish. His silver-streaked black hair hung nearly to his collar, his scuffed boots were spattered with mud, and his face was unusually weathered for a butler. But his bow to her was flawless, and when he met her gaze, his brown eyes were kind.

"And the housekeeper," Mr. Wright said. "Mrs. Thornton."

The housekeeper was exceptionally tall for a woman, nearly as tall as Mr. Wright, and heavyset, with graying auburn hair tightly coiled at her nape. She scanned Cecelia from head to toe, her pale green eyes narrowing. Her black dress was of good quality, but small grayish clumps of what appeared to be animal fur were stuck to the bodice.

"Alfred, our footman," Mr. Wright said, nodding to the young man who had opened the carriage door. "And Jenna, a housemaid."

The young woman smiled as she curtsied.

A scuffling sound near the open door caught Cecelia's attention. A small gray dog limped out of the house and dropped slowly down the half-dozen steps. The animal hobbled over and stopped at Mrs. Thornton's side. The dog panted as if it had just run a mile.

Other than Mrs. Thornton, whose stony gaze softened when she looked at the dog, no one, including Mr. Wright, paid the animal any notice.

"We received your message, sir," Long said. "We've prepared as best we could."

"Good," Mr. Wright said. "Thank you."

"You must be tired from our journey," Mrs. Stewart said to Cecelia. Her tone was softer than before, and her gaze now seemed more resigned than disapproving. Mrs.

Stewart glanced at the housekeeper. "Mrs. Thornton, please show Lady Cecelia to her room."

Mrs. Thornton nodded, her scowl deepening as she looked at Cecelia. "Come with me," she said. The housekeeper bent down, scooped up the dog, and cradled the animal against her chest. She glared at Cecelia as if daring her to comment.

Cecelia hid a smile and began to follow Mrs. Thornton inside. She adored dogs, but her aunt had never permitted her to have one and always scolded her for trying to pet them. Cecelia had never stayed in a home where dogs were allowed to wander freely, let alone where a housekeeper was permitted to carry one around.

Mr. Wright's household was certainly proving interesting. Much like him.

Before entering the house, she glanced back and saw Mr. Wright and his grandmother speaking quietly. She felt disappointed that he was not looking at her, which really was quite absurd. Truly, she needed a rest.

Mrs. Thornton led Cecelia inside, across a small entry hall, and up the stairs. Narrow as the stairway was, the wood gleamed with polish and a pot of fragrant wildflowers adorned the spotless windowsill at the landing. Despite the dog fur on her dress, the woman clearly kept an orderly house.

Mrs. Thornton shifted the dog to her other arm and led Cecelia down the hallway.

"Mr. Wright thought this room would suit you best," the housekeeper said, her tone disapproving, as if she believed Cecelia should be in the stables, or perhaps not here at all.

Cecelia followed Mrs. Thornton into a bedroom with two tall windows, a large bed canopied in white, and a small sitting area by a hearth. A vase of fresh flowers rested on a table by the sitting area. The room was a third of the size of her bedroom at Wareton, but it was pretty and smelled pleasant.

Cecelia stopped at one window and peered out. The room was above the garden, and the river was a short walk beyond.

The housekeeper stood before the cold hearth, watching Cecelia carefully. The dog struggled in her arms, and Mrs. Thornton stepped forward and put him down. On the bed. He immediately curled up into an indentation on the counterpane that was the exact shape of his body.

Cecelia's eyes widened. The dog was allowed to sleep on a bed in a guest room? Looking more closely, she noted a significant amount of dog hair on the bed cover.

"Do you need anything else?" Mrs. Thornton asked. The housekeeper glared at her, almost as if she wanted Cecelia to complain about the dog hair.

Cecelia truly didn't mind—she would be quite happy to have the novelty of a dog in her room—but she was shocked by the housekeeper's demeanor. Was the woman this rude to everyone? Surely they would not keep on such an ill-mannered housekeeper?

"Everything is fine," Cecelia said, forcing a sweet smile. "Thank you."

Mrs. Thornton frowned.

"And I love dogs," Cecelia added. She stepped close to the bed and stroked the dog's head. "I always wanted one, but wasn't allowed. How wonderful to have one in my room."

The housekeeper's frown deepened. "He's not staying." She swept up the animal in her arms, nearly knocking Cecelia over. "Now I've work to do." She strode from the room.

As Mrs. Thornton left, Reed hurried into the room with Cecelia's bag.

"Woman almost ran into me," Reed muttered as she set the bag down. "Although I can understand why she'd be disagreeable. I've learned there are only two housemaids and one cook. And the servants are regularly permitted time off to visit family."

"How kind," Cecelia said. Not every employer would be so gracious, but it spoke well of Mr. Wright and his grandmother. Even if the demeanor of their housekeeper did not.

"Only the one footman," Reed continued, "and no valet for Mr. Wright or lady's maid for Mrs. Stewart." Reed shook her head. "Although apparently they do employ a coachman, a groom, and a gardener."

Cecelia wasn't surprised. The house wasn't so large that it needed much staff, but no doubt Reed had been hoping for another lady's maid for company.

"It seems that they have very few guests," Reed added, "and Mr. Wright rarely goes out."

That would certainly fit what she already knew of him—never visiting Adrian and avoiding London. But did he not go out even near his own home?

"Apparently he hardly travels anywhere," Reed added. "Other than a trip to Plymouth now and again."

"Why Plymouth?" Cecelia asked.

"Not sure," Reed said as she began putting Cecelia's clothes away.

"But surely he must dine with other families? Attend assemblies and outings?"

Reed shrugged. "Not often, from the sound of it."

As Reed was about to lay a gown out on the bed, she stopped abruptly. She stared wide-eyed at the indentation and coating of dog hair.

"I don't think these bedclothes were changed," Reed said. "I will see to it at once that—"

Cecelia shook her head. "No, it's fine. Mrs. Thornton seemed to want me to complain, so I would rather not."

Reed raised her eyebrows, but she said nothing.

Mr. Wright might seem to lead a boring life, but his

home was turning out to be quite unusual. A rude housekeeper who carried around an elderly dog and a butler who looked and smelled more like a dockworker were hardly commonplace.

Most interesting of all, why would a young gentleman like Mr. Wright behave like a recluse?

Her thoughts returned to the time during their walk when he hadn't seemed quite so grave or judgmental. When he'd listened intently to her speak of traveling. When his voice had been soft, his expression warm.

When he'd smiled at her.

She felt a pang of…sympathy, yes, that was it. He had been through a great deal. The loss of his family. War. And likely romantic heartbreak as well. No doubt such troubles were behind his mercurial behavior.

He had saved her brother's life. Now he had done Adrian a great service by finding her in London and having her as a guest in his home.

In return for him being such a good friend to Adrian, perhaps she might help Mr. Wright. She needed some purpose to occupy her time at Westbury, anyway. Perhaps while she was here, she might learn the reason for his solitude and then attempt to draw him back out into society.

She smiled. Yes, she would do her best to help Mr. Wright. Surely no harm could come of it.

As soon as Mrs. Thornton began to lead Lady Cecelia inside, James dragged his gaze away from their new houseguest.

Yes, she was beautiful, perhaps the most distracting woman he'd ever seen if he were being honest. But he must not gawk like a fool.

"I never had the chance to ask if you saw anyone… familiar in London?" his grandmother said quietly.

"No. No one," he said. Or so he hoped. He reminded himself again that a decade had passed, and many of the people he had known in the city were probably gone. While he understood his grandmother's fear all too well, he could likely spend weeks in London and never be recognized. He would certainly not have her worrying needlessly. He added gently, "Nothing with which to concern yourself."

She sighed and her shoulders relaxed. "Thank heavens. I am so glad to be home again."

"I am as well," he said. "And I apologize again for our unexpected houseguest, but I could not refuse Wareton."

"I know." She looked at him intently. "But will she really stay an entire month? That is a long time for her to grow even more curious about you."

Curious about him? Lady Cecelia had asked him about Portsmouth, true, but it seemed an ordinary question, more to make polite conversation surely than showing any deep interest in him.

"I do not believe she is truly curious about much beyond her own concerns," he said dryly. "And certainly not about me."

His grandmother raised an eyebrow. "That is not my impression."

He shook his head. "Her interests seem to lie in courting scandal, and not much else." But as soon as the words were out of his mouth, he felt a twinge of guilt. Not only was he being too harsh, but also untruthful, speaking of her as he had thought of her before meeting her. Until yesterday, he had judged her based in great part on her letters, letters written when she was much younger.

He had thought her frivolous, assuming she'd written about matters of little substance because that was all she cared about. He hadn't considered that it was to distract herself—and her brother—from the bleak reality of his situation. Now it seemed foolish not to have thought of that possibility.

Many of his assumptions about her had turned out to be incorrect. The discrepancy made him quite uncomfortable. Likely because he was rarely wrong in his initial estimation of a person's character, and it bothered him that he had so misjudged her.

Though he had to admit that was not all that disturbed him about her.

She might be foolish in wanting to marry William Trent, but she had more interesting reasons than he'd expected. Her passionate words about wanting to travel and choosing her own husband had repeated in his mind during the journey home. He could not help but admire her determination and the way she had spoken about the unfairness of women not being as free to travel independently as men.

She had a point—an excellent point—he would not deny it. And as she spoke, she had also looked, well, so fiercely beautiful.

But even that was not the most unsettling aspect of their interaction.

When she'd shared her experience at sea, with such happiness in her voice and expression, it had sparked memories of his own, from a time when he'd felt very much the same. He'd felt a stab of envy, the deep envy of one who knows exactly what he is missing. Once, he too had thought the ocean a freeing and joyful experience. He had reveled in the sights, sounds, and adventure of sailing on the open water.

But no more. He could never return to the innocence of that age. He could never think of the ocean with anything now but heartache. Regret. And fear.

He snapped his attention back to the present to find his grandmother frowning at him.

"You do not have to worry about Lady Cecelia," he said quickly.

His grandmother stared at him silently for a few seconds, and then she nodded. "Very well. I've no strength for remaining angry with anyone, even her, for very long, anyway. And since I have little choice, I shall make the best of her visit."

"Thank you."

She smiled and touched his arm. "Now, I know you are tired too. Come inside."

"Not yet. Soon."

She nodded and turned toward the house.

He walked in the direction of the stables, taking deep breaths and reminding himself how the air here was so much more pleasant than in London. Westbury was fresh air, quiet, and peace. For years, he had desperately wanted such a life and now, finally, he had it. He did not need the clamor of London, the throngs of people, the many activities, the excitement—

No, not excitement, he reminded himself. London was unpredictability. Danger.

Although there had been a time when he was younger, when he'd reveled in the energy of the city. He'd loved the crowds, the marvelous and varied buildings, the extremes of life on full display, the sense that something unexpected could happen at any moment. He'd felt a similar excitement when he'd first gone to sea.

Of course, that was when he was young and foolish. Now he knew better.

Here in the shelter of Westbury was where he belonged. Safe from his past, and so far inland that the scent of the ocean never reached him.

As he strode into the stables, he scanned the stalls. He looked into the tack room and the office but found no one. Then he opened the door that led to the guest quarters above, which the groom occasionally used. He called up, but all was silent. Evans must be elsewhere at the moment.

James strode to the centermost stall and greeted his gray mare. As he began to saddle her, he heard someone approaching. He expected Evans, but instead Long appeared, stopping just outside the stall.

"How was everything while I was gone?" James asked.

"Fine," Long said. "But the news of a houseguest created quite a stir."

"I can imagine," James said. In the two years since he had purchased the estate, he seldom had entertained guests. A few bachelor friends from the army had visited on a handful of occasions. His grandmother had hosted no guests overnight, only the infrequent neighbor for luncheon or dinner. So a young woman staying at Westbury for a month was not only unexpected, but unprecedented.

"I was wondering if we should arrange for extra help while Lady Cecelia is here," Long said, a smile softening his weathered face. "Since you and Mrs. Stewart will likely be socializing more while she visits, perhaps another footman or maid would be of use?"

"Why should we need that?" Mrs. Thornton interrupted. She had come up behind Long without James hearing her approach. She cradled Urchin, who looked to be asleep. "We can certainly manage one guest who brought her own lady's maid."

Long turned to face the housekeeper, his smile gone. The butler straightened, but he was still forced to tilt up his head to look her in the eye.

"Mr. Wright or Mrs. Stewart might wish to entertain guests," Long said, "or attend more events in order to keep Lady Cecelia busy while she is here. She's a young lady accustomed to the excitement of London. She might be bored—"

"Then let her be bored," Mrs. Thornton said. She

gently patted the dog while she glared at the butler. "More likely, you're afraid with guests here that you'll have less time to run off and fish."

"Not true," Long said, scowling at her. Then he glanced at James. "I only fish when I have spare time, and then, Alfred is always here should anything be needed."

The housekeeper snorted.

Long glanced back at her and muttered something under his breath—something colorful—and then looked back at James.

James sighed.

"Perhaps while Lady Cecelia is here," Long said, "you will also be going out more, sir?"

Images of assemblies suddenly filled James's mind. Gatherings where he had to strive to not raise any eligible young woman's hopes while struggling not to appear rude.

James shook his head. "I have work to do." It was his standard excuse, although sometimes he simply claimed that he had no interest in attending. Sometimes he even convinced himself it was true.

Other times, when he had turned down yet another invitation to an assembly, picnic, or musicale, a sudden, powerful longing would hit him. A desperate desire to go after all, to enjoy the music and conversation, to talk and laugh with the people he barely knew but wished to know better—to simply forget his troubles and lose himself in the joy of such an evening.

On occasion he did attend such gatherings, but only often enough to not be completely rude and to establish the most basic of relationships with his neighbors. But he found he could never truly enjoy himself. Never really let down his guard.

Especially around marriageable women.

And sometimes, watching other men do what he could not—flirt and dance and court and fall in love—was simply too painful. Those nights he truly did wish he had stayed home.

At home he might be alone and bored, but at least he was safe from heartache.

Long knew enough about James's past to understand why James behaved as he did. Even so, the man repeatedly suggested that James attend assemblies, picnics, hunts, or any events to which the neighbors invited him. Long did not give up trying, even though he should realize how hopeless James's situation was. But James could never be too annoyed with Long for it, as he knew the butler meant well.

And Long was correct about Lady Cecelia's presence requiring more social activity. From what James recalled from her letters to her brother, Lady Cecelia loved to socialize, and she likely would be bored without many outings to amuse her. In any case, it would be up to his grandmother to keep her occupied.

"Ask my grandmother if she wishes to hire any additional help," James said, nodding to Long.

Long smiled. "Very good, sir."

Mrs. Thornton scowled.

"And if my grandmother does wish to hire anyone," James added, "tell her to ask the Talbots first."

"The Talbots?" Long said. "Are they new to town?"

"Yes," James said. "They've moved in with Mrs. Young, who is their cousin, having no place else to go. Mrs. Talbot is a widow with five children, four still at home. The eldest was in the navy and was supporting them, but he was recently lost at sea."

Long nodded and glanced at Mrs. Thornton, who had stopped scowling.

James hid a smile, knowing he had given her and Long something they could agree on—a rare event.

"Now, if you'll excuse me," James said, stroking the mare's neck, "it's time I took her for a ride."

He mounted the horse and set out to enjoy the sunshine and fresh air. Riding at a brisk pace, he followed his usual route that skirted the border of the estate. The fear and worry that had constantly kept him on edge in the city were all but gone now that he was home. Still, he found he was not completely at ease, not with the knowledge that Lady Cecelia would be his houseguest for a month.

An image of her walking flashed in his mind, of her face glowing as she spoke of traveling, and of the graceful beauty of her figure as she moved. But no matter how attractive she was, he must not allow himself to think of her too often.

At the crest of a hill, he slowed his horse. The view was lovely all around: the rolling hillside, the pond below, the fields and the river beyond. A flock of geese soared overhead. As their honks faded, he urged his horse forward again, continuing along the path as it sloped down toward the pond.

Sometime in the past year the reality that Westbury Park was truly his home had finally sunk in. Frequently he would still catch himself staring in awe at the house, or the landscape, and would wonder at the fact that it was all his.

He recalled Lady Cecelia's expression when she first realized the size of his home. Though she quickly hid her surprise, he knew she had expected it to be grander, more on the scale of those in her social circle.

But this estate was exactly what he wanted. Not even disappointment in eyes as beautiful as Lady Cecelia's could make him feel that Westbury Park was not perfect. Even so, her presence was a stark reminder of what he could never have at Westbury. A wife. A family.

And a family was the only thing that would truly make the estate a home.

He quickly reminded himself that even with that dream lost, he was still a fortunate man. Fortunate to have the means to purchase this estate. Fortunate to have survived to even five and twenty, after time spent in the London streets, at sea, and at war.

Compared to many of those he had fought with and sailed with, he was incredibly lucky. Unlike them, he had a chance to grow old.

James's chest tightened. As he always did, he pushed aside thoughts that would only lead to heartache. Even without the possibility of a family, what he had now was more than enough. His life now *had* to be enough.

As he neared the end of his property, where the path met the road by the entrance to his estate, movement through the trees caught his eye. Pausing, he looked through the thin woods at two riders moving slowly along the road, the men peering around as if searching for something.

He didn't recognize them, which was unusual. The only people who generally used the road were locals.

His pulse sped up. Could they be looking for him? What if while in London—

"I believe the house is further up," one man said. "My aunt described the journey in such detail, we cannot have gone far enough yet." His voice was refined, a gentleman's.

The other man nodded, and they started riding faster, quickly disappearing from view.

James let out a long, slow breath. Just a gentleman visiting family. Perhaps he was calling on Mrs. Marshfield, who lived farther down the road.

James turned his horse and began riding back toward the manor.

He must stop imagining threats everywhere. His past was behind him, and he finally had the peaceful and comfortable life of which he had long dreamed.

His greatest worry now was how to endure a month with an unwanted but attractive houseguest—a trying time perhaps, but hardly a great burden in the grand scheme of things. For no matter how distracting she was, in the end, Lady Cecelia's visit was unlikely to be a life-changing event.

CHAPTER SIX

CECELIA SAVORED A BITE OF roast lamb, trying not to stare at Mr. Wright too often across the dinner table.

"The food is delicious," she said to his grandmother.

Mrs. Stewart smiled. "I shall let our cook know you said so."

Since Westbury Park apparently had so few guests, Cecelia had been unsure of what to expect for dinner, but Long served efficiently, and all of the dishes were excellent and beautifully presented.

Mrs. Stewart had changed from her traveling clothes into an austere gown so dark blue it almost appeared black and a stark white mob cap. Her only jewelry was a silver necklace bearing an unfashionably large cross. However, her mood seemed more relaxed now that she was home.

While Mrs. Stewart smiled at Cecelia's compliment, Mr. Wright barely glanced up from his food. Since the start of dinner, he'd seemed to scarcely look at her, but she'd had difficulty tearing her gaze from him. He wore an elegant dark coat, trousers, a spotless white shirt, and an almost perfectly tied cravat. He had clearly shaved and bathed, and he smelled pleasantly of soap. Overall, he looked quite impressive, especially for a gentleman who lacked a valet.

Even her overly critical aunt might grudgingly approve of his appearance now.

Frowning slightly, Mrs. Stewart glanced between her and Mr. Wright.

"Lady Cecelia," she said, "I learned only today that you are apparently acquainted with one of our neighbors, Mary Mercer."

Cecelia frowned. The name was familiar.

"The daughter of Viscount Mercer," Mrs. Stewart added.

"Ah, yes," Cecelia said. "I recall now. We met several years ago in London." She remembered a very talkative young woman a year or two younger than she was.

Mrs. Stewart nodded. "I sent a message to the viscountess to let her know of your visit. Her reply conveyed that Mary has made your acquaintance before and that they both look forward to seeing you while you're in Westbury."

Cecelia smiled.

"In fact," Mrs. Stewart continued, "they are hosting a ball the day after tomorrow, and they have extended the invitation to you as well."

"I shall be delighted to attend." Once again, Cecelia's gaze was drawn to Mr. Wright. If he rarely went out, would he make an exception this time? "You will attend the ball as well?" Cecelia asked him.

He exchanged a glance with his grandmother before answering, "No."

"Why not?" Cecelia asked. Not that she cared deeply either way, but she wanted to hear his reason.

His grandmother said quickly, "I am afraid James's arm often troubles him, and dances can be especially difficult."

"Your arm?" Cecelia said. Adrian had mentioned that Mr. Wright had been wounded, but Adrian had said it was a minor injury. She had been under the impression that Mr. Wright had recovered full use of his arm. "I did not realize it bothered you."

Mr. Wright nodded and quickly took a bite of lamb. She suspected it was to avoid having to answer further.

"But it does not trouble you when riding?" Cecelia added. She knew he had been out riding earlier.

"Not usually," he said without meeting her gaze.

"I am afraid the Mercers are known for especially energetic gatherings with lively music," Mrs. Stewart said. "And last time, the dancing went on for ages. It was quite exhausting."

"It sounds wonderful," Cecelia said. She glanced at Mr. Wright. He was frowning and staring into the air in front of him while chewing slowly.

"Oh, yes," Mrs. Stewart said with a smile, "and the food is always unparalleled. Last time, there was a multitude of cakes that looked like live birds, and fruit arranged to look like Noah's Ark."

"How delightful." Cecelia looked at Mr. Wright again. He was still staring at nothing, his frown deeper. "And I imagine," Cecelia added, watching him carefully, "such an event must attract a lively crowd as well?"

"Indeed," Mrs. Stewart said, "there will be no shortage of excellent conversation, rest assured."

Sadness flashed across Mr. Wright's face and he reached for his wineglass. No, not just sadness, but something else…envy? Did he want to go to the ball?

He caught her gaze, his expression now annoyingly unreadable.

Mrs. Stewart cleared her throat, drawing Cecelia's gaze back to her.

"And since James will miss the ball," Mrs. Stewart said, "I would suggest that he accompany us on one of our other outings, but he is always terribly busy. Is that not correct, James?"

He nodded, his attention returning to his food.

Mrs. Stewart smiled at Cecelia. "So you will not likely see much of him. I had to decline nearly every invitation we received this past month for him, many because James is simply too burdened with estate matters."

Cecelia was almost certain that his being wounded or too busy were not his true reasons for declining invitations. Was he simply avoiding any situations that might lead to matchmaking? Or perhaps he was avoiding a particular woman who had broken his heart?

She took another bite of lamb, finding it suddenly not quite as enjoyable.

Even if Mr. Wright was suffering from heartbreak, his grandmother encouraging him to stay home was still peculiar. How often did grandmothers not want to see their grandchildren married?

Clearly, something unusual was going on, something they did not wish her to know about.

It was not that she cared *that* much about Mr. Wright. But if she was to help him by drawing him out into society, she had to learn the reasons for his reclusiveness.

Before she left Westbury, she must uncover his secret.

James wished that he had made some excuse to be absent from dinner. But as much as he wanted to avoid Lady Cecelia, it had seemed far too rude to miss her first evening meal at Westbury.

Dinners were usually peaceful. He generally ate with just his grandmother, and enjoyed pleasant conversation mixed with companionable silence. Tonight, thanks to Lady Cecelia's presence, everything was different. Polite on the surface, but underneath, so…tense.

As Long served the potatoes, James glanced to his right. His grandmother had finished speaking about the ball and was smiling politely across the table at Lady Cecelia. But he knew his grandmother well. She clearly disapproved of their houseguest in general and, he suspected, of the fact that Lady Cecelia looked especially lovely in her ivory silk evening gown. Ever since she'd first entered the dining room, he'd been trying not to stare at her.

While dressing for dinner, he'd even wondered if his shirt and cravat were fine enough before mentally rebuking himself. It wasn't a dinner party, and Lady Cecelia wasn't even truly an invited guest. He shouldn't feel the need to alter his attire. She was disrupting his life enough for the next month.

And now she had questioned him about going out, and about his arm. The way she'd looked at him when they'd been discussing the ball suggested she was suspicious of his reasons for not attending. He doubted that she was truly interested in him, but what else did she have to occupy her time while she was here?

"I understand you have no other family?" Lady Cecelia asked, looking at his grandmother.

"Sadly, we do not," his grandmother said. "James's mother died soon after his birth and his father—my son, Robert—died when James was ten."

"And he could not live with you?" Lady Cecelia asked.

It was a reasonable question, but one James hated to hear. Although she tried to hide it, his grandmother often looked pained when the topic arose.

"Robert had arranged for James to live with a distant cousin." His grandmother's voice was clipped, as it always was when she spoke of his father. "Robert disapproved of my second marriage and of my moving to Scotland."

"Mr. Wright mentioned you were out of contact," Lady Cecelia said. "How difficult that must have been." As she glanced at him, her beautiful eyes were soft with sympathy.

He quickly looked away, focusing on his food. He mustn't think about her eyes. Or any other part of her.

"Many years later," his grandmother said, "after I was widowed again, I was finally able to leave Scotland, and I sought James out."

And yet he couldn't help but look at Lady Cecelia again.

Her eyes were wide now. "You were not able to visit him all those years?" she asked.

His grandmother lifted her glass of wine, not meeting Lady Cecelia's gaze. "No."

"And you did not know where he was?" Lady Cecelia said, looking between him and his grandmother.

His grandmother glanced at him and then shook her head. "By the time I was able to leave Scotland, James was a grown man, off on his own. I only learned that he was not with his cousin." She paused. "It took some time, but finally I located him."

"For which I am very thankful," James said, smiling at his grandmother. For too long he had believed what he'd been told by his father's solicitor soon after his father died: that his grandmother had no interest in seeing him, let alone caring for him. That was why James had never attempted to contact her.

Other than the distant cousin whom he had never met, his grandmother had been his only remaining family, but he had been led to believe that she did not care about him. As a child of ten, he had quickly told himself it did not matter, but of course, it did. He had carried that pain of her rejection with him through many years that followed.

Then, only a few years ago, after so long without any family, to be reunited with her had been one of the happiest moments of his life. To have kin again, and someone with whom he could share his secrets, had been a relief beyond words. Most comforting of all, she had revealed that after his father's death, she had been prevented by the terms of his guardianship from caring for him, when in fact she had wanted to—dearly.

Lady Cecelia gazed at him. "Did you ever return to Portsmouth after you left?" Her voice was soft and pleasing. As beautiful as her face. Facts which he absolutely should not be dwelling on.

"No," he said.

Lady Cecelia opened her mouth, seemingly eager to ask more.

"Tell me, Lady Cecelia," his grandmother said hastily, "about your family. James has spoken often of Lord Wareton, but I understand you have another brother?"

Lady Cecelia smiled. "Yes, my brother Edmund…"

As she told his grandmother about Edmund, James listened quietly. Though he had never met Edmund Sinclair, he was already quite familiar with him from Wareton.

Lady Cecelia's voice was even more pleasant now: warm and full of affection for her brother. He found himself distracted by the way her mouth looked while she spoke, her full lips, and her pretty white teeth. And when she suddenly laughed at something his grandmother said, he found himself holding his wine in midair for a few seconds but forgetting to drink…

He tore his gaze away from Lady Cecelia and took a sip of wine. The trip to London had clearly fatigued him. No matter how attractive and interesting she might be, this was Lady Cecelia Sinclair, Wareton's troublesome sister. Even if he could marry, she was too far above him in situation, not to mention she had an understanding with another man. There were many reasons that he should pay as little attention to her as possible. Still, he found himself unable to look away from her for long.

"James," his grandmother said, "did you not hear me?"

He snapped his gaze to his grandmother's face. She was frowning, and the way her eyes narrowed when she looked between him and Lady Cecelia…. That look meant trouble. For him.

"Forgive me," he said. "What did you say?"

"I asked if we might use the carriage tomorrow."

"Of course," he said.

Once again, his grandmother glanced between him and Lady Cecelia, and her frown deepened.

His grandmother obviously suspected that he found Lady Cecelia attractive. Did she fear Lady Cecelia might break his heart? Or put him at risk of revealing his past?

Ridiculous. Yes, he did gaze at her a bit too often. But a man would have to be blind to not be distracted by her, and truly, he was in no danger of feeling anything more than a passing infatuation. He would never permit himself to develop any real affection for her, knowing full well that such feelings would be pointless. His grandmother, if she was worried about a serious attachment developing between them, was reading far too much into the situation.

The unfortunate truth was that no woman could change his fate. Not even a woman as incomparable as Lady Cecelia.

CHAPTER SEVEN

THE NEXT MORNING, CECELIA WAS enjoying a leisurely stroll alone at Westbury Park. The long walk felt especially wonderful after so many hours confined to a carriage over the previous few days. The freedom to wander by herself was also a rare pleasure. When Cecelia had mentioned her plan to walk at breakfast, Mrs. Stewart had frowned disapprovingly, but she'd stopped short of insisting that Cecelia have company, unlike her aunt did at home.

The weather was warm and sunny, and the path Cecelia followed beside the river was quite pleasant—shady in spots from the enormous willows, and fragrant from the blossoming hedgerows. Benches were placed in several especially lovely spots: one facing the river where it bent sharply and slowed, another beneath the largest willow tree, and a third next to a large group of boulders.

From what she had seen so far, Westbury Park was uncommonly beautiful. Mr. Wright had clearly chosen well when he had purchased the estate. And if his grandmother was to be believed, it was estate matters that had him gone before breakfast this morning and nowhere to be found since.

Cecelia followed the path as it curved into a tunnel of a half-dozen willow trees, lush and towering. When she strolled back into the sunlight, she caught sight of a man in the water beyond the rocky riverbank below. Long stood in the river holding a fishing pole, his trousers rolled up to his knees. His shoes and a large bucket rested on the ground nearby.

As she walked toward him, he turned and smiled. "Good day, milady."

"Have you caught many?" she asked.

"A few perch," he said, "just big enough to keep."

The line from the fishing pole dangled into the sparkling river. He looked so peaceful.

How nice it would be to join him. Of course, her aunt would say it was unconscionable to spend time with servants in such a manner. However, here at Westbury Park the atmosphere was far different from the grand estate of her brother. She would have hardly anyone to talk to at all if she followed her aunt's rules.

"May I sit with you?" she asked.

"Of course." Long smiled. "I'd be glad for the company."

She settled herself on a large flat rock a few paces from him.

For several minutes, she watched him fish in silence, enjoying the beauty of the sparkling river, the quiet rush of the flowing water, and the birds calling nearby.

Then a few quick splashes sounded and the line went taut. Long rose and started to reel it in when the line abruptly slackened again.

"Lost it," he said, but he was smiling.

"Now I understand why people enjoy fishing," she said.

He turned, wide-eyed. "You've never fished?"

"No."

He shook his head. "Of course you haven't, milady. Forgive me." He paused and added, "Would you care to try?"

"Try…fishing?" She imagined her aunt's reaction to such an idea. As if keeping company with a servant while he fished wouldn't upset her aunt enough, the idea of Cecelia herself fishing would give Lady Carlton palpitations. Cecelia resisted the ridiculous urge to search the landscape for her aunt.

Long was waiting silently, his expression kindly.

She slowly rose. "Actually, I…I would like to try. Thank you."

Long grinned. "You won't regret it, my lady." He reeled in the line, walked out of the river, and handed her the pole.

She grasped it awkwardly.

"Here, I'll show you, if you'll permit me." He motioned with his hands, as if he was holding the fishing pole. "Hold it so. Cast like this." He demonstrated how to swing the line out.

Her first cast barely made it to the water. He showed her how to reel it in. Her second cast was little better, but her third sailed well out into the river.

He nodded. "You have the idea of it. Now move it just enough to give the look of something wiggling in the water."

She let the line drift, but every few seconds she moved it as he had shown her. "Do you catch many fish here?" she said.

"Yes." The wrinkles around his eyes deepened as he smiled. "In fact, I caught a six-pound pike just a few weeks ago. Not right here, but at a bridge not far away. The water is calm there, where the river bends, and reedy. They like to hide there and ambush their meals."

"Will you show me?"

"Not until you catch some smaller fish first."

She had to wait for what seemed like a long time, but finally, something tugged at the line. She gripped the pole tightly, fumbling for the reel.

"That's it," he said, "not too fast, but steady. Don't let it go."

The fish pulled against the line with surprising strength. Her pulse sped up as she forced the reel to turn.

Seconds later, she lifted the pole and a gleaming fish rose out of the water.

He grabbed it quickly. "A perch," he said. "A fair size too." He slid it from the hook with ease and tossed it in the bucket. "Again?" he asked.

"Oh yes." She was enjoying this more than she had imagined. "Can you show me how to set the lure?"

He smiled and nodded.

After several more minutes of him teaching her about fishing, they fell into companionable silence.

"Do you have a family?" she asked after a time.

He nodded. "I did. A wife and son, but they are both gone now."

"I am so sorry," she said. "What happened?"

"My son was in the Royal Navy and his ship was lost at sea. A month after we learned he was gone, my wife died." He kept his eyes on the river as he added, "They said it was an infection of the lungs, but I believe it was heartbreak."

"Oh no," she said softly. "How long ago?"

He sighed. "Ten years now."

She wanted him to know that she understood just a bit of his grief.

"When I was very young, my parents were lost at sea," she said. "They were shipwrecked in a storm."

"Ah," he said, meeting her gaze. "I'm so sorry to hear that, but not surprised. The sea brings heartache to so many."

They fished and spoke a while longer before falling into silence once again. Eventually, her thoughts drifted to Mr. Wright and his seeming reluctance to socialize. Perhaps Long might reveal if Mr. Wright was suffering from heartbreak as she suspected.

"Does Mr. Wright dine with many families?" she asked.

"Not often," Long said. "He usually prefers to stay home." A hint of sadness had crept into his voice.

"Did something happen to make him so?" she asked gently.

He frowned, crossing his arms. "I'm not sure what you could mean, milady."

"That is, I wondered…if he had suffered a disappointment?"

He stared at her for a few seconds, blinking, looking as if he didn't understand what she had said. Then his stance relaxed. "Ah. Well, I cannot speak to that, but I do think he works too hard."

He could not speak to that, or would not?

"I always tell him," he said, "that the world wouldn't end if he stopped to fish for a few hours."

"Does he enjoy fishing?"

Long sighed. "I've tried to get him to join me, but he never does."

"Why not?"

He shrugged.

"Maybe he's never fished?" she said.

"Oh, he knows how to fish well enough," Long said. "I heard he once caught—" He glanced at her and shook his head.

Why had he stopped so abruptly?

"He used to fish, then?" she asked.

"So I have heard."

She wanted to ask him more, but he sat down and seemed intent on putting on his stockings and shoes.

He clearly didn't wish to speak any more about Mr. Wright. Much as she wished to learn more about Mr. Wright, she felt the loss of the ease they had shared when they started fishing.

"Do you catch more fish standing in the water?" she asked, to change the subject.

Smiling again, he looked up at her. "No. It's just cooler."

Standing in the water sounded delightful. Even in the shade, the air was quite warm today. Why should men so often be permitted to cool off and be comfortable, but not women?

Of course, a lady should not take her shoes and stockings off in public. She suspected Long wouldn't be bothered by it, but her aunt would be scandalized if she knew Cecelia had done such a shocking thing.

But for once in her life, her aunt was not around to control what she did.

She smiled. That alone was reason enough. While she was here, she might as well seize whatever small freedoms she could.

After rising early to visit a tenant, James rode home along the river later in the morning. Only a few moments had passed today without him thinking of Lady Cecelia, but at least he'd succeeded in avoiding her at breakfast. He rode beside the water for a time, made his way around a bend and stopped short.

Lady Cecelia stood in the river. The skirt of her pale walking dress was tucked into her sash to hold it up, and her bare legs were visible from knee to mid-calf, where they met the water. Her half-boots and stockings were placed neatly on the shore.

Long, standing nearby, turned and caught James's gaze. Long glanced at Lady Cecelia, looked back at James, and grinned.

She turned toward James. "I'm fishing," she said. Her eyes were wide and her face glowed with happiness.

"I...can see that," he said, trying not to stare at her gorgeous legs.

She motioned to the bucket. "Go see what I've caught."

Her smile and warm tone were so enticing that he couldn't resist. He dismounted, leaving his horse to graze higher up on the riverbank, and approached her.

"You've been fishing before," he said, peering at the half-dozen fish in the bucket.

"No," she said. "It never even occurred to me to try it. My aunt would never have allowed it."

From what he'd heard from Wareton about their fearsome aunt, Lady Carlton had been excessively controlling of her charge, so that wasn't surprising. No wonder Lady Cecelia seemed so thrilled with the simple activity of fishing. How often would a lady in her position be allowed such an experience? She had certainly never needed to catch her own dinner.

For a few minutes he watched her in silence, enjoying how beautiful and peaceful she looked.

Because he had been no more than five or six years old, he only vaguely remembered the first time he went fishing. His father had taken him to a pond and taught him how to bait a hook and cast a line. After that, he'd fished only occasionally, until he ended up at sea, where fishing had become a regular activity.

Perhaps that was why he'd lost his appreciation for it. Now he associated fishing with a time in his life he'd just as soon forget. But watching Lady Cecelia, he was not reminded of his time on the ocean, but of the earlier times fishing and of the simple joy of waiting peacefully for the fish to bite.

He was also reminded of how beautiful a woman's legs could look in the sunlight, something he'd rarely seen. And never before had he enjoyed it quite so much.

He wished she would pull off her bonnet, unpin her curls, and let her hair blow free in the wind. And what he wouldn't give to watch her draw her skirt up higher, until he could see all of her shapely legs and—

She froze abruptly, and the rod twitched as something pulled at the line. For a few seconds, she fought to reel the fish in. Then she pulled back hard and jerked the rod up.

The fish went sailing through the air, snapped free from the line, and smacked into his chest. Water spattered his face and coat. It took him a few seconds to realize what had happened. Ignoring Lady Cecelia's peals of laughter and Long's chortles, James retrieved the fish, scowled at it, and then dropped it into the bucket.

Was the universe chastising him for his wild thoughts? Perhaps it served him right. But it would take far more than a splash of cold water and a fish to keep him from noting Lady Cecelia's beauty. She looked at him with such happiness on her face, that he felt…a way he hadn't felt in a very long time. Or perhaps ever.

He quickly pushed aside the warnings that crept into his mind. He was tired of unremitting restraint. Damn tired. What harm could come of enjoying her company just a bit more?

He sat down and removed his boots and stockings. As Long helped her set the lure, the butler glanced at James and smiled. Before she could cast, James strode into the water.

"May I?" he said.

Her eyes widened, but then she smiled. "Of course." She handed him the rod.

"Thank you," he said as he cast out the line. Thinking again of her laughter a moment ago, he added, "Shall I see if I can fling one at you?"

Clearly startled, she tilted her head to look at him, but then she laughed. She had such a beautiful laugh.

"Only if it is a perch," she said. "They seem to hit their targets extremely well."

He held her gaze for a moment. In the sunlight, her eyes looked bright blue.

He felt a tug on the line and dragged his gaze from her. As he drew in the line, he could tell from the light resistance that it would be a small fish. When he lifted it from the water, the fish proved tiny, not even the length of his hand.

She glanced at him with her lips pursed as if she were trying not to laugh.

He gently tossed the pitiful fish back into the water and he cast again.

"So, tell me," he said, "what did you do as a child instead of fish?"

"I studied," she said, some of the joy leaving her face. "Music. French. Italian. Dancing. Voice. Painting." She sighed. "I was permitted archery and riding at least."

"You enjoyed only archery and riding?" He could see that she was a person who would prefer active, exciting diversions to more sedentary ones.

"And dancing," she said. "Although my aunt tried to keep me from learning anything new, any dance she deemed unsuitable."

"Tried to?"

She nodded. "Once we lived at Wareton Manor, my aunt had slightly less control over me. I managed to escape from her occasionally, anyway." She smiled mysteriously. "And what of you?" she added. "What was your childhood like?"

"Unremarkable." He shrugged and looked out at the river.

"Portsmouth must have been an exciting place to grow up, with so many ships arriving from all over."

He shrugged again, keeping his gaze on the water.

"The ships did not interest you?" she asked.

When he glanced at her, the genuine curiosity in her expression was so pleasing. What harm could there be in telling her just a small amount about his childhood?

"The ships did interest me," he said. "Nearly every day my friends and I enjoyed racing down to the docks to see who could get there fastest. Though we raced not just there, but all over the city."

She laughed. "That sounds wonderful." Her smile faded, and she sighed.

"It was," he said, "though we often got into trouble."

Smiling once again, she shifted closer. He breathed in her wonderful scent—lavender, fine soap, and now the outdoors as well.

"Tell me," she said softly.

He simply could not resist.

"One time when I was eight," he said, "a friend and I decided to race around the cathedral. We drew a large crowd, all cheering as they waited at the end, while we ran neck and neck along the whole length of the nave." He paused, and a wrinkle appeared in her brow. "Until we were almost finished racing, we couldn't make out that the man standing at the end, waiting for us, was the archbishop himself."

She gave a delightful gasp. "Oh no."

He sighed. "I wasn't allowed out again for a fortnight."

She laughed. But then her smile faded. "I did not realize the cathedral in Portsmouth was so large."

"It's not," he said quickly, "it only seemed so at that age."

"Ah." She nodded and her smile returned.

Fool. He'd slipped up, allowing himself to be distracted by a beautiful woman. A small detail this time, but if he wasn't careful, next time might be something far more difficult to explain away.

"Your childhood does not sound unremarkable," she said, "it sounds delightful. So…free." She looked at him as if expecting him to tell her more.

When he didn't respond, she tilted her head to one side. "What about before the army?" she asked. "How did you spend your time then?"

He met her gaze. If she only knew. Yet thankfully, she didn't.

"I fished a lot," he said.

She frowned slightly and opened her mouth, likely to question him again, when the line abruptly went taut. What felt like a good-sized fish fought him as he reeled it in.

This time, it was more than keeper size. The fish resisted as he tried to free it, forcing him to hold it against his chest as he removed the hook. He tried not to grin as he dropped it in the bucket.

"Not bad at all," she said as he handed the pole back to her. "And now I am not the only one who smells like fish." She looked up at him and smiled.

She stood only an arm's length away. Dirt smudged her gown, her hair was a mess beneath her bonnet, and at the moment she looked a bit more like a street urchin than a lady.

But her eyes sparkled with joy, and the way she had planted one hand on her hip pulled her gown tighter across her chest, drawing attention to her curves. Her lush lips were parted in a wide smile.

She was utterly beautiful.

And suddenly, he wanted to kiss her. He wanted to taste her lovely mouth. Feel her warm breath on his skin. Draw her into his arms until there was absolutely no space between them.

She stared back at him, her eyes widening and her smile fading. Had it grown oddly quiet? Then her face pinkened. Abruptly, she shifted and took a step backward.

"Ow," she said. She bent down and brushed what must have been a pebble from her foot. "Perhaps…I've had enough of bare feet for now. And the water is beginning to feel too cold." She turned and retreated toward the shore, in the direction of her half-boots and stockings.

More disappointment than relief filled him as she stepped onto the riverbank and paused to untuck her skirt. She smoothed it down, once again covering her wonderful legs. But he could still glimpse her bare feet as she sauntered over to the bucket and examined the fish.

Smiling again, she turned back to look at him. "I still caught the largest one," she said.

He knew he should not go near her. He should not allow himself to be drawn in by her warmth and beauty. But his body paid his mind no heed.

"Did you?" he said as he walked over to her.

It was difficult to tell which of the two largest fish was the biggest without lifting them from the water.

As he tried to grab a wriggling fish, the rough feel of the scales evoked a memory of the last time he had fished. He and Nate, his best friend at sea, had watched the sun drop into the ocean as they cast out their lines. Nate had talked about his mother and the village where he had grown up. James had told Nate stories of escaping trouble on the London streets.

James could still recall Nate's near constant jokes and his boisterous laugh. Looking back on it afterward, there was no way to have known that evening would be one of the last sunsets that Nate would ever see.

A lump formed in James's throat and a tightness grew behind his eyes. He pushed back the sorrow and regret, or he tried to.

He should have done so many things differently that day.

He released the fish and yanked his hands from the bucket.

And he should be behaving differently now. What was he doing, idling away his time, enjoying fishing? Even worse, he was flirting with a respectable young lady.

As he dried his hands on his trousers, he realized Lady Cecelia was watching him, a tiny wrinkle in her brow.

He had forgotten himself completely. Forgotten that even a few moments spent laughing and enjoying the company of a young lady was something in which he dare not indulge. Indeed, he had no right to do so.

"Forgive me," he said, straightening. "I must leave now."

As he turned to retrieve his boots, he briefly caught Long's eye. Long glanced toward Lady Cecelia, then back at him. The old butler's face, so happy only moments before, was now filled with sorrow.

"Is something amiss?" Lady Cecelia said to him, her voice somber. As he finished putting on his boots, she took a step toward him.

"Not at all," he said. "I just remembered that I have important matters to see to." His words came out sharper than he intended.

Her frown deepened, and she gazed at him much as she had in the carriage when he had told her that he had received no letters in the army. With something akin to pity.

His chest grew tight. "Forgive me, but I really must go," he said. "Good day."

He spun away and strode toward his horse, silently cursing himself for being so foolish.

CHAPTER EIGHT

THE NEXT AFTERNOON, CECELIA FROWNED into the mirror as Reed styled her hair for the ball at the Mercers' estate. Even the warm breeze scented with garden roses that floated through the nearby open window failed to cheer her at the moment.

"Have you learned anything new about Mr. Wright?" Cecelia asked. What she was most interested in, of course, was if Reed had learned about any romantic attachments. Several times during the past two days Cecelia had asked her the same question and so far, Reed had discovered frustratingly little.

Reed shook her head once again.

After yesterday, Cecelia was even more determined to learn what was behind Mr. Wright's strange behavior. Even before he'd arrived at the river, fishing had been delightful, but once he had joined her, it had become something more, something both joyous and unsettling. His usual serious manner had vanished and he had behaved like the carefree young man he should be, simply enjoying fishing and her company.

At one point when they'd been standing especially close, his stare had been so intense that her breath had caught in her throat. His gaze had dropped to her mouth, and he'd looked as if he wanted to kiss her. Even more shocking was her immediate thought that she might not mind if he did.

But that impulse was wrong. Wrong and reckless.

First of all, she had an understanding with another man.

Second, even if Mr. Wright was terribly handsome and rather interesting, and even if he had been wonderful company for a short time, he was not a suitable match for her. Not to mention he had no intention of marrying anyway.

So even if during those moments while fishing he had stared at her in a way that made her pulse quicken, her face warm, and her bare toes curl into the rocky riverbed, surely it did not mean that much?

He was far from the first gentleman who had looked as if he wanted to kiss her. Maybe her reaction was as much due to the thrill of fishing, being barefoot, and feeling gloriously free from her usual confining existence. No doubt that explained why his intense gaze was especially thrilling.

At any rate, all too soon the relaxed, happy Mr. Wright had vanished and Mr. Grim had returned. From that point on, he had seemed angry for having enjoyed himself. Long had said that Mr. Wright didn't permit himself much time for anything but work, and his behavior certainly confirmed that. His reserve seemed so wrong. What made a young and vibrant gentleman like him behave like an old vicar? Again, heartbreak seemed the most likely answer.

But how could she find out for certain?

She'd hardly seen him since his abrupt departure from the river yesterday. He seemed to be making himself scarce, only appearing at dinner last night. He'd barely looked at her during the meal, and he'd hardly spoken. When he excused himself for the evening, Cecelia felt quite dissatisfied. He'd permitted her a glimpse of how delightful he could be, but then retreated behind a wall of polite reserve. She wanted the company of the man she'd glimpsed at the river. The man who'd laughed freely and made her laugh as well.

Why had he so abruptly become so reserved? And why

was he so seemingly determined to deflect her attempts to try to find out more about him?

His grandmother was no help at all. Mrs. Stewart also evaded nearly every question Cecelia asked about Mr. Wright's background, so skillfully that Cecelia had the distinct impression she had been doing so for some time. Therefore, Cecelia had been left few options but to press Reed for any information she could learn about him from the staff.

Reed had gathered Cecelia's hair into a loose chignon, leaving some ringlets to hang free. Now she gently slid pins into Cecelia's blond curls to hold them in place.

"This morning," Reed said, "I had the chance to ask Alfred if Mr. Wright had his heart broken, as you suspect, but just like Jenna, Alfred seemed to know nothing." Reed paused to re-pin one curl. "Oh, but I did learn that Mr. Wright prefers to hire servants who have relatives who were in the Royal Navy."

"The navy?" Cecelia said. How interesting. "Like Mr. Long?"

Reed nodded. "Mr. Long and Mrs. Thornton both lost sons at sea, and Jenna and Alfred lost their fathers."

An odd coincidence, especially so far from the coast.

"Did they know each other," Cecelia said, "their relatives in the navy?"

"I don't think so. Mr. Long's son and Jenna's father both were lost at sea, but several years apart. Alfred's father died in a sea battle against the French."

"And Mrs. Thornton's son?"

"I'm not certain. Apparently, she almost never speaks of it, not even to Jenna. But Jenna told me that…" Reed glanced toward the door, as if listening for footfalls, then she whispered, "Jenna said that after Mrs. Thornton had been drinking a great deal last Christmas, she overheard her talking with Mr. Long about their sons. And thought she heard her mention that he died on the *Sentinel*."

"Oh no," Cecelia murmured. "How sad."

Every English citizen knew the tragic tale of the Royal Navy sloop *Sentinel* and its disastrous encounter with the now infamous merchant ship called the *Fortune*. Ten years ago, the commander of the naval vessel had stopped the *Fortune* as the merchant ship was returning to England. The navy commander intended to impress some of the *Fortune*'s sailors into duty on a large frigate nearby.

Shockingly, the captain and crew of the *Fortune* resisted. The encounter resulted in the deaths of over a dozen navy sailors, including the *Sentinel*'s commanding officer. Several dozen recently impressed men already on the *Sentinel* had taken advantage of the confusion to desert, adding to the chaos and allowing the *Fortune* to escape.

If Mrs. Thornton's son had been part of that tragedy, it wasn't surprising that the woman wouldn't speak of it.

"Yes, so sad," Reed said, speaking at a normal volume once again. "Oh, and apparently, Mr. Wright also gave Mr. Long instructions that for any new servants hired for your visit, he was to offer the job to a sailor's relative first."

Cecelia frowned. "Does Mr. Wright have family in the navy?"

Reed shook her head. "Not that I've heard."

He said his father had been a gentleman, not a sailor. And he had no other family now besides his grandmother. So why would he take such a particular interest in navy families?

"And he was never in the Royal Navy?" Cecelia asked.

"Only the army, at least as far as anyone says." Reed adjusted the final pin in Cecelia's hair. "It seems that Mr. Wright says it's all to honor a friend who was a sailor and died at sea, but he gives no more details than that. The servants think it's too painful for him to speak of."

Too painful to speak of? That must have been a very dear friend, indeed.

"Oh," Reed added, "but I did learn that he doesn't often attend balls because he was wounded in the arm while in the army. Supposedly the injury bothers him from time to time."

"Yes, that's what his grandmother told me," Cecelia said. "However, I've noticed that the injury doesn't seem to bother him while riding. Or building fences." That very morning she had seen him doing both when she just happened to go for a walk near him.

First, she'd strolled by the stables when he was preparing for a ride. He hadn't seemed to notice her as he'd started out, looking impressively athletic in his riding clothes. Later in the day, she had walked by a farm where he was helping a tenant and witnessed him swinging a hammer, looking anything but infirm. She had felt rather breathless herself just from watching him.

His every movement, no matter what he had been doing these past few days, was graceful and strong, with no hint of any injury. The more she pondered the matter, the more she believed he was lying about his reasons for not attending the ball.

He was clearly not socializing on purpose, and most likely because he was avoiding situations that might lead to matchmaking. But if she was to draw him out into society, which she was determined to do, she first had to understand what kept him away. Perhaps tonight at the ball she might discover more from his neighbors.

"There, milady." Reed smoothed one last curl and smiled at Cecelia's reflection. "Now, which gown will you wear?"

Two trunks of clothing had arrived that morning from Wareton Manor, providing far more options than the few dresses Cecelia had taken with her to London.

"The white floral," Cecelia said. The white floral was fashionable but not too daring, and therefore an excellent choice in an unfamiliar setting. It was also similar to the walking dress she'd worn while fishing. Mr. Wright had seemed to admire that dress. She had caught him glancing at her figure more than once, though he had tried to hide it. But that was certainly not why she had decided upon a similar gown tonight. Indeed, he might not even see it.

Reed smiled as she helped Cecelia into the gown. "You look so beautiful," Reed said. "No one will be able to take their eyes off you."

She helped Cecelia with her jewelry: dangling sapphire earrings and a silver necklace that drew attention to the gown's low neckline. Cecelia dabbed lavender perfume on her wrists and neck. She was looking forward to the evening, even if Mr. Wright would not be attending.

"And you'll be dining with the others tonight?" Cecelia asked Reed. At breakfast, she'd heard that the servants were planning a special dinner together while she and Mrs. Stewart were out.

Reed's smile faded. "I…am not sure."

"Why not?" Cecelia frowned. "They did include you?"

"Yes. Mr. Long invited me."

"Well then, do you not wish to go?"

Reed briefly met her gaze before looking away and pursing her lips, as she often did whenever she was reluctant to say something.

"What is it?" Cecelia said. "You might as well tell me now, for you know I'll have it out of you anyway."

Reed said quietly, "Please do not make a fuss."

Cecelia crossed her arms. She would make no such promise, and Reed knew it.

Reed sighed. "Most of the staff are welcoming, and Mr. Long, especially so. It's only…the maid hired to help while we're here. She has an aunt from my village and so…she knows about me."

"Does she?" Cecelia said, her pulse speeding up. "What happened?"

"Nothing. I don't think she has told anyone else, not

yet, anyway. But she made a point of mentioning to me where her aunt lived, and I could tell she doesn't think highly of me and…well, it simply might be best if I didn't go tonight."

Cecelia uncrossed her arms. "Help me with my shoes and gloves, please."

"Milady," Reed said quietly as she laid the shoes out for her. "There is no need to do anything."

"Do what? I cannot imagine what you mean." Cecelia stepped into her shoes a bit more forcefully than usual. Reed helped her slide on her gloves, and Cecelia added, "I think I shall go downstairs early." *And have a word with someone.*

With any luck, she might even kill two birds with one stone.

Cecelia headed to the library, where Jenna had said she would find Mr. Wright. Normally when she had this type of problem, she could rely on others, such as Edmund, to help her. But here in Westbury, she alone must defend Reed. At least no one she would face at Westbury, not even Mrs. Thornton, was as fearsome as her aunt. Perhaps she could even resolve the problem with Reed and use it as an opportunity to learn more about the enigmatic Mr. Grim.

She stepped into the library and immediately spotted Mr. Wright's tall form across the room. He stood with his back to her, apparently reshelving some books. He must have heard her shoes on the carpet because he paused, a book in hand, and turned to face her.

As his gaze fell on her, he appeared startled, but then his expression softened. He favored her with only the briefest smile, and yet she suddenly found it oddly difficult to breathe.

Why exactly had she come in here?

"Lady Cecelia," he said, in his delightfully deep voice, "is there something I can do for you?"

Go fishing with me again and this time, kiss me.

What on earth? No, she was not here to entertain such…inappropriate thoughts. She had a serious purpose. First, she must help Reed.

"Yes," she managed. "I do need your help."

He raised an eyebrow and gently slid the book onto the shelf. Then he strolled closer, pausing only a few feet away and leaning with one arm against a nearby chair. His gaze slowly swept over her body before settling on her face. His expression was annoyingly inscrutable.

How could he possibly look even more handsome now than yesterday? And did he like her gown or not? She did not care, truly.

"How may I be of assistance?" he said.

Another shamefully inappropriate thought threatened her traitorous mind, but she ruthlessly squashed it.

"It is a matter of some delicacy," she said.

His shrewd gaze remained fixed on her. "I am quite intrigued."

Despite the unlit hearth, the room abruptly felt far too warm.

"It is…regarding the new maid," she managed.

"The new maid?" He straightened. "Have you spoken with my grandmother about it? Or Mrs. Thornton?"

"No. I wished to speak with you first."

He frowned. "I fear I have been a neglectful host. I have not ensured that your needs have been met, but instead I have left it all up to others."

She shook her head. "No, it is not from any neglect that I wish to speak with you. It is because, well, at the heart of the matter is a subject that you might best address."

He looked bewildered. "And what subject is that?"

"Military service."

His eyes widened and then very slowly, he crossed his arms.

"You see," she continued, trying not to speak too quickly, "Reed did not wish me to say anything, but I learned that the new maid has a connection to Reed's village and was speaking ill of her."

His dark eyes narrowed as he waited silently for her to explain further.

No doubt the entire household would learn about Reed soon enough. Therefore, she should present Reed's story as it ought to be told and recount it directly to Mr. Wright, whose opinion would likely carry the most influence.

"Reed is the eldest of three," she said quietly, to lessen the chance any servants might overhear, "and she lost her mother as a child. Several years ago, her father became unable to take care of the family, so it was left to Reed." Cecelia paused. "She was caught stealing, but it was only to help them."

His brow furrowed. "Is this what Reed meant when she said in London that she would gladly suffer worse for you?"

He had a remarkably good memory.

She nodded. "Yes. I employed her when my aunt was against it. I felt it wrong that Reed be kept from honest work because of her past, especially when her transgression was done solely to help her family." She paused and added, "Besides, once she had work, she would no longer need to resort to stealing."

He was still frowning. Was he displeased that someone who was the subject of such gossip had been brought to his home?

"Why couldn't Reed's father take care of his family?" he asked.

"He was in the army. He was wounded and discharged, but there were rumors that he had been injured…while attempting to desert. No cowardice was ever proven," she added quickly, "but the rumors persisted and made life difficult for him. He drank heavily, and eventually…he took his own life."

Surprise filled his expression for an instant before his eyes narrowed once again.

She clasped her hands together nervously. She'd hoped that he would be especially sympathetic about such matters. So much about him, including his own military service, Adrian's regard for him, and his concern for sailors, suggested he was a gentleman of great compassion. But as he continued to stare at her silently, her pulse sped up. What if she was mistaken about him?

She drew a deep breath. Well, if she had to defend Reed further, she would. She usually found a way to defend others, even to her aunt, though she might not dare to do so directly. After her aunt had railed against employing Reed as her lady's maid, Cecelia had told Edmund. Edmund was a fierce believer in second chances, and he had joined her in arguing Reed's case to Adrian. Together they had won him over, and in the end, Adrian had forced her aunt to concede.

But here in Westbury, there was no one else to enlist to speak up for Reed. Cecelia must defend her alone.

Mr. Wright stared at her, his face like a mask. "How unfortunate," he finally said, "that Reed and her family should suffer so greatly for her father's behavior."

"Yes." She let out a long breath. He did agree with her, thank heavens. But there was an odd edge to his tone.

Perhaps she should have ended the conversation there, but more words seemed to flow of their own accord. "But even to judge her father seems unfair," she said, desperate to gain his further understanding. She wanted reassurance that he was truly as compassionate as she'd hoped.

He raised an eyebrow. "But desertion is a grave offense."

His voice was strangely slow and deliberate. "Do you mean because there was no proof?"

She shook her head. "Even if there were evidence, whatever happened, no one else can know what was in his heart, what he suffered…" Once she had started, the words flooded out. She had argued this point before when discussing Reed and her father with Edmund and Adrian. "I believe no one else can truly judge such matters," she said, "at least not someone who has not been in similar circumstances. I know that I cannot."

She met his gaze again. He was looking at her oddly, with one eyebrow still raised, but now with a hint of a smile.

"I admire your compassion," he said softly. "Very much."

His tone and the way his gaze slid over her as he spoke made her feel warm. Likely her face was turning pink, as it often did when she was embarrassed.

She hardly deserved his compliment, truthfully.

"I must confess that played only a small part in hiring Reed," she said. Of course she felt compassion for Reed and bristled at the injustice of her situation, as many would, but Cecelia was acting in self-interest as well. Reed was highly competent, being both naturally skilled and having worked as a lady's maid before being unfairly dismissed. Even more so, Cecelia simply liked her.

"Whatever her past," she said, "she was who I wanted for my lady's maid." Cecelia had also insisted that Reed receive the respect of being addressed by her last name, as befitted an exceptionally skilled lady's maid. "She was best suited to the position."

"Of course," he said. "Although it seems that Reed has fallen short in one regard." His expression was now grave.

She stiffened. "What do you mean?"

"She lacks your defensive skill with bags." He grinned.

He was joking, after all this? If she had a bag in her hand this instant, she would be tempted to wallop him with it for allowing her to fear, if only for a moment, how he'd react.

But then he took a step closer, and her pulse quickened again.

His smile faded. He was gazing at her as he had during that moment while fishing, that moment when she'd thought he wanted to kiss her.

Would he dare do something so inappropriate? Would his hair feel as silken as she imagined if she held him close for a kiss?

Heat rose in her face, and she forced her gaze away from him. What was the matter with her? She had an understanding with another gentleman. She should not be having such thoughts about anyone else.

She tried to focus. What else had she sought him out for? Oh yes, to ask him about—

Noise from the hall interrupted her thoughts. Slow, scuffing sounds, growing louder.

The dog appeared in the doorway and shuffled into the room. He looked odd, his fur darker and shinier than usual.

"Why is he…wet?" she said.

"Urchin likes to cool off in the river sometimes." Sadly—no, thankfully—Mr. Wright was no longer looking at her. He moved to the dog, crouched down, and began scratching behind Urchin's ears. "Don't you, old boy?" he said softly.

She followed him and stopped a few feet away. "He can walk that far?"

"It takes him a while, but yes, he still manages it. He's always loved the water." Mr. Wright sighed and sorrow filled his expression as he continued to pet the dog. He was gazing at the animal with nearly as much affection as Mrs. Thornton did.

"Mrs. Thornton dotes on him so much," Cecelia said, "almost as if he is her child."

"Yes, Urchin is the closest thing she has left to one." He frowned, as if he regretted what he'd said, and he abruptly stood.

Before she could ask another question, footfalls sounded in the hall—heavy, determined steps. Mrs. Thornton marched into the room.

"Oh, there he is," the housekeeper said, her voice soft. "He needs to dry off by a fire." She bent down and scooped up the dog. "Not in this drafty library."

"Before you go, Mrs. Thornton," Mr. Wright said, "I must speak with you."

Still patting Urchin, Mrs. Thornton said, "Yes?"

More footfalls sounded in the hall and Mrs. Stewart glided into the room. She had not yet changed into her evening attire.

"There you are," Mrs. Stewart said, stopping beside the housekeeper. "If you would be so kind as to help me with my gown, Mrs. Thornton." Mrs. Stewart frowned as she glanced between Cecelia and Mr. Wright.

"Certainly," the housekeeper said. "After I finish speaking with Mr. Wright."

"You should hear what I have to say as well," he said, looking to his grandmother. He cleared his throat. "Lady Cecelia has informed me that the new maid is aware of some unfortunate events in Reed's past, and the maid implied to Reed that she might share them." He then recounted the details. As he spoke, both Mrs. Thornton and Mrs. Stewart's eyes widened, and they glanced between Cecelia and Mr. Wright.

"I am certain," he continued, "that we shall all ensure the matter is handled correctly. Reed has suffered enough hardship, and I'll not have her treated badly here. However, the new maid may stay, so long as she understands we'll not tolerate unkind gossip."

Cecelia couldn't help but smile. He was showing kindness to Reed and kindness to the other maid. The perfect response. Truly, he was a good man. A very good man.

Mrs. Thornton frowned, but she nodded at Mr. Wright.

"Of course, James," Mrs. Stewart said in a rush. "I shall make sure of it. But now, enough about that…" She took a deep breath and turned toward Cecelia. "I see you are dressed for the ball." Her voice still held a tremor of some strong emotion. "You look lovely."

"Thank you," Cecelia said. From the corner of her eye, she could tell Mr. Wright was staring at her, but she resisted the urge to look at him.

"I cannot wait to introduce you to our neighbors," Mrs. Stewart said, her voice normal once again.

"I am looking forward to it," Cecelia said sincerely. "I always enjoy music, and dancing, and meeting new people." She finally allowed herself to glance at Mr. Wright.

She swore that longing flashed in his expression, just as she'd noticed that first night at dinner.

"I'm so pleased," Mrs. Stewart said.

At that moment, Long entered the library.

"This just arrived for you, milady," Long said, handing Cecelia a letter.

As Cecelia thanked Long, Mr. Wright turned and strolled several paces away. Mr. Wright appeared to be scanning the bookshelves, but he seemed to watch her out of the corner of his eye. Was he curious about her letter?

After Long left, Mrs. Stewart and Mrs. Thornton continued to stare at Cecelia, both still frowning.

Cecelia scanned the writing on the outside of the folded paper. The somewhat messy script was distinctly William's.

"Is it from one of your brothers?" Mrs. Stewart asked.

"No," Cecelia said. "It is from Mr. Trent." Despite their understanding, Cecelia wondered if Mrs. Stewart might disapprove of her receiving a letter from a gentleman. But Mrs. Stewart smiled. It seemed the welcome reminder that Cecelia was romantically involved outweighed her usual sense of propriety.

"How lovely," Mrs. Stewart said with a sigh. "If you will excuse me, I must finish dressing, so I'll leave you to enjoy your letter." She glanced at Mrs. Thornton. "If you could please assist me, Mrs. Thornton."

"Of course," the housekeeper said.

Mrs. Stewart started to turn away but paused, her gaze darting between Mr. Wright and Cecelia.

"James," Mrs. Stewart said, "I believe Alfred was looking for you earlier."

"Yes," he said, not looking away from the bookshelf. "I'll find him shortly."

"I think it was a matter of some urgency," Mrs. Stewart said.

Was she concerned about leaving her alone with Mr. Wright? Cecelia's face warmed. How ridiculous.

"I said I will speak to him shortly," Mr. Wright answered, an edge to his voice.

"Very well." Mrs. Stewart slowly turned and left, with Mrs. Thornton close behind her.

Cecelia considered returning to her room to read the letter. She glanced at Mr. Wright, who still appeared engrossed in searching for a book. Hadn't he been scanning the same shelf for a long time?

If he had simply been curious about who the message was from, he knew now. She would have expected him to go find Alfred. Was he truly merely interested in looking at books?

She found herself oddly reluctant to leave. It wasn't so much that she wanted to be near him, no, but the chair by the closest window did look quite inviting. So she sat, smoothed her gown, and then gently broke the wax seal on the letter.

Out of the corner of her eye, she could see that Mr. Wright had shifted closer. He had selected a book and was now slowly leafing through the pages. He looked so handsome.

But why was she so distracted when she had a letter from William?

She forced her thoughts from Mr. Wright and began to read.

Lady Cecelia, I must beg your forgiveness for not going to London as planned.

She gasped. William hadn't merely been late? He had never gone to London at all?

She tightened her grip on the letter. Her face suddenly felt hot. Without looking directly toward him, she could tell Mr. Wright had turned to look at her.

Perhaps she should have taken the letter to her room to read after all. Well, she would not flee now. She took a deep, calming breath and tried to force a placid expression. But her pulse raced.

How on earth could William have abandoned her, after she had traveled to London to meet him?

"Is everything all right?" Mr. Wright asked.

"Yes," she said, glancing at him. "It's fine." At least he didn't look pleased that she was upset at William's letter. She forced her attention back to the page.

Shortly before I was to leave for London, my father learned of our plans and forbade me from eloping. I sent an urgent message to you, but the messenger was unable to reach you.

She took another deep breath. Yes, she was angry, but she must remember that William's father was a formidable man who had a reputation for always getting his way. He also controlled the purse strings for the entire family, so William could not easily defy him.

Still, she was shocked that William had not traveled to London himself to tell her about the change of plans, even if only to escort her safely home. Then again, perhaps she should be more understanding. She certainly knew what it was to lack the fortitude to stand up to someone, and Mr. Trent was one of the few people who seemed as fearsome as her aunt. She must put her anger—no, her annoyance—aside, and not allow this disappointment to ruin her plans to marry William.

Still feeling Mr. Wright's stare, she tried to appear calm as she continued to read.

My manservant did receive the messages you left for me in London, and he relayed them to me. I was naturally overjoyed to learn your brother is considering giving us his blessing. However, soon after, my father made it clear that he will not support our plans to travel. Please know that I tried to persuade him, but he is immoveable on the matter. I cannot go against his wishes, nor can I ask you to give up your cherished dream of traveling. Therefore, though it pains me deeply, I must release you from our understanding. Since almost no one knew of it, I believe this can be done without harm to your reputation.

William was ending their understanding?

Her heart began to race. She read the rest of the letter.

I am deeply sorry. Knowing your kind and generous nature, I hope it is not too much to ask that you consider forgiving me for disappointing you.

Your devoted friend,

William Trent

She stared at the paper, stunned. Knots seemed to form in her stomach. Not long ago, William had said that he wanted to travel as she did, and he spoke with such passion as to be utterly convincing. Yet he had conceded to his father so quickly?

Adrian's warnings about him leaped to mind. How she did not know him long enough to be fully aware of his faults. She recalled Edmund's words that Trent was unworthy of her.

No, they couldn't be correct. Could they?

During those weeks before they tried to elope, she

had imagined all the wonderful new places they would discover together and the beginning of what she hoped would be a quite satisfactory marriage. William had truly seemed to share her determination to travel. And yet, his father had quite easily convinced William to abandon their plans.

Then she recalled what Mr. Wright had said about William during their trip to Westbury. How he threw himself enthusiastically into different pursuits, but only for brief periods of time. His desire to travel had apparently proved just as short-lived.

Her face felt hot again as realization burned through her.

She had liked William in large part for his agreeable nature, not considering that perhaps he was too agreeable, too easily led by others, and especially by his father, who apparently intended to control his son in all matters.

What a fool she was.

Adrian had been right. And Edmund. And even Mr. Wright. Perhaps their reasons were different, but they were correct—William Trent was not the right husband for her.

Forcing back tears, she refolded the message. As she stumbled to her feet, Mr. Wright strode forward and stopped close to her.

"Are you quite well?" His gentle tone only made her feel worse. "Your letter seems to have upset you."

"No, I…" She met his gaze. His dark eyes were full of concern. "Yes. It has." What was the point in pretending? He could tell she was lying. Not to mention that he would learn soon enough, anyway. "I…have something I must tell you."

"What is it?"

"I…appreciate all that you and your grandmother have

done for me," she said quietly, "but it seems that I shall not have to impose on you much longer."

He frowned and stepped even closer. "What do you mean?"

"Because," she said, meeting his far too intense gaze, "I am not marrying Mr. Trent."

CHAPTER NINE

I AM NOT MARRYING MR. TRENT.
James stared down at Lady Cecelia. No doubt surprise was showing on his face, but hopefully little else. He concentrated on not looking too pleased at her words. Or too alarmed.

"So tomorrow," she said, "I shall write to my brother and let him know, and I will make arrangements to leave Westbury."

"Mr. Trent," he said, still disbelieving. "Ended the engagement. To you."

She nodded.

"Why on earth?" he asked.

She took a deep breath. "He said that…his father did not approve of our plans to travel. He will not go against his father, and he knows how much it means to me, therefore he felt it only right to release me from the understanding."

He frowned. "If anyone learns—"

"That is unlikely. Our understanding was a secret, and his father will wish to conceal any hint of scandal."

"I suppose that is true." Hopefully she was correct and her reputation would be untouched.

"I am relieved, actually," she said. "Even if we could travel, I would not be content married to him, not when he is so easily ruled by his father." She shook her head. "I have lived long enough under my aunt's control. I'll not accept it in a father-in-law."

Her forehead wrinkled and her eyes shone with

determination. She'd looked the same when he'd seen her preparing to do other difficult tasks—stand up to Mrs. Thornton, attempt to pry information from his grandmother, or question him about his past. Once again, he admired her resolve.

"And," she added, an edge to her voice, "it seems that while I waited for Will—Mr. Trent—in London, he never even left his home."

"He…what?" Trent was even less trustworthy than James had believed.

"He did send a message to let me know." But her tone made clear that she knew that was not enough. A decent gentleman would have gone himself to ensure her safety.

"Inexcusable," he muttered.

"Perhaps." She sighed. "Anyway, apparently my brothers—and you—were correct about me being foolish for wanting to marry him." Her voice wavered, as if she was holding back tears, but she tilted up her head and held his gaze. "Go ahead and say so and be done with it."

He stared back at her in silence.

Yes, he had thought her foolish. And of course, he was glad she was not going to marry the scoundrel, but did she expect him to gloat over her disappointment?

Perhaps she had reason to believe that he would. He had often been too blunt and outspoken with her. Even now, he was somewhat tempted to rail against Trent as a prospective match and remind her how much better off she would be without him. But seeing the pain and disappointment in her expression, what he really wanted at the moment was…to ease her sadness.

He should not give in to such soft emotion. Her heartache was not his concern, and he *must* keep his distance. He should be civil but, above all, reserved. Others might comfort her over her disappointment—it need not be him.

Except that he very much wanted it to be him.

"Mr. Trent is the foolish one," he said, "for not eloping with you when he had the chance."

She smiled briefly before the sadness returned to her expression. Her gaze again dropped to the floor. She clearly believed he was only being kind, when in truth, he meant those words. Deeply.

The pain in her eyes suggested that she had formed an attachment to Trent—the wretched, undeserving scoundrel.

His chest tightened as jealousy washed over him.

While fishing with her yesterday, he had felt more happiness than he had known in years. Until he had remembered that he never should have allowed himself to be so unguarded in his behavior.

So this morning he had risen early to avoid seeing her at breakfast, and he'd kept away from the house most of the day. Only at dinner last night had he allowed himself to briefly indulge in her company. After all, it would be rude to completely avoid her. But he was careful not to let his guard down as he had when they had fished together.

Perhaps he was becoming a bit infatuated with her, but still he had felt in control of his emotions.

Until today.

The moment she'd walked into the library with her hair artfully arranged in curls that begged to be disheveled by his hands, and in her stunning pale gown with the delightfully low neckline, he'd been distracted enough, finding it difficult to not stare at her like a fool.

When she'd said she'd sought him out and that she'd wanted to speak with him first, he'd been ridiculously intrigued. But even that paled in comparison to when she'd defended Reed and her father. The passionate earnestness in her voice and expression had magnified her beauty, striking him to the core.

Confusion and longing had engulfed him—to do what

exactly, he wasn't sure. Learn her secrets. Make her laugh. Kiss her. And when he'd stepped toward her, she had seemed startled, in a way that suggested she might have noticed him gaping at her. At least she had no idea how deeply her words had affected him.

How could she?

Ardently defending her maid for stealing was kind and admirable enough, but she had not stopped there. She had defended Reed's father with equal fervor. She had evidently pondered the man's suffering a great deal, and her compassion was so genuine, James could not help but be deeply moved.

He had tried to hide it. Tried to hide that her words moved him so because of his own memories of similar circumstances. And most of all, he'd tried to hide his realization that his efforts to distance himself from her had failed. Spectacularly.

Since he first set eyes on her he'd found her distracting, but now he knew too much about her to dismiss her as merely an attractive woman who he longed to bed. He felt as if he were standing at the edge of a precipice—one he imprudently wished to jump off.

"Trent is a fool for letting you go," he said. "I will also say, that while I agree ending it is for the best, you are wiser than your family in at least one regard."

Her eyes widened and she met his gaze. "What is that?"

"The Trent family is growing in influence," he said, "and a background in trade matters far less than it once did. I agree that in that regard, such an alliance could have been of great benefit."

She gazed at him in silence for a moment, then slowly smiled. "Thank you," she said softly.

That his small acknowledgment of her foresight could have such an impact on her suggested how little her opinion was valued in her family. That also annoyed him, far more than he had any right to feel on her behalf. If it had only taken him a **few days** to realize how insightful she was, how could her own family not see it?

She continued to gaze up at him with such warmth that he had to resist the desire to step even closer to her. Her effect on him was…intoxicating. And alarming.

Then all too soon the warmth in her gaze faded, and her expression was again sad.

"Despite your disappointment," he said quietly, "you will still attend the ball?" Not only had she admitted that she'd been foolish, painful as it was, now she apparently refused to give in to self-pity.

She tilted up her head at him. "Of course I shall attend. I have been looking forward to it, as has your grandmother, and the Mercers are expecting me." She paused. "Even after such a disappointment, I'll not miss such an exciting evening, not hide myself away. That would be—" Her gaze stopped on him, her lovely blue eyes widened, and she quickly glanced away. "That is to say, the evening will be the distraction I need."

But he knew what had stopped her, what she'd been thinking. That hiding away would be cowardly, that it was not the way to deal with problems, as he was doing. Perhaps she wrongly believed a romantic disappointment had him avoiding socializing, but in essence, she was correct. He was hiding. As he should. For just this one evening, however, he very much wanted not to hide.

He wanted to go to the ball. With her. He wanted to indulge in what many other gentlemen took for granted—enjoying an evening out without reservation, including the company of a captivating woman.

Although in just these past few moments, since she had announced the end of her understanding with Trent, she had become far more dangerous. Now she was an eligible young lady—precisely the type of woman he should avoid.

A jolt of apprehension shot through him, which he promptly ignored.

Soon she would leave Westbury, likely never to return. She was too far above him in circumstances to seriously consider him as a suitor. Furthermore, she clearly wanted a husband who was eager to travel—something out of the question for him.

So what was the harm in letting his guard down for just one evening? She was, after all, his friend's sister and she'd suffered a great disappointment. If he could ease her distress by distracting her from her troubles, he should. He was not behaving imprudently, not really. Or even if he was, he was risking no one's feelings but his own.

Pushing aside all the wisdom that had kept him safe these past years, he said, "I believe that I will attend tonight after all."

Her beautiful eyes widened. "You will?"

"I will." He recklessly added, "If you will dance with me."

Then she smiled, fully and brilliantly, a smile that made him feel ridiculously happy.

He knew immediately that he'd made a terrible mistake. Even worse, he did not care.

CHAPTER TEN

CECELIA HAD NEVER ENJOYED POOR dancing until tonight.

While Mr. Wright seemed somewhat familiar with the quadrille, he was clearly out of practice. He quickly improved, however, working through the complicated steps with good humor and without throwing off the pattern. From the way many other young ladies nearby were watching him intently, Cecelia suspected they would also forgive his less-than-perfect dancing.

He looked especially handsome, dressed more formally than she'd seen before. His dark jacket and trousers were tailored flawlessly to his muscular body, and his hair appealingly disheveled.

But what made him even more striking this evening was his happiness and lack of reserve. His manner was as open as when they fished together. And his behavior was clearly out of character, evidenced by the surprised and intrigued looks of many people around them—and the increasingly displeased glances from his grandmother.

Mrs. Stewart had seemed quite put out by her grandson's decision to join them, and she had barely spoken during the carriage ride to the ball. Once inside the candlelit ballroom, Mrs. Stewart had assumed a pleasant demeanor, but whenever she looked at Cecelia and Mr. Wright, her eyes narrowed.

His grandmother was wrong, though, if she believed Mr. Wright had any serious interest in her. He was only being kind because of her message from William. If he occasionally cast a lingering glance her way, it was no different than what many gentlemen did, signaling a notice of her appearance, but nothing deeper.

After all, they were hardly a suitable match even if Mr. Wright intended to marry, which he clearly did not. And soon enough she would be leaving Westbury—which would make Mrs. Stewart exceedingly happy once she learned of it—and in the meantime, Cecelia was determined to enjoy herself. She refused to let even her disappointment with William ruin what was likely one of her last evenings in Westbury.

And she was enjoying herself far more than she had expected. She was even feeling more relieved than sad about William. Only because it had allowed her to recognize William's true character, of course, not for any other reason. It certainly had absolutely nothing to do with Mr. Wright, pleased as she was that he'd decided to accompany them tonight.

She kept thinking about how, rather than gloating over her broken engagement as she'd feared, Mr. Wright had seemed genuinely sympathetic. Even more surprising was his acknowledgment that she was correct about the benefits of an alliance with the Trent family. He hadn't done it merely to cheer her up either, as he had seemed quite sincere.

And now, not only had he suddenly decided to attend the ball, but even though he said he never danced, he had asked her. He was obviously attempting to distract her from her disappointment with William. The idea that Mr. Wright was going to such lengths to cheer her up pleased her. And the way he gazed at her as they danced, with such openness and warmth, made her feel almost giddy.

Over the last few years, she had enjoyed more than one evening when the dancing had been particularly agreeable. Even a few nights that had seemed close to magical. But tonight, this otherwise seemingly ordinary country ball with mostly strangers and now a less-than-polished dance partner, was somehow outshining the happiest of those evenings.

She tried not to dwell on the possibility that a good part of the reason was because whenever Mr. Wright took her hand or moved close, she was intensely aware of him. Each time such thoughts threatened to overwhelm her, she quickly pushed them away. The emotional tumult of the day no doubt had her confused. That was surely the reason for the intensity of her feelings, feelings that were difficult to sort through at present.

One thing was certain: she was even more determined to help Mr. Wright. Before this evening was over, she must learn why he was usually so reclusive. In the short time she had left in Westbury, she must do all she could to help him enjoy more wonderful evenings like this one.

When they paused dancing, waiting to the side while other couples had their turns, she gathered her courage.

"Tell me why," she said, "when you so clearly enjoy balls, you usually avoid them? And please do not say it is about your arm."

He frowned. Perhaps she had been too bold and he was about to close himself off again. But thankfully, his smile returned.

"That is why," he murmured, glancing toward a group of young ladies and their mamas watching them. "Surely you see them closing in."

"Yes. And now that you've proven you will dance, you will be expected to have the good manners to partner with many others."

His smile faltered, but only for a moment. "I was hoping my poor footwork might frighten them off." He leaned closer until his arm brushed hers, sending a delightful shiver through her.

Trying not to be distracted, she quickly said, "It will

take a great deal more than that to frighten them off." Did he truly not realize how attractive he was?

He sighed. "Very well. I will do my duty and dance with more ladies." As they rejoined the dance, he added, "But I am certain that no other partner shall prove as enjoyable as you."

His startling words caused her pulse to speed up even before she'd taken a step. She nearly forgot the pattern for a dance she'd known for years. Another moment passed before she realized that he hadn't truly answered her question. He was once again distracting her from asking about him.

"Why do you usually avoid gatherings?" she said when they danced close.

"As I have told you before," he said, "I have no plans to marry and no wish to raise false hopes." There was an edge to his voice and a hint of sadness in his expression that made her certain there was more to it.

"But could you not simply make it clear you are a confirmed bachelor and still enjoy yourself?" she asked.

"I am this evening."

True enough. She should not press him when he clearly didn't wish to speak of it, but she could not help herself.

The next time during the dance when she had the opportunity she asked gently, "Did someone…disappoint you?"

He glanced at her, silent for a moment. "No," he finally said. He smiled, but for the first time that evening, his smile did not reach his eyes.

Was he lying, and he was in fact suffering from a broken heart? He certainly seemed to be hiding something. And he was quiet for the remainder of the dance and smiled less often, implying that she had gone too far with her questions.

But when the dance ended, he kept hold of her hand and shifted closer.

"If you are not already engaged for the waltz," he said, "will you dance with me again?"

She stared at him in surprise. Although they were an unlikely match, with his uncharacteristic behavior this evening, no doubt there was already speculation about them. To dance a second time would make an attachment, or at the least a flirtation, a certainty in many people's eyes. Even though no one had claimed that dance, prudence dictated that she should decline. If her aunt were present, she would be furious if Cecelia danced twice with a gentleman whom she would consider so unsuitable. No doubt Mrs. Stewart would be equally displeased.

"I believe," he added, "that you are one lady with whom I might dance without any danger of raising false hopes."

He was saying she was safe. She should be relieved. Instead, disappointment rippled through her. But of course, he was correct.

Wonderful as his company was tonight, he was an unsuitable match for her. While he was a gentleman, he was one of modest wealth and few connections, not someone who would be considered a fitting husband for the sister of an earl. Furthermore, even if they had been well-matched, and even if he wished to marry, he wanted a completely different life than she did.

He clearly desired a quiet existence in the country without even regular trips to London. Much as she enjoyed the country at times, the idea of a lifetime without travel was horribly depressing. And imagining Mr. Wright spending many more years in such a fashion made her truly sad—though she knew she had no right to feel so.

"Is dancing with me again such a momentous decision?" he asked with a hint of a smile.

No. Of the many mildly rebellious and gossip-inciting things she had done in her twenty-one years, this was perhaps the easiest decision of them all.

She returned his smile. "I would be delighted to dance with you again."

He nodded and opened his mouth to respond when a strident voice interrupted.

"Lady Cecelia!" Mary Mercer, daughter of Viscount Mercer, was approaching quickly through the crowd, her gaze fixed on Cecelia. Cecelia had only spoken with her briefly after they'd been introduced earlier.

Mr. Wright inclined his head at Miss Mercer, but he turned away as a gentleman nearby drew him into conversation.

"I am so pleased to have a chance to speak with you further, Lady Cecelia," Miss Mercer said, stopping in front of Cecelia. She had chestnut hair and warm brown eyes, and she was the same height as Cecelia. "We may have only spoken briefly three years ago, but I recall enjoying our conversation very much. You were, of course, Miss Sinclair, then."

Cecelia stiffened. People rarely reminded her that she had become Lady Cecelia only recently, after her brother had inherited the earldom from a cousin. Eventually she had been officially granted the same title and precedence as if her own father had been an earl. When people did remind her of that fact, it was often done unkindly. Yet she sensed no malice in Miss Mercer's dimpled smile.

"How delighted I was," Miss Mercer continued, "to learn you were the Lady Cecelia visiting Westbury."

Cecelia smiled. "I am delighted to be here—"

"We were all quite surprised to hear of your visit," Miss Mercer said in a rush. "No one knew that Mr. Wright and Mrs. Stewart were at all connected to the Earl of Wareton."

Cecelia nodded. "By now, you have no doubt heard that Mr. Wright served with my brother—"

"Indeed," Miss Mercer said, "and how like Mr. Wright to be modest about such a connection. We are so glad to have you in Westbury to liven things up. It can get so dreadfully dull here." Miss Mercer leaned closer. "Of course, you must meet so many fascinating gentlemen in London. How I envy you being able to go so often! I am forced to remain here most of the year. My father says the city air is harmful." She sighed dramatically. "However, I am journeying there within a fortnight, for the first time in ages. Will you be in town soon?" She finally paused for breath.

Cecelia smiled again. "I am not certain."

Miss Mercer looked briefly disappointed before her smile returned. "And how delightful that Mr. Wright is here tonight too. So unexpected."

The opening Cecelia had been waiting for.

"Mr. Wright does not often attend balls?" Cecelia asked, as if she did not already know.

"Hardly ever," Miss Mercer said, leaning even closer and lowering her voice. "Unfortunately, as he is one of the more handsome gentlemen around." She sighed again, looking wistful.

Cecelia had liked her so far, but now she suddenly felt…annoyed.

"Oh," Miss Mercer continued, "I did fancy him a bit when he first arrived in Westbury, naturally, but my parents soon set me straight on that account. My father insists I marry a gentleman of high rank or at the least great fortune." She rolled her eyes. "Still, Mr. Wright is quite respectable, and many ladies would be quite pleased to have him. If only he would not hide himself away."

Irritation pricked at Cecelia over Miss Mercer describing James as unworthy of anyone—although she was correct in the practical sense that he was not a suitable match for either of them. But the words still grated, and Miss Mercer apparently wishing to play matchmaker for him was no less annoying. Which was ridiculous. She also wanted to help him come out of his social isolation, did she not?

"Has Mr. Wright been more social in the past?" Cecelia asked.

Miss Mercer shook her head. "At least, not since he moved to Westbury. He has joined the board of several charities and attends certain events. But he makes an appearance only occasionally at balls and assemblies, and he is always reserved. He certainly shows no interest in finding a wife."

For several more minutes, Cecelia listened to Mary Mercer speak with barely a pause for breath. But Cecelia's attention was only half on her and half on watching Mr. Wright.

As he continued to speak with a nearby gentleman, a group of six women edged closer to him, clearly waiting for the right moment to approach. Three were young ladies, and the other three were likely their mothers.

Cecelia looked away, stifling a stab of annoyance. Not about the ladies clamoring for his attention tonight, no. She was simply frustrated about being unable to solve the mystery of his behavior.

She and Miss Mercer continued to linger by the windows. Miss Mercer shared an astounding number of details about the ladies and eligible gentlemen present. She seemed to know everything about everyone and was eager to relay as much information as possible. Cecelia made a mental note to be extremely careful in what she shared with her.

Cecelia listened to her ramble on, squeezing in a polite response when she could, but her mind returned to what Miss Mercer had said about Mr. Wright.

If Mr. Wright had been reclusive ever since he moved here, maybe his heart had been broken before then. That would fit with what Reed had learned from the servants, who also claimed to know nothing of an attachment since he lived in Westbury. Although if his disappointment was from before then, two years seemed a long time to still be so heartbroken.

Could his strange behavior be explained by heartache from a more recent, secret affair?

Miss Mercer's chatter once again turned back to Mr. Wright, and Cecelia seized the chance.

"Perhaps Mr. Wright seems uninterested in finding a wife because his heart is already taken?" Cecelia said.

"Perhaps." Miss Mercer lowered her voice. "At one point, there was speculation that he had an attachment in Plymouth. It seemed that he sent many messages there, and he visited somewhat regularly—one of the few occasions he went anywhere. When he was asked about his business there, he was also always oddly vague."

Was that the answer? Had a lady in Plymouth broken his heart?

"But," Miss Mercer said, "it turned out to be nothing interesting."

"Then what was it?" Cecelia asked, feeling strangely relieved.

"It was all about an orphanage, not a lady."

"An orphanage?"

"Apparently, he is a benefactor." Miss Mercer's tone suggested this was a great disappointment.

"How kind," Cecelia said.

Miss Mercer shrugged. "Indeed, but an orphanage is hardly as interesting as an attachment."

Having been orphaned himself, it made sense that he would be drawn toward such a charitable endeavor. But why in Plymouth?

"Did he once live in Plymouth?" Cecelia said.

"Not that I know of."

"Do you happen to have any connections in Portsmouth, where he first lived, that know him?"

Miss Mercer shook her head. "No. In fact, when he first

came here, naturally people tried to learn more about him, but no one from Portsmouth seemed to know of him."

The same results Cecelia had from her cousin.

"Perhaps because he left when he was so young?" Cecelia asked.

"I do not believe so," Miss Mercer said. "No one seemed to know anything of his family. And he seems reluctant to speak of it."

"How odd."

"I thought so too, at first. But then it was decided that it was because, well, his family likely did not move in the same circles."

"What do you mean?" Cecelia asked.

"It's believed his background is likely far more modest than a gentleman of his situation should wish to admit to." Miss Mercer lowered her voice even further. "Apparently, every so often he slips into, well, rougher speech. At least that's what some gentlemen say."

Was Mr. Wright not the son of a gentleman as he claimed? It would explain his lack of connections and reluctance to speak of his past. And yet, it did not seem to fit his character to be ashamed of modest beginnings. The fact that he had no desire to build a larger house, though he almost certainly could afford to do so, and the fact that he seemed uninterested in many of the trappings of wealth, suggested he was not especially concerned with impressing others.

She thought of his tale about the race he'd run as a child, and his mention of the cathedral. His story had seemed not quite right for Portsmouth. It had made her think of a cathedral in a different city, a cathedral distinctive for its long nave. But his explanation had made sense. Somewhat.

Or…had he been covering up a mistake?

Her pulse sped up. What if the reason no one knew

of his family in Portsmouth was because he was actually from another city? But if so, why would he conceal that fact?

Perhaps she was being fanciful, imagining such deception. But she decided that tomorrow she would write to a friend in a different city inquiring about Mr. Wright. And in the meantime, she must try to coax more information from the enigmatic Mr. Wright himself.

She glanced in his direction. The young women and their mothers had succeeded in surrounding Mr. Wright and engaging him in conversation. One young woman whose gown was far too tight seemed to be practically throwing herself at him. For all his apparent avoidance of such situations, he certainly did not look ill at ease now.

For the next hour or so, as she and Mary Mercer shifted through the crowd, speaking with and occasionally dancing with others, Cecelia was acutely aware of how much Mr. Wright was enjoying the evening. He chatted with dozens of people, and he was frequently smiling and laughing. He enjoyed two glasses of punch and a fig biscuit. He danced with six women, including seeking out two ladies who were obviously short of dance invitations.

He was unquestionably a kind and thoughtful gentleman. And his happiness this evening made him mesmerizing to watch. She was only one of many women who were paying close attention to his movements.

Well…good. Seeing him socializing was exactly what she had wished. If she suddenly was feeling a touch dissatisfied, it was only because she still had no answers to why he seemed to avoid attachments.

The time finally arrived for their second dance together. As the music started, he slid his warm fingers around hers, met her gaze, and smiled.

Heavens, he was handsome.

Although her gloves prevented a genuine touch, her

body reacted as if he had laid a bare hand on her naked skin. She missed a step and forced herself to look away from him and focus on the dance. His own dancing had become, while not flawless by any means, much smoother.

She must remember her purpose.

Since he would not answer her more direct questions, she would try a different tactic.

"I learned something very interesting about you," she murmured once he drew her close. The waltz allowed for more intimate dancing than their first dance, and being held in his arms was having an alarming effect on her pulse.

"Oh?" He raised one eyebrow.

"You are involved with an orphanage?"

His eyes widened. "How do you know that?"

"Miss Mercer."

"How does *she* know that?" he asked, frowning.

"She seems to know everything."

He laughed. "True." That laugh had been too rare until this evening.

"You are more interesting to people than you realize," she said. "After all, there is not much to occupy people here in the country besides following their neighbors' lives."

He laughed again. "Why, thank you. I think."

She had not even meant to insult him, but…she met his gaze and could not help but smile in return.

"But why in Plymouth?" she asked. "Did you live there once?"

"No." His smile faded. "However, I learned there was a particular need in that city. Too many children whose fathers were lost at sea, and their mothers gone as well, without a decent place to live."

Lost at sea. Like her own parents. But children who, unlike her, were left with nothing and no one to care for them. She deeply admired his concern for them. She felt a pinprick of guilt that she did not do more to help others as he did.

"They are all children of sailors?" she asked.

"Yes."

"I have heard that you have an affinity for helping sailors and their families."

His lips thinned, and his eyes narrowed slightly, the same look he had whenever he was avoiding questions.

"You do not wish to speak of it?" she said.

"Not especially."

"You enjoy being mysterious." She tried not to be distracted by how wonderful it felt to be in his arms.

"Mysterious?" He raised an eyebrow again. "That makes me sound…far more interesting than the truth."

"Which is?"

"That I am quite dull."

"You certainly try to be."

He laughed and drew her closer. She caught the light scent of his shaving soap, and she discreetly shifted just a bit nearer to breathe it in again.

"Not tonight," he said softly, his face close enough to hers that his breath warmed her forehead. "All thanks to you."

For a few delightful seconds, he caressed her hand that was clasped with his own. His touch was little more than a brush of his fingertips. Even so, her breath caught.

That small intimacy, a touch that he'd likely done without much thought, had her feeling more lightheaded than any of the kisses she'd shared with Mr. Trent.

Mr. Wright had wanted to distract her from her disappointment, and he was succeeding—to an alarming degree. And she would not pretend that she was not enjoying his attentions, meaningless as they no doubt were to him. Then the realization hit her: she would likely never dance with him after tonight. Unless she journeyed to his estate in the future, in a short time, she might never set eyes on him again.

The dance came to an end too quickly. As he released her hand, he met her gaze and frowned.

"Now you look sad," he said. "And I thought I was distracting you from your disappointment."

"You were." She forced a smile.

He believed she was sad about William. And she was, but perhaps not nearly as much as she ought to be.

A short while later, it was time to leave. As they exited the manor, Mr. Wright offered Cecelia his arm. When his grandmother turned back to speak to a friend, he and Cecelia continued outside without her, caught up in the sea of departing guests.

Once outside, they moved away from the crush of people and began strolling toward their carriage, far down the line. The night air was marvelously refreshing, and a strong breeze rustled the trees and hedgerows.

She relished the strength of his arm as she leaned closer to him, grateful for the excuse to touch him. Thanks to him, the evening had been a delight. Being in his company was wonderful. *He* was wonderful.

Guilt pricked at her as she thought of how irritated she had been with him in London and during the journey to Westbury, and of how severely she had misjudged him.

When he'd found her in London, he had been doing her brother a great service. He was not only a good friend, but he had saved Adrian's life. He had a kind heart, for those he employed, for orphans, and for everyone. And this evening he was being so considerate, distracting her from her sadness over William when she hardly deserved it.

He was likely only being kind, and his behavior this evening meant little else. Still, she could not help but wonder, would he miss her when she left Westbury?

They continued to walk in silence until they had almost

reached the carriage. A dozen or so paces from the coach, she stopped. They were just outside the light cast by the coach's lantern, still in the shadows, and the driver did not seem aware of their approach. She glanced back. His grandmother still had not followed them.

"Is something wrong?" he asked. His deep voice sounded delightfully concerned.

She turned and looked up at him. "Mr. Wright, I must thank you for this evening, and for having me as a guest in your home. If I have ever seemed ungrateful, I am sorry. I know you were only doing what my brother asked," she said, "and that my visit has been an inconvenience for you." As she finished speaking, the breeze grew stronger. She raised her hands and grasped the hood of her cloak, preparing to pull it up.

"Indeed," he said, "a serious inconvenience."

Startled, she dropped her hood without lifting it. Her gaze flew to his face. Here she was apologizing, and he responded by being rude—

Except he was smiling. A teasing smile that made her want to move even closer to him.

"But not entirely unwelcome," he added softly. He stepped nearer.

The next thing she knew, his strong hands brushed against her face as he gently lifted the hood of her cloak, settling it over her head.

Those few, brief touches sent shivers through her. The effortless way he adjusted her cloak had her wondering… was he equally experienced at handling other articles of female clothing? From the way he was staring at her now, she suspected the answer was decidedly *yes*.

His gaze slid from her eyes to her mouth and lingered a moment before returning to her eyes.

Her heart began to pound. She wanted him to kiss her. She wanted to kiss *him*.

No. No matter how handsome he was, no matter that

he was suddenly warm and charming, she simply could not indulge in a flirtation with him. But oh, how she wished that she could.

She should step back. But she simply couldn't look away from him.

He seemed to remember himself and dropped his gaze. He appeared about to step back when she reached out and took his hand, stopping him. Though his eyes widened in surprise, he did not pull away.

His fingers felt wonderfully strong and warm around her own.

"Thank you," she said softly, holding his gaze. "For making me laugh. For dancing with me. For making my disappointment easier to bear."

Then she intended to look away from his too-intense eyes and handsome face and to move toward the coach. Instead, she lifted onto her tiptoes.

And she kissed him.

She gently pressed her lips against his, and he went completely still. He tasted warm and delicious and sweet and lemony—he must have enjoyed one of the lemon biscuits from the dessert table not long before.

Kiss me back, she thought. *Please kiss me back.*

He shifted his hands toward her, as if he was about to draw her close, but then…then he abruptly drew away, so quickly that she nearly lost her balance.

His face was expressionless, but his stiff shoulders and clenched jaw made it clear—he was appalled.

Mortification filled her.

He glanced back toward the manor, likely looking for his grandmother, who still had not appeared. Then he turned back to face her.

"Lady Cecelia," he whispered, "I have enjoyed your company…more than I can express." His voice was rough. "And I do not mean to presume anything. However, I must let you know that…I can never marry you." He took a deep breath. "I can never be the gentleman that you deserve."

They were perhaps the politest words he'd ever spoken to her, and they only added to her embarrassment.

"I am so sorry," she whispered. "I should not have—"

What must he think of her? Merely because he had been kind to her, she should never have acted so impulsively.

Footfalls sounded on the path, and Mrs. Stewart appeared.

The footman, who had been chatting with another footman at a nearby carriage, hurried to their coach and opened the door.

The three of them settled into the carriage and they started back toward Westbury in silence. Mrs. Stewart glanced between Mr. Wright and her, frowning as if she suspected something unusual had happened.

No doubt after tonight, Mrs. Stewart would be greatly relieved by her grandson's behavior during the short time remaining of Cecelia's visit. Now that she had made such a muddle of things, Mr. Wright would likely avoid her as much as possible.

CHAPTER ELEVEN

JAMES IGNORED HIS GRANDMOTHER'S DARK looks during the carriage ride home. Once they had arrived and he'd handed his coat and hat to Long, James strode to his study. He paced the room for a few minutes and then dropped into the chair at his desk.

After such a long evening, he should be exhausted. Instead, he felt wide awake—wide awake and far too agitated to sleep anytime soon.

He'd enjoyed a wonderful evening, the happiest he could recall. At least until the end, when the depth of his mistake in attending the ball had become shockingly apparent.

He tore open the first of a stack of correspondence waiting for him and he stared at the letter about a charity wishing for his assistance without reading more than a few lines.

How had he allowed himself to be so captivated by Lady Cecelia that, against his better judgment, he'd actually flirted with her?

And then he'd danced with her. Twice.

Still, he'd regained some control, and all might have been fine if only she had not kissed him.

He could still hardly believe it. *She* had kissed *him*.

She was certainly not the first woman to surprise him with a kiss, but hers had been far more than the simple, pleasant warmth of a yielding female mouth against his.

She'd tasted of berry punch, and her lips had been

lusciously soft and warm. Sweeter and more intoxicating than any other woman he'd ever kissed.

Her taste, scent, the brush of her skirts against him, everything that was uniquely her, had devastated him.

He'd wanted to not only kiss her in return, but to deepen their kisses. Deepen them until he pushed her up against the carriage and kissed her so thoroughly that her hair and gown would be hopelessly disheveled.

Miraculously, his sense hadn't completely deserted him, and—against every desire—he'd somehow pulled away. After that, he simply hadn't known what to say. He didn't want to lie to her, but neither could he be truthful.

But if he had been truthful, he would have told her that he wanted very much to kiss her, that he rarely went more than a few minutes near her without thinking about kissing her, but that he should not, could not, kiss her, because he could offer her no future.

Not that she would ever want a future with him.

Tossing the unread letter onto the desk, he let his head fall into his hands. He immediately regretted it; his coat still smelled like her lavender soap. He quickly straightened.

She was beautiful. And kindhearted. Clever. Caring. And funny. And damnit, she smelled wonderful and felt wonderful in his arms. She made him feel…alive in a way he hadn't felt in so long. Or perhaps ever.

And she was absolutely, positively not for him. So he had to stop thinking about her. Now.

Snatching up the discarded letter, he once again tried to read it and failed.

He should never have let his guard down, never flirted and danced with her. Especially now that she no longer had an understanding with William Trent.

Footfalls sounded in the hall and his grandmother glided into the room. She pulled the door shut behind her more forcefully than usual.

She turned to face him. "Forgive my intrusion, but we must speak about Lady Cecelia." Her expression was funereal.

He sighed and shoved the letter aside. "If you wish."

She sank into one of the chairs by the hearth and folded her hands in her lap.

"Please explain," she said, "what on earth happened this evening."

He paused. Naturally he had no wish to discuss what had occurred, but his grandmother would learn soon enough. Or at least, she would learn some of what happened. Thank heavens she didn't know about the kiss. Hopefully she never would.

"Very well," he said. "In the letter Lady Cecelia received from Mr. Trent, he ended their understanding."

She paled. "He ended it? Why?"

"It does not matter why, but it is no reflection on her. Trent is a fool."

"That's unfortunate. Most unfortunate."

"That is why I attended and why I danced with her. To take her mind off it."

She raised one eyebrow and leaned back in her chair. "Really? Do you honestly believe that is the only reason? Why you danced with her *twice*?" She shook her head. "She looked anything but disappointed at dancing with you."

She stared at him silently.

"Your worry is unfounded," he finally said.

"Is it? Whenever I am alone with her, she quickly turns the conversation to you. She has been asking too many questions."

"Has she?" He shrugged. "No doubt she is bored." But he felt a burst of pleasure at his grandmother's words.

She sighed. "You underestimate yourself."

He crossed his arms. "I don't imagine her interest in me, if it even exists, will last." Likely her questions about him were merely to pass the time. And as for her kissing him…well, he doubted she had any idea of the reaction it ignited in him.

Her kiss had been impulsive and kind, nothing more. Even without the matter of her wishing to find a husband who desired to travel, it was almost unthinkable that a lady of her situation would seriously consider him as a suitable romantic prospect. Likely, she had merely been thanking him for all his help, and he had embarrassed her by rejecting her sweet gesture so harshly.

Yet he had no choice.

"What if you are wrong?" his grandmother said. "And what if she is determined to find out more about you?"

"You need not worry," he said. "Since she is no longer to be married, her reason for visiting Westbury is gone. She told me she will write to her brother tomorrow and make arrangements to leave." That idea should fill him with profound relief, but it did not. He refused to examine why.

His grandmother sighed and nodded. "Good. The sooner she leaves, the better off we shall all be." Her eyes narrowed. "And in the meantime, you must behave with far more reserve."

"Of course. But as I said before, I only attended tonight and danced with her to take her mind off her disappointment." His words were unconvincing, even to himself.

The annoyance vanished from his grandmother's face. She looked profoundly weary. And sad.

"You try to hide it," she said quietly, "but I see the way you look at her, the way you have looked at her ever since she arrived. And the way you were tonight with her…" She shook her head. "I have never seen you so happy."

The words were like a knife twisting in his chest.

He stood and strode to the window. "You are imagining

things," he said. He doubted she would believe him, but he must try to convince himself.

"Am I?" she said. "James…"

He turned back and met her gaze. She looked at him with such sorrow that he knew he did not want to hear what she had to say. Likely heartbreaking words about him being unable to marry.

Such truths were hard enough to bear in his own thoughts, let alone hear them spoken aloud.

Her eyes seemed to shine with unshed tears, but thankfully, she kept silent.

She dropped her gaze and wiped her eyes. Then she took a deep breath, stood, and turned to leave. Just before reaching the door, she stopped and looked back at him.

"Please, *please* be careful," she said. "You have far too much to lose. And I…could not bear to lose you again." She paused. "To a woman like Lady Cecelia, your heart will never be more than a plaything. And she will never, ever deserve you."

CHAPTER TWELVE

A WEEK AFTER THE BALL, CECELIA decided to take an afternoon stroll alone beside the river. She stopped after a while and sat on a bench, gazing out at the water and land beyond, admiring the slow-moving shadows cast by the scattered clouds.

Westbury was so beautiful. She had enjoyed her visit more than she'd ever expected. Over the past week, Mrs. Stewart had arranged for several outings with various neighbors. They had picnicked on Viscount Mercer's estate, explored centuries-old ruins, viewed several beautiful churches, and visited many interesting shops in nearby towns.

All the outings were quite pleasant, but Cecelia's enjoyment was dampened by the fact that Mr. Wright had declined to join them.

In the first days after the ball, she had been relieved to not have to face him. At the same time, she could not stop thinking about him and about their kiss. Mortification coursed through her whenever she recalled his reaction. And yet the kiss had been so pleasant, brief as it was. She kept imagining what it might have been like if he hadn't pulled away, but instead had returned her kiss…

Of course, she should not dwell on such pointless thoughts. She should instead be thinking about her own future and of what she should do next.

Whenever her mind turned to William, she felt only an ever-lessening twinge of sadness followed by an increasingly large amount of relief. The more she'd contemplated it, the more certain she was that she'd been saved from making a terrible mistake. Marrying William would not have brought the freedom that she'd once imagined. It likely would have been another gilded cage—this time with William's father, a man as controlling as her aunt, guarding the door.

She was grateful, however, that William recognized how dear that freedom was to her. A less trustworthy gentleman might have tried to hold her to their understanding. And because their agreement had been based on practical reasons, at least no hearts had been broken. But now she must search for another eligible gentleman who shared her desire to travel and whom she would be content to marry.

If only Mr. Wright wished to travel.

What a foolish thought. He did not even want a wife. And even if he did wish to marry, and even if he wished to marry her—which he clearly did not—her aunt would have palpitations if she were to choose a husband of no rank and relatively modest fortune, with no connections to any other prominent families beside their own. Even Adrian, as much as he esteemed his friend, would likely be against such a match. Indeed, compared to Mr. Wright, William Trent was a far more eligible suitor. Even if earned through trade, the Trent family had tremendous wealth and with it, growing power and influence. Mr. Wright had nothing of the sort.

And even if Mr. Wright had been an eligible match for her, as much as she was drawn to him and had grown to respect and admire him, he wanted a very different future than she did. He wished for a quiet life in the country and to never even go to London, let alone travel overseas.

Now it seemed that their incompatibility was just as well. Whatever interest she'd imagined in his eyes before, he'd made it quite clear on the night of the ball that he lacked feelings for her beyond friendship.

I can never be the gentleman that you deserve.

In this matter, at least, he'd proved quite tactful. She had said something very similar when she'd rejected many gentlemen. *It's not you who is unworthy, it's me. Truly.*

Ha.

So the morning after the ball she had written to Adrian, informing him that she and Mr. Trent had ended their understanding, and asking him to respond with arrangements for her return. Yesterday she had received his reply that he still wished her to stay the month as planned. He had added that he would arrive a few days early if possible in order to enjoy a visit with Mr. Wright before taking her home.

Despite all that had happened, she had been strangely relieved that she was not to depart early. Not because she wished to be near Mr. Wright—well, not entirely—but because in the time that she had left at Westbury, she still wished to help him.

She had yet to learn why he was reclusive. The day after the ball, she had also sent a message to a friend in Winchester, a city with a cathedral known for its long nave. If she was correct that Mr. Wright was concealing where he was really from, her friend might know something about his family. But she was uncertain when she might receive a reply.

Though she dared not mention her suspicions, perhaps there was still hope Mr. Wright himself might reveal more.

He'd avoided her for several days after the ball, but then two days ago, he'd abruptly stopped hiding. He had joined his grandmother and her for every meal, not only for dinner. The past two evenings he sat with them to play cards, and he even seemed reluctant for that time to end. Yesterday he had also sought out her company repeatedly throughout the day, much to the displeasure of his grandmother.

Cecelia put on a good front, struggling to achieve the correct balance of friendliness and reserve, doing her best to behave as if that kiss and his rejection had never happened. She tried not to meet his gaze for too long. She tried not to notice how good he smelled when he leaned close. She tried not to notice how pleasing was his form, his smile, his laugh—everything about him.

She tried repeatedly not to think about the kiss—and failed.

He was little help. Now that he was in her company again, she was both annoyed and terribly pleased at the same time.

And to confuse matters further, just this morning at breakfast, she'd caught him staring at her with an intensity that had made her forget all about her food. She'd been so distracted that she'd even spilled half her chocolate.

But she must not read too much into his odd behavior. Perhaps he'd simply decided he did not need to be so reserved any more. After all, he had made his feelings clear a week ago and she was only here a short time longer. Soon enough, she would return home and once again plan her future—a future in which Mr. Wright would have no part.

If only Mr. Wright—

She heard a noise behind her and turned to see Urchin shuffling along the path. The dog was moving at a crawl, yet panting as if he was running at full speed.

"You have walked far, Urchin," she said. She glanced around, half-expecting Mrs. Thornton to be following the animal, but there was no sign of her. She smiled. No Mrs. Thornton, and no aunt to admonish her for going near a dog.

Urchin finally reached her. He stopped, looking up at her with his soft dark eyes, his pink tongue hanging out as he continued to pant. She reached out and patted his head, and he wagged his tail. She continued to stroke his soft gray fur until his panting eventually stopped. His mistress might be disagreeable, but he was quite the opposite. She resolved to give him a treat later if she could.

Urchin eventually lost interest in her and turned his attention to the river. He shuffled to the water's edge and then made his way in, inch by inch, until his legs were half in the water. Then he paused and began to drink.

After a moment, he lifted his head and edged forward, farther into the river. The water was up to his chest now. She frowned as the dog seemed to twitch in the water and then started swimming.

No, not swimming. The current had grabbed him. He whimpered as he began to be pulled downstream. She rose and hurried to the water's edge as the river carried him toward a cluster of boulders.

Urchin stopped against one of the rocks, the water pushing him against the stone as the current split around it.

"Climb up!" she called, as if he could understand her. "Up!"

Urchin seemed to be trying, but he couldn't pull himself out of the water. His whimpers grew louder. Then his head began to bob, each time sinking a little lower.

She clenched her hands into fists, willing the poor animal to somehow gather his strength. The dog was paddling hard to keep his head above the water. Splashes erupted near him as he tried to gain traction against the rock and haul himself out of the river. He turned and looked toward her, letting out a loud whimper. Then his head dipped almost completely beneath the surface.

He was going to drown.

She frantically looked around for a sign of anyone nearby. She called out for help, but was answered with silence. No one else was close enough, only her.

Her heart pounding, she tore off her half-boots and stockings, and she rushed into the water.

As James strolled alongside the river, every time the path curved he wondered if Lady Cecelia might be around the next bend. He knew she was somewhere nearby. She'd mentioned earlier that she intended to go for a walk. Of course, he should not be out searching for her. He should be keeping his distance.

He'd forced himself to stay away from her after the ball. For a few days, he'd settled for glimpses of her from a window as she left the house, for hearing her laughter from a distance, and for inhaling the faint lingering scent of her perfume only after she'd left a room.

Torture that it was, he'd kept away from her—until he simply couldn't resist his desperate need to be near her any longer.

Very soon she would leave Westbury and his life would return to normal. No more being distracted by her conversation or laughter or beauty. No more hearing her quick steps throughout the house or smelling her lavender soap. No more wondering what color gown she would be wearing for dinner and how low the neckline would be.

No more disapproving glares from his grandmother. In a terribly short number of days, his peaceful life would return.

He had never wanted Lady Cecelia in his home, and her imminent departure should fill him with relief. Instead, the idea of her leaving filled him with a horrible emptiness. Ever since the ball, he'd spent nearly every moment thinking of her and feeling an ever-growing confusion. He alternated between an odd sort of happiness and feeling completely out of sorts.

No longer could he pretend that he wasn't infatuated

with her. But it wasn't only that—he was also increasingly dissatisfied with…well, everything.

Her presence was like a light cast on his existence, revealing how dull and predictable his life had become. After so many tumultuous years, he'd been comforted at first by the quiet routine of his life at Westbury. Anytime restlessness threatened, he'd ruthlessly banished it, reminding himself of how lucky he was to at last have a peaceful life, and of the dangers that awaited beyond the shelter of his current situation.

Such reminders had mostly worked—until her arrival.

Now, the memory of her kiss haunted him constantly. One moment he felt shock and relief at his restraint all over again; the next moment, he would feel a deep stab of anger.

He'd been fortunate enough to have a woman as incomparable as her kiss him, and he hadn't kissed her back? What in blazes was wrong with him?

No, he was right to have gained some sense. He had been a fool to let his guard down at all. Any attachment was pointless. And of course, she deserved far better than him.

And when she did leave, surely his infatuation with her would end soon enough. His feelings for her would fade in time, just as they had for others—even if his longing for Lady Cecelia seemed far more intense than any attraction he'd felt in the past.

He had almost reached the river, but there was still no sign of her. Where was she? Fishing again?

He turned onto the path that skirted the water. A spot of bright white in the center of the river stopped him cold.

A bonnet. Her bonnet. She clung to a rock near the center of the river, clutching something small and gray against her chest. Urchin.

What the hell had happened?

He tore off his hat, jacket, boots, and stockings. He strode into the water, his gaze never leaving her. How long had she been there? It was one matter to stand in the river to fish on a hot day, but to be immersed in the chilly water for too long could make her dangerously cold and exhausted. From this distance, he could not tell how tired she might be and whether she might be in danger of losing her grip.

Why did she not let go of the dog and grab the rock with both hands?

As he pushed across the river, he shouted at her to let Urchin go.

She shook her head.

Damn foolish woman. But he was also deeply impressed that she kept hold of the creature.

He yelled at her again, but she only seemed to clutch the animal more tightly.

Please let her hold on, he prayed as he pushed through the frigid water. The current was stronger than it appeared, and he fought to cross without being pulled too far down the river. If he missed her, it could take too long to try again.

As he struggled to move closer, he could see that she was shivering, and her skin was paler than usual. He reached a large rock and rested for just a few seconds before moving forward again.

Crossing the last stretch of water seemed to take an eternity, but finally, he reached her. His heart pounded as he drew both her and the dog into his arms. The current pushed at his back and legs, and he dug his bare feet deeper into the stony bottom.

Even if they let go now, he could hold them, for a little while, anyway.

A shout came from the shore. He turned his head and saw Reed on the riverbank. She must have been nearby and heard his shouting. She was yelling something about a boat, but there wasn't one in sight. She must be talking about getting a boat from the pond.

He wasn't going to wait that long.

"Take Urchin," Lady Cecelia said, shifting against him. "I can hold on."

"No." He wasn't going to leave her. If she weakened, if she were swept away—

"Can you climb up?" he asked. She shook her head. The rock was barely out of the water, anyway. If he tried to put Urchin on it, the poor creature might be dragged off.

"You can't take us both at once!" Her fingers were white where she clutched the rock, and now her whole body trembled.

"The hell I can't," he said. "You hold the dog, I'll hold you."

She met his gaze, and she actually smiled.

Clutching the trembling dog even closer, she lifted its head onto her shoulder.

He pulled her against him. "Hold on as tightly as you can."

She slid an arm around him and gripped him like a vise. Even with the smell of wet dog and the fact that she felt like an icicle, having her press against him almost made him forget his purpose.

He drew several slow, deep breaths. Then he let go of the rock. Together they slowly and carefully moved toward the shore.

The water at last grew shallower. They stumbled out together with her leaning heavily against him. He lowered her onto the grass just past the water's edge. The dog slipped from her arms.

Mrs. Thornton appeared on the path nearby, running toward them. She dashed past Reed and scooped up Urchin.

"Ready Lady Cecelia's room," he shouted to Reed as

he stumbled to his feet. "A fire, blankets, and something hot to drink. I'll bring her. Go!"

Reed nodded. "Yes, right away!" She turned and hurried off.

Mrs. Thornton stood rubbing the dog to warm it. She glanced at him.

"You saved Urchin," the housekeeper said, her voice breaking.

He shook his head. "Lady Cecelia went in after him, and she kept him from being swept away. I only helped them back."

Mrs. Thornton looked at him, wide-eyed in disbelief. "I…I better warm him up," she finally muttered. Then she turned and strode toward the manor, clutching Urchin in her arms.

He looked back to Lady Cecelia. She lay on the grass with her eyes closed, still breathing heavily. She was pale and shivering, but likely she'd be fine once she warmed up.

"What the devil were you doing?" he said, moving to loom over her.

Her eyes popped open. "What do you mean?"

"How in the blazes did you end up in the river?" Why was he shouting?

"Oh," she said, "I thought it would be a lark to take the dog for a dip." She yanked the ribbon of her bonnet, loosened it enough to pull it from her head, and dropped the sodden hat in the grass. "What do you think? Urchin became trapped in the water. No one else was nearby, and I couldn't let him drown." She pushed a clump of wet hair from her forehead. "I didn't realize the river became so deep farther out."

He fell to his knees beside her. Her pale, wet gown clung to her, the outline of her stays and a great deal more visible against the fabric. Her trembling had stopped, though her lips were still tinged with blue.

"You could have drowned!" Why was he still shouting? His hands were trembling, but he wasn't really cold anymore.

As she turned her head to meet his gaze, he raised a hand to her cheek. Her blue eyes widened.

"A foolish thing to do," he added, his voice softer. He slipped his other arm beneath her back and lifted her up against him. She only stared at him, her lips slightly parted.

For once, she seemed to have nothing to say. He, on the other hand, had plenty to say.

Instead, he kissed her.

She'd nearly drowned, and he chose *now* to kiss her?

Cecelia might have been annoyed if he wasn't so… delicious. And it was no proper, restrained kiss either. She slid her arms around him. Some parts of her were still freezing, but other parts were becoming delightfully warm.

Yet it was wrong, all wrong, to be kissing James Wright in this manner.

Except it did not feel wrong at all.

He deepened the kiss, and she opened her mouth to him, clutching him tighter. He had a wonderfully broad chest and strong arms and oh—

Still kissing her, he fell back, pulling her tightly against him. And the next thing she knew, she was lying on top of him there in the grass, pressed against the whole wet heavenly length of him. He wrapped one hand in her hair, keeping her mouth tight against his, and his other hand was on her back, sliding downward…

He groaned, gave her one last deep kiss, and rolled her off him. Feeling dizzy, she sat up and pushed damp hair from her face. Her skirt was halfway up her legs. When had that happened?

"Damn it!" he whispered. He was kneeling beside her, breathing hard, almost as breathless as when he'd dragged her from the water. Next to him was her now flattened bonnet, which they must have crushed when they—

Movement down the path toward the house caught her eye.

Mrs. Stewart stood there, staring at them. Even from that distance, she likely had seen everything. Cecelia's face warmed.

Mr. Wright leapt to his feet. He offered her a hand, helped her to stand, and then quickly stepped away.

She smoothed her skirt and then busied herself retrieving her bonnet from the grass, avoiding his grandmother's horrified stare.

What would Mrs. Stewart do now?

Normally, being caught in such a compromising situation would mean one thing: she and James would have to marry.

CHAPTER THIRTEEN

WHEN CECELIA ARRIVED BACK AT the house, Reed already had a fire warming her room. Reed quickly helped her into dry clothes and settled her in a chair close to the hearth.

Cecelia enjoyed the heat of the coals despite not feeling the least bit cold. Not since Mr. Wright had kissed her. Just thinking about their kisses made her feel warm all over. Warm and breathless.

Reed frowned as she handed her a cup of tea. "Are you sure you're well, milady? You look flushed."

"I am fine. Thank you." Cecelia smiled and inhaled the soothing aroma of the tea before she took a sip.

"Thank heavens Mr. Wright found you," Reed said. "What were you thinking, going in after the dog?" Reed shook her head. "Forgive me, but I didn't think you liked Mrs. Thornton."

"I don't," Cecelia said. "But she wasn't the one in the river."

Reed laughed and pulled a letter from her pocket. "In all the excitement, I nearly forgot. This arrived for you." Reed handed her the folded paper.

Cecelia opened the letter and scanned the first few lines.

"It's from my friend, Lady Margaret," Cecelia said. "I wrote to ask her if she knew of the Wright family." If her suspicion was correct, maybe she would finally learn more about Mr. Wright's past.

"Ah." Reed walked over to the hearth to tend the fire. "Anything interesting?"

Cecelia frowned. "She writes that she knows of several families named Wright in Winchester, but none that matches the details I shared with her."

"Winchester?" Reed said. "I thought Mr. Wright was from Portsmouth."

"So he says. But he told me something that made me wonder."

Cecelia continued reading silently.

Many years ago there was a family with a different name that matches some of the details you mentioned, including an orphaned ten-year-old boy. That child also had a grandmother in Scotland who was passed over for guardianship of the boy upon the father's death. The boy apparently ran away before his more distant relatives could collect him.

Ran away? That couldn't be correct; Mr. Wright had gone to live with a cousin. Even if Lady Margaret was wrong about the name, other details didn't fit.

Cecelia continued to read.

That child was said to have never been recovered by his family, although there were rumors he ran off to London and eventually was impressed into the Royal Navy.

Impressed into the navy? Even if it was somehow true and Mr. Wright was the person described in the letter, why would he conceal having been in the navy? And yet he seemed to have an affinity for sailors and their families. Was that merely a coincidence?

Of course, so much time has passed that some of these details might be incorrect, but I believe the child's name was James Wyatt.

Also James. But it was such a common name. Could the man she knew as Mr. Wright really be James Wyatt?

A knock sounded. As Reed went to open the door, Cecelia folded up the letter and slipped it into a nearby drawer.

"It's food," Reed announced with a grin.

Mr. Long entered carrying a covered tray. "From the cook, on orders from Mrs. Thornton," he said, winking at Cecelia. "We are all quite glad you're well, milady." He placed the tray on a table and left.

Reed lifted the cover. "Look at this! Sandwiches, fruit, and biscuits—even the special ones Mrs. Thornton usually hides and only gives to Mr. Wright."

"Special biscuits?" Cecelia asked.

"Here, try one." Reed handed her a small plate covered with scrumptious-looking chocolate biscuits.

Cecelia bit into one and moaned. The biscuit was flaky and sweet and far better than any she'd had since her arrival at Westbury. Or nearly anywhere else, for that matter. And she only had to risk her life to get one.

Another knock sounded. This time, Mrs. Stewart marched into the room.

Cecelia swallowed against a sudden lump in her throat. No doubt she would soon learn what Mrs. Stewart intended to do about having witnessed their scandalous behavior.

"Thank you, Reed," Cecelia said, forcing a smile.

Reed nodded and left, closing the door behind her.

Mrs. Stewart lowered herself into the chair beside Cecelia, but sat on the edge, her back rigid. "How are you feeling, Lady Cecelia?"

"Much better, thank you."

"I am glad to hear it," Mrs. Stewart said quickly. "So, I will be direct. I must ask you…do you wish to marry James?"

"Oh…I…no."

Mrs. Stewart seemed to relax slightly. "I suspected as much," she said, managing to sound both relieved and angry.

She wished Mrs. Stewart didn't look quite so relieved. Not that she wanted to be pressured to marry James, of course, but why was the idea so unappealing to his grandmother?

"It was only…the excitement of him rescuing me from the water," Cecelia said. "I could not marry him, no matter how…" *No matter how wonderfully he kisses.*

And, oh, it had been wonderful. The entire walk back to the house, she could think of nothing else. Could she ever look at him again without recalling how delicious his kisses were and how delightful it felt to be pressed against him?

Mrs. Stewart sighed. "It is for the best, anyway. As you may already be aware, James does not plan to marry."

"Yes…but will you tell me why?"

Mrs. Stewart stared at her for a moment. Then she leaned forward, lifted the poker from beside the hearth, and stirred the coals.

"You said you do not wish to marry him," Mrs. Stewart finally said, not meeting her gaze, "so why does it matter?"

"I still wish to know," Cecelia said quietly. For a young gentleman to not want to marry and have an heir for his estate was unusual. It was none of her concern, she knew, but she still wanted to know.

"Did someone break his heart?" Cecelia asked. "Is that why? Or…is he waiting for someone?"

"No." Mrs. Stewart returned the poker to the stand next to the fire with a loud clang. "Some men are just destined to remain bachelors."

Mrs. Stewart turned toward her again. "Truthfully, I'm relieved that you do not wish to marry him. Even if he did intend to marry, and even if your family approved the match—which I find highly unlikely—I do not believe that you would suit in the long term." Her gaze drifted away from Cecelia, and she added quietly, "And giving into to such…emotions can lead one to make terrible mistakes."

Cecelia frowned. Was Mrs. Stewart speaking only about

her and Mr. Wright? But before Cecelia could respond, Mrs. Stewart cleared her throat, met Cecelia's gaze again, and said, "You two simply do not suit."

Cecelia said nothing. Mrs. Stewart was correct, of course. They did not suit. And marriage—at least for a lady in her position—was best decided upon for practical reasons. Infatuation often led to long-term misery. She'd certainly seen enough examples of that with her aunt's husbands. But tightness grew in Cecelia's throat and behind her eyes, as if tears threatened. It was from exhaustion more than anything, surely.

"I am prepared to never mention again what I witnessed today," Mrs. Stewart continued. "However…" She shifted in her chair and the heavy cross at her neck glinted. "As you know, James is careful not to raise any lady's hopes. He has shown no particular attention to any woman." She paused. "Until now."

Warmth spread through Cecelia at those words.

"You have clearly captured his interest," Mrs. Stewart said. "Try as he might to hide it, I could tell even before I witnessed…such definite proof."

Cecelia no longer felt like crying. What happened on the riverbank *was* undeniable proof that she had captured his interest. Perhaps some of his emotion might be from the excitement of having rescued her, but surely not all. Those odd, intense looks he'd given her lately suddenly seemed quite different. Perhaps he'd been so upset about her possibly drowning that he had finally let his guard down. To kiss her with such passion, he must find her attractive. He must care for her at least a small amount.

Speaking of which, would he ever kiss her again?

Wrong as it might be, she wanted very much to kiss him again.

She also, even more now, wanted to solve the mystery of his background.

As she held his grandmother's gaze, Cecelia's pulse sped up. Fierce as Mrs. Stewart had shown herself to be, however, she was nowhere near as frightening as Cecelia's aunt. Mrs. Stewart might reveal nothing, even if Cecelia pressed her, but she could at least try.

"I have something to ask you," Cecelia said.

"Yes?"

"By any chance, are you familiar with Winchester?"

"Very little." Mrs. Stewart's expression did not change.

"You have visited the city?"

"A few times. Long ago."

Had her face paled slightly? Cecelia expected Mrs. Stewart to ask why she was inquiring. It would be a typical response. But she did not. Was she simply too angry about finding James and her in a compromising position? Or had the question about Winchester upset her as well?

The woman was sometimes frustratingly difficult to read. Just like her grandson.

Cecelia's heart still raced, but she forced the question out. "Do you happen to know of a family from Winchester named Wyatt?"

Mrs. Stewart's eyes widened for an instant, before she shook her head. "As I said, I know little of Winchester. Now, back to the most pressing matter," Mrs. Stewart added with a scowl. "Given the circumstances, you must agree that it would be best if you left Westbury as soon as possible. I imagine your brother would understand if you went home immediately and did not wait for his arrival."

The prudent choice was indeed to leave now, before something even more scandalous happened. Not to mention politeness dictated she should leave at the time her hostess suggested. But in spite of everything, Cecelia felt an intense determination not to leave, at least, not yet.

"That is kind of you to consider my welfare," Cecelia said, "but I will wait for my brother to arrive."

"You might wish to reconsider," Mrs. Stewart said, her voice tighter.

"My brother wishes to see Mr. Wright."

Mrs. Stewart's eyes narrowed. For a few long, awkward seconds, she stared at Cecelia silently.

"Much as I do not approve of the reason for your visit, Lady Cecelia," Mrs. Stewart said at last, "I was nonetheless sincerely pleased to have your company. However, my grandson's well-being is more important to me than anything else."

"Of course, and it does you credit. But I am not—"

"Please." Mrs. Stewart lifted one hand. "Let us speak plainly. You know your own power. It is hardly surprising that a woman of your beauty and position would… indulge in flirtations to amuse yourself."

Cecelia's throat went dry.

"However," Mrs. Stewart continued, "he deserves better than to be the plaything of a lady who will never think him worthy of her."

Nausea burst in Cecelia's stomach. "I do not…that is, I am not—"

"Then you would marry him?" Mrs. Stewart raised one eyebrow.

Cecelia could not answer.

"Exactly." Mrs. Stewart smiled grimly.

There was a long silence. "I can see that I have offended you with my bluntness," Mrs. Stewart said, a slight tremor in her voice. "But I cannot say I'm sorry. I was not able to protect James in the past when I should have been there for him. But now, I will defend him no matter what."

The steeliness in her tone was so unlike her usual demeanor, Cecelia was speechless.

Mrs. Stewart rose, her lips pressed into a thin line. "Now, I have matters I should attend to," she said briskly. "I will leave you to rest."

She spun around and strode from the room. Her footfalls quickly faded. Her words did not.

He deserves better than to be the plaything of a lady who will never think him worthy of her.

Cecelia dug her fingers into the chair. She could see why Mrs. Stewart might believe that but, truly, it was not like that. He did not want to marry her, or anyone, so it was not as if she was toying with him. Not to mention, he was the one who started kissing her—this time, anyway. They were both behaving imprudently, but the idea that she was…misusing James was simply not true.

Mrs. Stewart was likely, and understandably, truly angry about their scandalous behavior. Or perhaps not only about that, but also possibly Cecelia's questions… Mrs. Stewart had looked alarmed, even if she'd quickly concealed it. Had Cecelia discovered their secret? Was Mr. Wright not who he claimed to be?

To learn the truth, perhaps she would simply have to ask him.

After returning to the house, James bathed, changed into dry clothes, and went downstairs to his study. He stood and stared at a pile of documents on his desk. Then he turned away and began pacing by the windows.

For days now, he had imagined kissing Lady Cecelia. Nothing he'd envisioned had come close to the reality.

If he had any sense, he would send her home as soon as possible, before something even more disastrous happened. Something even more disastrous than kissing her wildly while pressed against her in wet clothes on the riverbank.

He cursed. He must not allow himself to think too much about those moments, and how flushed with pleasure she'd been, and her delightful soft gasps and moans, and how afterward she had seemed happy about what they'd done. Exceedingly happy.

They were immensely fortunate that, other than his grandmother, no one else needed to ever know about the scandalous incident.

He curled his hands into fists and continued to pace. The honorable thing would be to confess to Wareton. The next step would be to marry Lady Cecelia, something he could not do, even if her family supported the idea, which they would not.

He strode to his desk and dropped into the chair with a sigh. He should not keep such a transgression from Wareton, but if he did tell him, it could very well end their friendship. Also, he must consider Lady Cecelia's feelings about informing her brother. But that was one conversation he absolutely did not wish to have with her. He wanted to pretend the entire madness had never happened.

However, he must decide how to deal with her presence for the time that remained.

First, he needed to apologize for his behavior. No doubt now that time had passed, she was embarrassed, and apologizing would be uncomfortable, but it must be done. After that, he would put the whole matter behind him. She undoubtedly wished to do the same. Then for the rest of her visit, he would keep himself as busy as possible and away from her company.

And he would try to forget the most wonderful, most intoxicating moments of his entire life.

He heard someone approaching in the hall. His grandmother marched in and shut the door. Forcefully.

"How could you?" She stopped on the other side of his desk and glared at him. "What were you thinking?"

"Clearly, I was not."

She leaned forward and slapped her hands onto the polished wood. "I knew something would happen! Yet

I never imagined I would see such…" She shook her head, apparently deciding against finishing whatever she was about to say. She took a deep breath and asked, "How long has this been going on? How…far have you compromised her?"

He could hardly believe he was having this conversation with his grandmother. Yet he could not deny that what he did affected her as well. She had a right to ask.

"What you saw today," he said, forcing himself to meet her gaze, "is the most that has happened between us, I swear."

"That was more than enough," she replied. She alternated between frowning and looking astonished. "I almost fainted. And I have never fainted in my life!"

"I am sorry. But she nearly drowned. And after I pulled her from the water, I…I lost control." He'd never abandoned restraint like that before. Of course, he'd never saved someone from possibly drowning before either. Now that the rush of emotion he'd felt over saving her was fading, surely his control would return.

"Indeed," his grandmother said, her eyes narrowing. "And what do you intend to do now?"

Avoid dinner, for one thing, he thought. A meal together would be horribly awkward.

"I shall ensure nothing of the sort happens again," he said. "And I will keep my distance for the rest of her stay."

His grandmother shook her head. "It has already gone too far. She must leave as soon as possible. If anyone else had seen it…" She sighed. "Thankfully, Lady Cecelia made it quite clear that the last thing she wants is to marry you."

The last thing? Had she phrased it that way exactly? He scowled. Though of course he should not care. He certainly couldn't marry her.

"I tried to persuade her to leave early," his grandmother continued, "but she refused. She said she wanted to wait for Lord Wareton to take her home. But you must do something because this…situation simply cannot continue."

She opened her mouth, paused, and then, in a much quieter voice, she said, "She asked if I knew a family in Winchester by the name of Wyatt."

His heart seemed to stop beating.

"She what?" he whispered.

"It seems she received a letter today from Winchester. I believe she must have written to someone in the city and asked about you. How she thought to ask in Winchester, I have no idea. Perhaps you might." She paused to glare at him. "But you see why it is even more imperative that she leave as soon as possible." She cleared her throat, and suddenly she looked more frightened than angry. "Although, it may already be too late."

"What do you mean?"

"This morning," she said, "when I…found you together, I was returning from visiting Mrs. Harvey. She mentioned that her groom said that a week ago someone had been asking about you in town. A stranger."

A chill went through him.

"What stranger?" he asked.

"He called himself Smith. Said he was interested in finding the gentleman who had hired a coach from Westbury to London a few weeks past. As far as she knew, the man didn't say why."

"What did the man look like?"

"I don't know," she said with a sigh. "I don't know any other details. I didn't want to ask too much and have Mrs. Harvey think even more about it. But I am returning to town tomorrow to try to find out more from the groom. Discreetly, of course."

James cursed.

"Let us hope it is nothing," she added. "Just an odd coincidence."

But they both knew it would be an odd coincidence indeed.

She opened her mouth as if she wanted to say more, but then quickly closed it again. After giving him one last distraught look, she turned and marched from the room. He leaned back in his chair as her steps faded.

Lady Cecelia had discovered his secret. Likely his story about the race and the cathedral had given her the idea.

Damn his idiocy. As if kissing her wasn't bad enough, now this.

And as to the man asking about him… Perhaps he had been recognized in London. He wished it might simply be an odd coincidence, as his grandmother said.

One thing was certain. Each day Lady Cecelia remained here was dangerous, and now it was perhaps dangerous in more ways than one. His grandmother was correct. He must convince Lady Cecelia to leave—as soon as possible.

CHAPTER FOURTEEN

THE NEXT MORNING, AS CECELIA sat alone at the breakfast table, someone gently spoke her name. It took her a moment to recognize who it was—Mrs. Thornton had never before addressed her in anything close to a kind tone.

"Lady Cecelia," Mrs. Thornton said, "I want to thank you for saving my Urchin." The housekeeper had paused just inside the doorway with Urchin cradled against her chest. For once she wasn't scowling at Cecelia. Cecelia hadn't seen her since rescuing the dog yesterday.

Cecelia smiled and lowered her cup of chocolate to the table. "I am so glad he is well."

Mrs. Thornton moved closer and stopped next to her. Urchin caught sight of Cecelia and started wagging his tail.

"May I pet him?" Cecelia asked.

Mrs. Thornton nodded.

Cecelia pushed back her chair and was about to reach out to pat him, when to her shock, Mrs. Thornton gently placed the animal on her lap.

Cecelia couldn't help but smile. Urchin smelled faintly of rosewater. Mrs. Thornton must have given him a bath. Cecelia rubbed gently behind his ears and his tail thumped against the edge of the table.

"I know you wonder why he's so dear to me," Mrs. Thornton said. "Well, you've earned the right to know." The housekeeper's eyes shone. "He was my son's dog. My son who died. When Mr. Wr— that is, when I got the news, I learned that Urchin had shared my son's berth."

Had she started to say that Mr. Wright had told her?

"Urchin was your son's dog?" Cecelia cradled him more tightly.

Mrs. Thornton nodded.

No wonder the woman doted on the creature so.

"Will you sit with me?" Cecelia motioned to the chair beside her.

Mrs. Thornton's eyes went wide. "Sit. With you."

"Yes. Please."

For the first time in Cecelia's memory, the housekeeper looked uncertain. She slowly moved forward and lowered herself into the chair, staring at Cecelia warily.

"What was your son's name?" Cecelia asked. She continued to pet Urchin as his tail slowly stilled and his eyes drifted shut.

"Nate," Mrs. Thornton said softly. The stiffness left her shoulders.

"How old was he?"

"Sixteen," Mrs. Thornton said, her voice cracking. "It was…a decade ago." So her son had been close to Mr. Wright's age.

"How terrible." Cecelia was even happier that she had helped to save Urchin, if it had spared an already heartbroken mother more grief.

"I'm sorry if I was ever rude," Mrs. Thornton said, meeting her gaze. "I…I was upset Mr. Wright had to go to London because of you. And I was sure you would bring trouble to this house and to him. But now I'm truly sorry. And I want you to know…when you saved Urchin, it's as if you saved a bit of my son."

Tears filled Cecelia's eyes, but she forced them back.

"And I'm also sorry," Mrs. Thornton added, "because I heard you lost your parents to the sea when you were very young. Is that true?"

"Yes."

The housekeeper's expression softened even more. "How old were you?"

"Two," Cecelia said. "I don't remember them."

Mrs. Thornton nodded sympathetically.

Cecelia paused, gathered her courage, and asked, "Will you tell me something?"

"If I can."

"Was it Mr. Wright who told you about your son's death? Were they at sea together?"

"I…couldn't say." Mrs. Thornton dropped her gaze to the table.

Which Cecelia took as a yes. But if so, that could mean…

Cecelia took a deep breath. "Did your son…die on the *Sentinel*?"

Mrs. Thornton's eyes widened. She leaned back and looked directly at Cecelia. "Why would you think that?" she whispered.

"I heard a rumor," Cecelia said gently.

Mrs. Thornton briefly closed her eyes. Cecelia waited, hoping the housekeeper would reveal more, but she remained silent.

"And Mr. Wright," Cecelia said, "he was with your son?"

Mrs. Thornton shook her head. "It's not my place to tell you about Mr. Wright's past."

The hollow look in her eyes suggested Cecelia had at least hit close to the mark. She thought back to that day in the library, when she had spoken about the unkindness Reed and her father had faced because of the rumors of his desertion, and the peculiar way Mr. Wright had reacted. Was it because something similar was true for him?

If Mr. Wright had been on the *Sentinel* and concealed that fact, it probably meant one thing: he had been a deserter. Likely he had been one of the impressed sailors who never wanted to be on the ship in the first place, and he had fled when the opportunity arose. He would have been fifteen at most. Press gangs were not supposed to take boys that young, but it happened anyway. It was no wonder if he'd chosen to run, and no different than what many others had done.

Desertion was a crime, but given his young age and many years having passed, he might not have to fear punishment now. That was, if it hadn't involved the *Sentinel* and that infamous encounter when so many sailors had died.

If it was true, what a terrible burden for him. But it would explain so much. Why he helped the families of sailors. Why he might change his name and hide himself away in the country, for fear of his past being discovered. And perhaps even why he would never marry.

Sadness washed over her, and she took a deep breath. Perhaps her suspicions were correct, but unless Mr. Wright chose to tell her himself, she might never be sure of the real story.

However, one thing was certain: now she understood why he employed the less-than-well-mannered Mrs. Thornton, and why the woman had no fear of losing her position for being rude. Mr. Wright must have hired her as housekeeper because he'd sailed with her son.

Heavy, fast steps sounded in the hall—Mr. Wright's.

As he stepped into the room, his gaze fell on her and then Urchin in her lap, and his eyebrows shot up. His expression wavered between apprehension and a smile. The smile won out.

"Good morning, Lady Cecelia," he said, walking closer. He wore simple clothes—a dark coat and breeches, and a plain cravat. He looked far less disheveled than yesterday.

"Good morning, Mr. Wright," she said.

He stopped next to her and reached out to pat Urchin,

his arm brushing against her own. Then he stroked the dog's back, allowing his hand to come so near to her legs that she held her breath.

He was almost as close to her as yesterday, when he'd been pressed against her, when they had—

"I'll take him," Mrs. Thornton said, swooping toward her.

"Allow me," he said. As he slid his fingers under Urchin to pick him up, the backs of his hands brushed against Cecelia's thighs.

He frowned, looking flustered, as if he hadn't meant to touch her. But as far as her body was concerned, he might as well have kissed her as passionately as he had yesterday—that was how heated and shaky she suddenly felt.

He quickly turned away and handed Urchin to Mrs. Thornton. He paused to pat the animal again and murmur something kind.

Cecelia sighed. He was so gentle and caring. He had such a good heart. If any woman ever did convince him to marry, she would be most fortunate.

And Cecelia would be…horribly jealous. Yesterday by the river had been so—

No. She must stop thinking about him in that way. How pointless.

"Mr. Wright," she blurted, focusing on her plate while she spoke. "Will you join me?" If she looked into his dark eyes, he might sense what she had been thinking.

"No, thank you," he said. "I already ate."

"Your grandmother already went out," she continued. "Apparently, she had errands to run in town."

Cecelia had been surprised to be left unchaperoned, especially after yesterday. According to Reed, Mrs. Stewart had seemed distracted and nervous this morning. Cecelia couldn't help but wonder if it had anything to do with the events of yesterday.

"Yes, I know she went out," Mr. Wright said. She finally dared to look at him; his expression was grave. "I wondered if when you are done with your breakfast you might join me for a stroll?"

"Certainly." She even managed to sound somewhat normal. As if she hadn't been caught only yesterday in a highly compromising position with him. And as if she wasn't longing to behave imprudently again.

He nodded. "Please take your time and enjoy the rest of your breakfast. I will wait in the garden."

He spun around and strode away, leaving her with a pounding heart.

As if she could eat another bite now.

Soon after, Cecelia gathered her courage to go out to the garden. She found Mr. Wright pacing near the rose arbor. He looked almost impossibly handsome.

Her chest tightened, and her pulse sped up. She wanted to…do scandalous things with him. This instant.

Oh dear. This infatuation could be disastrous—if she allowed it to be.

Not long ago, she might have permitted herself to get swept away by attraction and emotion, but she'd grown wiser. She'd vowed never to allow romantic notions to lead her to marry imprudently. While a certain amount of affection was good in a marriage, the most important factors must be practical.

Sadness threatened, but she pushed it away.

He did not even want to marry. So why must she think about suitability and marriage at present? Why not simply appreciate his company and worry about the future later?

He stopped pacing and watched her approach. Warmth filled her whole body as she thought yet again of their intimacies yesterday. What were the chances that he would kiss her again like that, right now? Pull her behind the cover of trees, kiss her even more thoroughly, and hold her against him—

She tripped on a stone in the path and quickly caught herself. Pushing away the deliciously distracting thoughts, she focused on walking the last few paces toward him without stumbling again.

Sadly, he did not look like a man who intended to kiss anyone right now. He appeared horribly somber.

"Thank you for joining me," he said. "Shall we walk by…" He frowned. Perhaps he had been about to suggest they walk by the river but thought better of it after yesterday. "Shall we take the path by the pastures?"

"That would be lovely," she said. They began strolling away from the gardens toward the stables.

"You are up early this morning," he said.

"I had trouble sleeping." She paused. "I kept thinking of yesterday."

His eyes widened and he almost missed a step. Did he expect she'd not speak of what happened between them?

"Lady Cecelia," he said softly, shifting his gaze to the ground. "I am sorry. What we did was—"

"Wonderful." She stopped and turned toward him.

He paused but did not face her, so she moved to stand before him. His eyes widened again. As he met her gaze, he seemed about to step back. But he did not.

"It was wrong," he said, frowning. "If he knew, your brother would be furious. And rightly so."

She said nothing. Adrian might have better intentions than her aunt, but even he sought to influence her too much. She was tired of others dictating her life. She was also tired of stifling rules of behavior.

Tilting her head, she looked up at him. His brow was furrowed, and his hair was disheveled in a way that only made him look more handsome. Oh, how she wanted to stare into his gorgeous eyes for the rest of the day. And kiss him. And—

What a muddle she had gotten herself into.

Mr. Grim, she'd thought when she'd first met him. How wrong she'd been. He was kind and clever. Witty, too. Warm and caring. And so handsome. And his kisses were heavenly…

She wanted more than anything to slide her fingers into his thick hair, pull him closer, and taste his mouth once again. She eased forward until only inches separated them.

"You are determined to create scandal?" he murmured.

"I am not interested in scandal. I am interested in choosing what I do." Such as traveling if she wished. Or kissing a gentleman if she chose, without having to marry him.

Her pulse sped up as she shifted even closer until her skirt brushed against his legs.

She asked softly, "You…do wish to kiss me again?"

He closed his eyes. When he opened them, she saw his restraint fall away.

"God, yes." He reached out and clasped her hand. "Of course, I do."

His warm, strong fingers slid around her own, his bare skin pressing against hers. He lifted her hand, bent down, and kissed her fingers. The brush of his lips made her knees threaten to buckle. She had to concentrate on remaining upright, rather than collapsing onto the grass.

As he straightened, he smiled wickedly. "If it were up to me," he whispered, "I would kiss you as I did on the riverbank, all over again, but for far, far longer. And I would kiss you everywhere."

Heat washed through her.

He brushed his mouth against her fingers one more time, but then sadly, he released her hand and stepped back.

"And that is exactly why," he said, his voice rough, "it would be best if you left Westbury. As soon as possible."

Did he truly want her to leave?

He met her gaze again and her heart raced even faster.

No, he did not want her to go. The way he stared at her made that apparent. But he was clearly trying to choose the honorable path.

But she couldn't leave. Not without knowing why he was the way he was. And who he truly was.

"You see," he added just above a whisper, "if we should be caught…in another compromising situation, I cannot do what honor demands. No matter how much I might desire it, I can never marry."

She frowned. He could never marry, even if he wanted to?

"I do not understand," she said.

He motioned to a bench a short distance away, not far from the stables. "Perhaps we should sit."

She nodded.

Once they settled on the bench, she angled toward him. He inched away and remained facing forward.

"When my father died," he said, "I'd hoped to live with my grandmother. But I soon learned that I was to be sent far away, to live with relatives I'd never met."

"Yes, you went to live with your cousin?"

"No, I was supposed to live with a cousin, and that is what I allowed people to believe. But I ran away." He glanced at her and added, "I ended up on the London streets."

The London streets. That explained how he'd known of that alleyway. And how his grandmother had lost contact with him. Perhaps Lady Margaret's letter had been accurate about what had happened to him after all.

"I survived on the streets for a time," he continued, "but eventually, when the city became too dangerous, I had to leave." He took a deep breath. "I'd been working for a man, pinching cargo at the docks, and he wrongly believed that I'd stolen from him. He wanted me dead."

He met her gaze, as if to gauge her reaction. Did he think she would be horrified?

If he'd stolen in order to survive, he'd only done what so many others had done. Like Reed.

"Where did you go?" she asked.

"I went…to sea." He added quickly, "After my time at sea, I made a new life in the army, and I hoped I'd put my past behind me."

"You changed your name?"

He nodded. "When I joined the army."

"Your real name is James Wyatt? And you are from Winchester, not Portsmouth?"

He nodded, not seeming surprised that she knew. "My grandmother said you asked her questions. I assume my story about the cathedral gave it away?"

"Yes," she said. "What you told me about the cathedral with the long nave made me think of Winchester, so I wrote to my friend who has lived there for decades. That name was the closest match she knew of, to the details I provided."

He said nothing.

"Is this…why you have never married?" she asked softly.

He glanced at her and nodded. "Marrying under a false name would not be a legal marriage. Nor would I endanger…a family." His voice hitched on the last word.

The pain that she'd glimpsed when he'd spoken of marriage, the pain she'd once assumed to be from heartbreak over one woman, was not that at all. It was heartbreak over the wife and family he would never have.

No wonder he avoided attachments.

Tears filled her eyes. She swiftly wiped them away. She wanted to reach out to him, to touch him, to comfort him, but she feared his reaction.

"So," he said, not looking at her, "I hope now that you will understand why I cannot…why you must leave."

"I do understand," she said. But there was so much more she wanted to know, so much he had skipped over. "Will you tell me what happened at sea?"

He stiffened and curled his hands around the edge of the bench. "I've shared enough."

They sat in silence for several minutes. He was clearly not ready to tell her more. But how painful it must be for him.

She finally gathered the courage to reach out to him when the sound of horses stopped her.

They both rose. Hoofbeats crunched on the drive that led to the house—several horses were approaching rapidly.

Three riders appeared, men wearing rough clothes. The men scanned the surrounding landscape for something. Or someone.

"This way," Mr. Wright whispered. He gently took her arm and started to lead her behind the stables. The fear in his expression sent her pulse racing. He clearly believed these men were dangerous. But in only a few seconds, they would be out of view.

One of the riders turned and caught sight of them.

The man called out to the other two, and they all urged their horses toward her and Mr. Wright. The men stopped a dozen paces from them and slid off their horses.

The one who had first spotted them stepped forward. He was tall and burly, with red hair curling out from beneath a worn, dark cap. Something bulged beneath his coat. A pistol?

"James Wright?" the man asked. He glanced at her, then kept his gaze on Mr. Wright.

"Yes," Mr. Wright said.

The men swept past her and set upon Mr. Wright. She watched in shock as they struggled. Mr. Wright landed two impressive blows on the larger one and managed to knock the smaller man to the ground. The third man joined them, and the three of them finally succeeded in shoving Mr. Wright against the wall of the stables and holding him.

She looked around for help. They were out of sight of the house, and unless someone happened to be in the stables, they'd be unlikely to hear the struggle. If only there was something close by that she could use as a weapon to help him. A tree branch or—

"Go!" Mr. Wright shouted at her. His hat was gone. Blood trickled from his mouth.

She should run and scream for help. Mr. Long or another servant might be close enough to hear if she shouted—

"Not so fast," the red-haired man said as he grabbed her by the arm. "Keep quiet, and I'll not harm you."

She struggled, but the man was too strong. He swung her around until her back was toward him, and he pinned her against his chest. He reeked of stale sweat and horses.

"Don't hurt him!" she said.

"Don't worry, I won't. Not much, anyway." The man laughed. Then he shouted to his men, "Turn him around. Let me see his back."

His back? She stopped struggling.

The ruffians tried to force Mr. Wright around. He got one arm free and landed a hard blow to the larger one.

"Do that again," the man holding her said, "and I'll hurt her."

Mr. Wright stilled. He allowed them to take his coat and waistcoat, all the while glaring at the man holding her.

"And the shirt," the man holding her said.

The other two men stripped off Mr. Wright's cravat and shirt and spun him around, shoving him roughly against the wall.

She stifled a gasp. Mr. Wright had a thick, straight scar

that ran from just beneath his right shoulder down to his waist. A scar from a wound that must have been agonizing.

Her throat felt dry. What in heavens had happened to him?

The man holding her moved forward, dragging her with him. "How'd you get that scar, Mr. *Wright*?" he said, sounding pleased.

"In the army," Mr. Wright answered tightly.

The man holding her let out a sharp laugh. "Right. You can let him go," he added to the men holding him.

The men released Mr. Wright. They both stepped back quickly as he spun around. Mr. Wright kept his fists at his side, his gaze on her.

The man holding her abruptly freed her. She rushed to Mr. Wright. He caught her and pulled her behind him, wrapping one muscular, bare arm protectively around her.

"I'm to let you know that you have three days," the red-haired man said, staring at Mr. Wright. "Three days to get your affairs in order and make your way to London. To the Black Bell."

Mr. Wright remained silent.

The man stared at Mr. Wright a few seconds longer then, smiling, he tipped his hat. "Good day, *Mr. Wright*," he said. He and his men turned away.

Within seconds, the men were back on their horses. They headed onto the road and disappeared toward the main entrance to the estate.

Once they were out of sight, Cecelia realized her heart was still pounding. Mr. Wright held her protectively for a few seconds longer, then he abruptly released her. He silently retrieved his shirt from the ground.

"What on earth just happened?" she said.

He didn't meet her gaze as he slipped his shirt over his head. Then he pulled on his waistcoat.

"Where in the blazes is my cravat?" he snapped. He quickly spied it on the ground, grabbed it, and tied it on haphazardly. Then he picked up his crumpled coat and began brushing the grass from it. Other than narrowed eyes, his manner was as calm as if he were preparing to go into dinner.

"Tell me," she said.

He put on his coat, and then he strode over to retrieve his hat from beside the stables.

She followed him. "Will you not answer me?"

He shoved his hat on, turned, and stopped in front of her. His expression was the grimmest she'd seen.

How had he been scarred so badly, if not in the army? She'd never heard of such an injury from Adrian, only of his arm.

"You are still bleeding," she said, stepping closer. He must be in pain too, where they had struck him and shoved him against the wall. "Who were those men?"

"I do not know," he finally said. "But one of them—the red-haired one—I've seen him before."

"When?"

He paused before answering. "A few weeks ago."

A few weeks ago?

"Where?" she asked.

He silently met her gaze. The anger in his eyes made the answer horribly clear.

That night in London when he'd found her, she vividly recalled his words, and the guilt they'd sparked in her.

After all I have risked to find you… You put us all in danger.

Had he not only been speaking of being robbed?

"You saw him when you were searching for me?" she asked.

He gave a curt nod.

"Then…this is all my fault," she whispered.

He said nothing.

"What…what do they want?" They obviously had

been confirming his identity but wanted him alive. "Let me try to help." She reached for his hand.

He jerked away. "You've done quite enough." He would not meet her gaze. "The only helpful thing you could do now is leave."

He turned his back to her and strode toward the manor.

CHAPTER FIFTEEN

CECELIA STARED IN SHOCK AT Mr. Wright as he strode toward the house. After a few seconds, she found her bearings and hurried after him.

Did he truly believe she would simply leave? Whatever crisis he faced, perhaps she and Adrian could help him—if he would let them. Indeed, if his trip to London to recover her had brought this about, she owed it to him.

As Cecelia followed him into the house, Reed and Mrs. Thornton met them in the entryway.

"What happened?" the housekeeper said, her brow furrowed. "We heard riders leaving just now. Are you—"

"It's happened," Mr. Wright said. He swept past them and strode up the stairs, two at a time. Halfway up, he turned, met Mrs. Thornton's gaze, and gave a slow nod. The housekeeper looked as if she was about to cry.

"Tell Long I need to speak with him immediately," he added. He spun around and continued upstairs.

"He's injured," Cecelia said. "I'll need warm water, and—"

"There's a kettle on now," Mrs. Thornton said.

"I'll fetch what's needed," Reed said, already turning away.

"Since Mrs. Stewart is out, I'll tend to him," Mrs. Thornton said to Cecelia. The housekeeper's voice cracked, and her eyes shone with tears. "I'll just speak with Mr. Long first."

Mrs. Thornton started to turn away, but Cecelia grasped her arm. "I will care for him."

Mrs. Thornton's eyes narrowed. She scowled at Cecelia as fiercely as she had in the past. "This is all because he went to London to search for you, isn't it?"

Cecelia's stomach churned as she held Mrs. Thornton's gaze. "Yes."

"I knew you would bring trouble."

"Please, let me tend to him. I must speak with him to see how my brother and I might help him."

Mrs. Thornton gazed at her silently. Some of the anger faded from her expression. "Very well," she finally said, her voice still sharp.

"Why would those men wish to harm him?" Cecelia asked quickly, before Mrs. Thornton could turn away. "Does this have anything to do with him being at sea? With your son?"

After a second's hesitation, Mrs. Thornton nodded.

Cecelia took a step closer. "Will you tell me what happened, so I might help him?"

Mrs. Thornton bit her lip and frowned.

"I know this is my fault," Cecelia said. "But now I only want to help him if I can. Please tell me."

Mrs. Thornton sighed. "I suppose there's no more hiding from it now, anyway." She took a few deep breaths, clearly trying to fight off tears.

"For years now," Mrs. Thornton said, "he's felt badly about what happened that day. And that he ran off. But he only did what he had to do to survive."

Sadness washed over Cecelia. Then he was among the deserters, as she'd thought. But what did those men want with him now? Blackmail?

Rapid footsteps sounded and Reed appeared holding a basin of warm water and several folded cloths.

Sniffing loudly, Mrs. Thornton spun around and hurried away.

Reed frowned after the housekeeper and looked back at Cecelia. "Would you like me to help, milady?"

Having Reed with her would be more proper. But Mr. Wright would be even less likely to tell her anything with Reed there.

"No," Cecelia said, taking the basin and cloths from her. "Thank you."

Reed nodded and turned away.

As Cecelia approached Mr. Wright's room, her steps slowed. Would he even let her tend to his injuries, let alone tell her the truth about his past?

She took a deep breath and knocked briskly. He called for her to enter.

His eyes widened as she stepped inside. He had clearly been expecting Mrs. Thornton. He straightened from leaning against the mantel. He wore the same shirt as earlier, but untucked and open at the neck. Dried blood still marred his lip, and fresh blood trickled from his brow.

He scowled. "You should go—"

"Sit," she said. Tilting up her chin, she stared at him, refusing to look away first.

He stared back, frowning. After a few seconds, he muttered something that could have been "very well" or "bloody hell." He sighed and dropped into the armchair by the fire.

She marched over and placed the basin and cloths on the small table beside him. As she turned back toward him, her gaze fell on the enormous bed.

She was in his bedroom. Alone with him.

Not that anything scandalous would happen. The door was wide open, and anyone could walk in at any moment. She was only tending to his injuries.

She recalled the look of him shirtless only moments ago—the sculpted muscles of his arm, the scattering of dark hair across his chest. What would it be like to touch him beneath his shirt? To—

She forced the inappropriate thoughts away. How shameful, to be so distracted at a time like this. Her face felt hot as she dipped a cloth in the warm water and turned toward him.

The chair creaked as he leaned back and looked up at her. His expression was dark. He was clearly a man with a troubled past, a past she intended to learn more about.

"First," she said, lifting the cloth to his forehead, "tell me what happened at sea."

He raised an eyebrow but said nothing.

She gently wiped away the blood, his breath warming her bare forearm. "Please tell me."

"If I tell you, will you leave afterward?"

"I will make no promises." She dropped her hand and stepped back.

He stared at her, appearing annoyed and something else she couldn't quite place. Then he shook his head and looked away. The anguish on his face made her heart ache. He clearly wasn't ready to tell her and pressing him about it would likely prove fruitless.

She rinsed the cloth in the washbasin and turned back to him. Gently, she dabbed at the blood on his lip. Having his mouth pressed against hers had been so delicious. She wanted to kiss him again. Now.

He tilted back his head and looked up at her, his gaze seemingly focused on her mouth.

Was he also thinking about their kisses?

He reached up and drew her hand away from his face. "Enough." His voice was hoarse.

She let her hand fall. "Are you in pain?" she said, taking a step back. "Where they struck you—it must hurt."

He shrugged. "I've had worse."

She thought of his scarred back. "Clearly." She paused. "What will you do now? What did they mean about three days to get to London?"

"I assume they will find me there."

"You could alert the authorities."

"If I do, the truth about my past will come out. I will

be arrested, or worse." He shook his head. "My only choice is to run."

"What do you mean?"

"I mean that I cannot stay here." The resignation in his voice made her breath catch.

She stepped closer to him. "But your estate…" Dear heavens, had searching for her in London cost him so much? "Let me, and Adrian, try to help you. Tell me what happened, so we can—"

"No." He rose. "I will not have you mixed up in this any further."

She only wanted to help him. But it seemed that he would not let her. Soon he would leave, and she would most likely never see him again.

Her throat tightened. Her chest ached. He had tried to do right, to escape his past, and now everything he had worked so hard for was ruined. And because of her.

He sighed and looked down at her. "Now you know enough," he rasped. "So leave me in peace."

"No." Her heart pounded as she stepped closer, reached out, and took his hand. She expected him to push her away, but he didn't.

"Please allow me to help," she whispered. "Do not send me away."

James stared down at Lady Cecelia. He wanted to remain angry with her, but the warmth and compassion in her eyes made that difficult. Her longing for connection with him only made her even more beautiful and tempting. Before she'd taken his hand, he'd already been tormented by her closeness. Her gentle caresses as she tended to his wounds. The delicious scent of her hair and skin as she leaned near to him. The heat of her body mere inches from him.

Even though his life was shattered, and even though she

was part of the reason, he still wanted her. Desperately. Perhaps it was easier to focus on his desire for her than on the reality of what had just happened.

He gently slid his fingers through hers, holding her hand more tightly. His gaze fell on her warm, sweet mouth. She had responded so passionately to him at the river. If he pulled her against him right now, and kissed her, would she react as intensely?

If anything could take his mind off his wreck of a life, it was her. How he'd love to kiss her again. To see what her breasts looked like free from her stays. To taste the rest of her gorgeous body, as he'd tasted her mouth and neck, and to know what it was to have her naked and breathless beneath him.

But to do so would be not only reckless but dishonest. She did not know the truth about him. If she did, she almost certainly would not want anything to do with him.

And if he had any sense, he would want nothing to do with her. Especially now.

Reluctantly, he released her hand and strode to the hearth. He leaned against the mantel, taking deep breaths to slow his racing pulse. He forced himself to look at the glowing coals, fearful that staring at her too long would shatter his fragile restraint.

He must remind himself of the danger to both of them. It wasn't difficult, as what had happened outside a short time ago was seared into his mind.

When the men had attacked, those horrible moments had felt like an eternity. When that big one had held her, and threatened to hurt her…

He swallowed on the tightness in his throat from the memory of the rage that filled him. He'd been overcome with fury and a fear just as powerful. Fear that was different, but as potent as the dread he had felt in the army when the lives of his comrades had been in danger.

A fear of losing something irreplaceable.

His chest tightened and again that nearly overwhelming fear of something happening to her filled him. The dread was quickly followed by a wave of anger.

He had become so infatuated with her. Never mind how impossible the situation was and had been even before today. Never mind that she was part of the reason his life had just fallen apart. And yet he could not stand the idea of any harm coming to her.

He had to leave soon, but before he did, he should tell her of his past—at least enough of the truth that she would finally leave.

"You must go," he said. "Today."

"I do not want to." Her lovely voice was confident, determined.

He turned to face her. "You would feel differently, if you knew the truth."

She stood by the chair, one soft hand resting on its back. Her face was delightfully flushed. "I think I do know," she said.

He almost laughed. She could not possibly know. Not and still look at him as she did now.

"What do you know?" he asked.

"That you were a sailor." She stepped closer. "And that…you survived when others did not."

How did she know that?

"Is that not true?" she said.

"It is." But surely, she could not have learned everything?

"On the *Sentinel*," she said, her voice almost a whisper.

Hearing that ship's name sent a horrible tumult of emotions washing through him.

"Whatever happened a decade ago," she said, "it does not matter to me. If you ran away from impressment, it was only what many others have done."

Somehow she had reasoned that he'd been impressed and deserted?

"The man you are now is what matters," she continued, "and I wish to help you." Her beautiful eyes and voice were full of such genuine concern, he could almost weep. "Indeed, I owe it to you. It was because of me that you were recognized in London."

He shook his head. "That does not mean you should be involved."

"I am already involved," she said gently, moving even nearer. "I wish to be involved." She was only an arm's length from him.

Close as she was to the mark, she would likely never guess the full, horrible truth. Why not let her go on believing as she did now? Her version of his past, awful as it was, was still better than the reality.

The idea was tempting. He could keep her sympathy and compassion, for a short time at least. And such a deception might not be entirely selfish, for he'd be protecting her from the shock and possible danger of knowing the truth.

Except that without that truth, she would never understand the true peril of his situation. Only the real story would likely convince her to leave immediately, and to distance herself from him, where she would be safer.

And guarantee that she would never wish to touch him again.

He allowed himself to drink in the way she looked at him—the warmth and sympathy in her eyes, her longing to comfort him. When he revealed the truth, he knew those soft emotions would be gone forever.

"I did desert my shipmates," he said, "you have that part right. But not the rest."

She tilted her head to one side, her beautiful gaze never wavering from his face.

He forced out the horrible words. "I wasn't a deserter from the *Sentinel*. I was on the crew of the *Fortune*."

As shock blossomed on her face, he stepped to the side.

He strode toward the door. Coward that he was, he would not watch her shock turn to revulsion. He paused in the doorway, but he did not look back toward the silence.

"Now you truly understand why," he said, his voice breaking, "you must leave. Immediately. I will see the carriage is made ready."

And then he fled.

CHAPTER SIXTEEN

A S HIS STEPS FADED, CECELIA stood frozen.
I was on the crew of the Fortune.
Several long seconds passed before she comprehended the full, terrible weight of his words. Then her legs began to tremble. She managed a few steps and lowered herself into a nearby chair. She leaned forward, hugging herself.

Dear heavens. He had not been a Royal Navy sailor, but a crewman on one of the most infamous ships in the British Empire. The ship whose captain and crew were responsible for the deaths of a dozen Royal Navy sailors.

She felt as if she could barely breathe. She forced out a long, trembling breath.

When the commander of the *Sentinel* had tried to impress sailors from the *Fortune* and Captain Grey and his men had resisted, some recently impressed men on the *Sentinel* had deserted in the chaos. She had assumed James to be one of those men who fled. She had never imagined he'd been among the merchant crew that killed the navy sailors and then escaped out to sea.

After the massacre, the *Fortune* and her crew had apparently sailed to the Barbary Coast and turned pirate. About a year later, the ship was said to have been badly damaged after a battle with a Spanish ship and had reportedly sunk. None of Grey's crew had ever been found alive.

Until now.

Her pulse raced faster. She could not remain in his room for a servant to find. Or worse, for him to return.

She dragged herself to her feet and stumbled out into the hallway toward her room.

The door was open, and Reed was taking clothes from the wardrobe.

"Mr. Wright said to prepare to leave right away," Reed said.

Cecelia nodded.

"Are you well, milady?" Reed stepped forward. "It's no wonder if you're upset, after those men…well…. Does Mr. Wright think they'll return?"

"I do not know." Cecelia wasn't ready to speak of it yet, even to Reed. "I…need to walk."

Reed nodded. "I'll fetch you a bonnet."

A few minutes later, Cecelia was striding alone down the path toward the river.

She had no idea where James had gone, but she hoped she would not run into him. What on earth did one say to such a revelation?

Though she wanted to somehow convince herself that it must all be a fantastic lie, in her heart she knew that his words were true.

No wonder he had changed his name and hid away from society. No wonder he carried such guilt toward Royal Navy sailors, and he made such an effort to help their families. Not because he had been impressed into the navy and had deserted, but because he had been among the crew that slaughtered over a dozen of them.

Nausea churned her stomach.

His past was nothing like she'd imagined. It was far, far worse.

She kept walking until she reached the end of the estate. Then she turned back, walking more slowly. Her shock gradually faded. Her thoughts calmed from the chaos of trying to comprehend what she had just learned about him, to what she knew of him before.

He'd fought for king and country in the army, risking

his life. He'd saved others, including her brother. He'd rescued her from the river. Heavens, the man even helped orphans.

He could have let her believe that he was a deserter from impressment, could have kept his secret and her sympathy. Instead, he'd chosen the truth, horrible as it was.

And it was horrible. But he was not.

Whatever his past actions, she was certain that now he was a man of deep compassion and honor. And yet no amount of heroics could erase his involvement in that dark event. He'd said she should leave immediately, and he was correct. Distancing herself from him as soon as possible was the prudent thing to do. Except…

When he went to London to look for her, he'd risked discovery to help her brother. And now because of her, his peaceful life was lost. Tears filled her eyes. She walked faster, until she was almost running.

She would not leave without helping him. But first, she had to learn more.

When Cecelia returned to the house, Long was out front, speaking with Evans. Long seemed to be giving orders to prepare the carriage to take her home.

"Where is Mr. Wright?" she said.

"I believe he's in the stables, milady," Long said. His usual smile was gone, but he did not look at her unkindly, as if he blamed her for what was happening. "The carriage will be ready for you soon."

"Thank you," she said. As she was about to turn away, she paused and glanced between Long and Evans. "However, I will not need the carriage. At least, not yet."

Long's eyes widened and his face softened. It wasn't quite his usual smile, but it was something close.

"I have to run errands for Mr. Wright," Long said, "to help him settle his affairs. Jenna must go out too. I was going to have Evans keep watch by the road, just in case those men return. But if you need him here—"

"No," she said. "I have Alfred, Reed, and Mrs. Thornton. We'll be fine."

Long nodded.

She thanked them both, and then turned and strode toward the stables. When she stepped through the open doors, she spotted Mr. Wright just inside a stall, speaking softly to his mare.

Would he take the horse with him, or was he saying goodbye?

Cecelia moved into the doorway of the stall, and he lifted his head. He met her gaze, and all the breath seemed to leave her body.

He looked utterly heartbroken. But he quickly composed himself, gave his horse one last pat, and straightened.

"Was there something you needed before you leave?" he asked, his eyes focused on some point beyond her.

Was he simply too angry to look at her? Or was he not meeting her eye because he feared her reaction to having learned about his past? What horror he must have endured. How painful, and how lonely it must be, to live with such secrets.

"Yes," she said softly. Curling her hands into fists to hide her shaking fingers, she stepped toward him, not stopping until she was only an arm's length away.

"I will not leave," she said. "At least, not until you tell me more of what happened at sea."

He lifted his gaze to meet hers, his eyes wide. He stared at her as if she was an apparition.

"You must leave now," he finally said. "To stay is… beyond foolish."

"No." She forced herself to sound far more confident

than she felt, and she squared her shoulders. "Tell me about the *Fortune*."

He gazed at her in silence. If he refused to share any more, she simply would not leave until he did. But from the way he was staring at her, his eyes wide with a glimmer of hope, he clearly wanted to tell her.

"It is not right to burden you with it," he said.

"You will want my brother to have an account of what happened, will you not? A truthful account?" She tried to keep her voice even. "I presume he knows nothing of this?"

He nodded. "I do owe him the truth."

"Then tell me, and I shall convey it to him." If that was the excuse that he needed to tell her, so be it.

He stepped toward her, brushing against her skirt as he moved past her through the doorway. She turned and followed him. He took a few steps and paused, apparently scanning the building for anyone else.

"Mr. Long sent the groom to keep watch by the road," she said. "And he was going out as well. You can speak without much chance of being overheard."

He nodded and turned to face her.

"How long were you on the ship?" she asked.

"Nearly a year." His voice sounded almost normal. He began strolling toward the back of the stables. "When I needed to escape London, I ended up in Newhaven. But I wasn't sure how long I'd be safe there, so when I was invited to join the crew of a merchant ship, I jumped at the chance." He stopped walking as they reached the end of the stalls, just before the open doorway to outside.

"The *Fortune*?" she asked.

"Yes. The crew told me how good a ship it was, of the many places they'd sailed, how they were all treated well, much better than in the navy." He smiled sadly. "And when I met the captain, I was hooked."

"Captain Grey?"

He nodded. "His crew respected him, many even idolized him. He had been quite successful, and he was charming too." He leaned one shoulder against the wall, his gaze on the floor. "Grey spun fabulous tales of adventure, and, well, it was exciting."

She thought of the way his eyes had lit up when she'd spoken of how much she'd enjoyed being at sea. Of how he'd said he understood.

With the toe of one boot, he nudged a piece of hay on the otherwise cleanly swept floor. "That is," he continued, "it was exciting, until one night as we were nearing port, the commander of the *Sentinel* caught us just outside the harbor, intending to impress some of the crew."

He straightened, crossed his arms, and fell silent.

"And?" she said.

"And you have no doubt heard the rest." His eyes narrowed. Meaning that was all he would share at present.

While he was speaking, her heart had sped up. In the silence, her pulse slowed again, almost to normal. So much about him finally made sense.

"This is why so many people who work here have relatives who were sailors?" she said.

He nodded.

"Do…they all know of your past?"

"Long does," he said. "I told him when I offered him the position. Alfred and Jenna don't know. But I thought if I had positions to offer, why not help the families of sailors?"

He spoke as if it were the obvious choice. As if any man would have done the same.

"Mrs. Thornton knows, of course," he said. "I went to see her afterward. I had to tell her what had happened to her son, and I wanted to give her Urchin."

If they'd been friends, then Mrs. Thornton's son must have been on the *Fortune* too. No wonder Mrs. Thornton rarely spoke of him. Not only because his loss was too painful, but because he sailed with Grey.

"What happened to her son?"

"Nate died that night when we were caught by the *Sentinel*," Mr. Wright said, his voice tight.

"He died fighting the navy sailors?"

"No." He shifted and crossed his arms more tightly. "Nate died at Captain Grey's hands."

She frowned. "I do not understand."

"We were hiding that night as the *Sentinel* searched for us," he said slowly. "Grey had spotted them earlier that day and knew they were a press ship. He'd said we should use the cover of darkness to hide and hopefully escape. It wasn't difficult to convince most of the crew. No one preferred impressment to working on a ship like the *Fortune*."

Of course. The merchant marines enjoyed far better pay and conditions.

"But Nate didn't think it right to hide," he continued, "and he feared it would be all the worse for us when they inevitably caught us. He also thought the press gang might pass over the two of us for being too young. So he stole up on deck that night, intending to light a lantern to alert the navy ship." He paused. "Grey realized what he was planning and killed him."

"How terrible," she said.

He turned and strolled back toward the other end of the stables, pausing at a stall. After a moment's hesitation, she followed him.

He stared into the empty stall, seemingly focused on nothing. His expression was so dark that she longed to reach out and offer some comfort. But she feared her touch might send him retreating into himself and he would stop sharing his past. At the same time, she dreaded what he might reveal next.

"What happened after your friend was killed?" she finally asked.

He turned and met her gaze. "I had followed Nate on deck to see what he was up to. After I saw Grey kill him…I wasn't thinking clearly, I was so filled with rage…I lit the lantern." He shook his head. "Grey quickly smashed it, but it was too late. We'd been spotted. Grey tried to kill me too, but I jumped overboard and swam away from the ship. When the navy sailors boarded, I watched from the water. I was shocked when Grey and some of the crew fought back. Then I saw men begin to jump from the *Sentinel*. I swam to shore as they did, along with Urchin."

A sigh of relief escaped her. "So…you did not…"

"No. I did not have a direct hand in the attack." His voice was leaden with anguish.

She fought back tears. He'd witnessed his friend's murder, and then everything else… She could not imagine what he had suffered.

"After that," she said, "you became James Wright?"

"Yes."

"But what do those men want now?"

He shook his head. "I've told you enough. Enough details to convey to your brother."

She stepped closer. "But you did not kill His Majesty's sailors. You did not—"

"I might as well have." He curled his hands into fists. "I was the cause of it all. If not for me, the *Sentinel* might never have found us. None of those sailors would have died. And the crew of the *Fortune* would not have become outlaws." He paused and then said quietly, "You once asked me why I chose to help the orphanage in Plymouth. It's because I learned that several of the Royal Navy sailors who died were from there."

"Oh," she whispered. "Of course."

"Not," he said, his tone harsh once again, "that anything could ever make up for what happened."

"But…it is not your fault that Grey and the others chose to resist. And you did not resist, you only fled to save yourself. Surely if you went to the authorities, you would not be punished."

"I was part of Grey's crew for almost a year before that," he said, his voice tight. "And as it became well-known later, Grey was a free trader."

Indeed, and the punishment for smuggling was death. Was there truly no hope for leniency?

A terrible silence followed.

She was so far out of her depth. All she could focus on was that he was in pain and she wanted to help him. But she had no idea what to say or how to help. So she remained silent, her heart aching for him.

"For years now," he said quietly, "I've lived in fear of the truth coming out. At least now, I suppose that worry is gone." But there was no real relief in his voice, only sorrow.

She asked, "In three days, those men want you in London—why?"

"Most likely, to bring me to him."

"Him?"

"Captain Grey."

He stared at her as if he expected that now she might finally turn and run.

"But…Captain Grey is dead."

He shook his head.

"But his ship was lost… Are you certain he is still alive?"

"About two years ago, I first suspected he might be alive," he said. "And after today, I am certain."

So he did not only hide out of fear of the authorities learning he had been on the *Fortune*'s crew. He hid from something even worse.

A chill swept through her. Her hands began to tremble.

He was being targeted by a man who had been—who apparently still was—one of the most wanted villains in

England. Any prudent person would advise her to flee this instant. Her aunt would be horrified and would insist she leave at once.

But her aunt was not here. She was free to make her own decisions.

Ignoring her pounding heart, she let out a long breath and stood straighter.

"So, is that all you have to tell me?" she asked.

He lifted one brow. "Is that…not enough?" That familiar expression and the sardonic edge to his voice gave her hope. Hope that despite everything, his spirit hadn't been crushed.

She nodded. "However, you are wrong. About me leaving." Stepping closer, she slid her arms around him and rested her head against his chest. "You need friends more than ever," she murmured.

He kept his arms at his sides, not pushing her away, but not embracing her back. She could hear his heart beating through his waistcoat and shirt, thrumming fast.

"I will not leave," she added, "not without trying to help you. I cannot begin to imagine what you have gone through, but it must have been awful beyond words. And now, when you thought you had left it all behind you, to have this happen…" She shook her head, her cheek brushing against his soft coat.

She had to do something to help him. Perhaps she could not solve his problems, but she could for a brief time at least help him to forget everything else.

She shifted even closer until she was completely pressed against him. She slid one arm out from around him, lifted her hand to his face, and traced the line of his jaw.

"Before you leave, James," she whispered, "let me… comfort you."

CHAPTER SEVENTEEN

JAMES, LET ME…COMFORT YOU.

The prudent choice, the honorable choice, would be to push her away. Now.

But James couldn't. His anger and sorrow were suddenly a fading memory. All he could think of was that she was warm and sweet and soft—a dream come to life in his arms. He wanted to lose himself in her.

"Lady Cecelia—"

She shook her head. "Cecelia."

"Cecelia…" How good it felt to say her name. Even more wonderful was her wide smile at hearing it.

"I want to." Her warm fingers traced along his mouth.

"You risk your reputation," he said. "Your future."

She tilted her head and kissed along his jaw. "It's my choice to make," she murmured, her breath warming his skin. "It's what I want." She ran her fingertips along his neck. Pressed her breasts against him. Sighed against him.

"Besides," she added, just above a whisper, "no one else need ever know, and I know there are things we might do that are…not completely reckless."

He stifled a groan. She was beautiful, devilishly seductive, and apparently not completely ignorant of such matters. What man could blame him for accepting her shocking proposal?

That was, beside her brother, one of his closest friends.

He took her hands and looked down into her beautiful blue eyes. "I am trying to…" She lifted their clasped hands and pressed her mouth against his fingers. "Behave with honor," he added raggedly. The heat of her mouth was so delicious and suggestive that his heart raced even faster.

I know there are things we might do that are not completely reckless… Those words had ignited a firestorm of ideas in his mind.

She knew the truth about him, and she still wanted him. Amid his heartache, that knowledge brought him intense joy.

Telling her much of what had happened at sea had been half-relief, half-torture. Other than Mrs. Thornton, he'd never shared so many details with anyone, not even his grandmother. It had been difficult enough to relive the events in his mind, never mind recount them to anyone else. But he did want Wareton to know the truth and he'd wanted Cecelia to know at least some of the story, even as he dreaded telling her.

He now realized that he wanted her to know, but had feared her reaction, believing she would be horrified and would quickly distance herself from him. It was a sensible response. Any ordinary person likely would do so.

But she was anything but ordinary.

He had never known a woman so intriguing, so desirable. And what she was offering him… Risky as their behavior was, she would likely ensure it did not interfere with her future. She was so clever and so determined to get what she wanted.

She was the most beautiful, exciting woman he would ever know. And his life was likely almost over. No matter what happened, he would never have another chance to hold her in his arms. If he gave up that chance, he could not imagine a moment would pass during however many days he had left on earth, that he would not be full of deep regret.

So he would allow himself a bit of heaven, an exquisite memory of her to hold on to.

He dragged her against him and kissed her.

As they kissed, Cecelia's heart pounded, and her body heated with anticipation.

She couldn't help but compare James to William. Though she had kissed several other gentlemen before James, only with William had she shared more than a brief embrace.

For too long she had simply been *so* curious. Over the past few years, from discussions with more experienced ladies who were willing to speak freely, she had learned far more about intimate matters than an unmarried lady was supposed to know. And once she had an understanding with William, it had seemed reasonable to finally satisfy her curiosity just a bit more. He had been happy to oblige.

William's kisses, however, while pleasant, had always been gentle and restrained. While their intimacies had been nice, she had always felt in control of herself. She had been motivated by curiosity and the thrill of doing something rebellious far more than anything else.

But James's kisses were so different, so intense and passionate. And the way they made her feel was quite the opposite of being in control.

After one more heavenly kiss that made her ache all over, he drew away.

"Not here," he murmured.

"Where?" she whispered.

"Come with me." He took her hand and drew her toward the center of the stables, slowing before a door.

He yanked the door open, and she followed him through the doorway and up a narrow flight of stairs. At the top, he shoved open another door, and they stepped into a large room. Light streamed in through two small windows, illuminating a simply furnished bedchamber with a small bed. A wide, threadbare carpet covered half the floor. The room smelled of dust and was empty of any personal belongings, but the bed was made up.

"The groom's quarters?" she asked.

"Yes, but Evans almost always stays in the village. No one is likely to look for us here." He strode over to the door and locked it. Then he turned and fixed her with a stare that made her heart race. "Do you trust me, Cecelia?" he said as he walked closer. Hearing her name in his wonderfully deep voice made her shiver.

She smiled. "Yes, I trust you."

The bed creaked as he sat down and then he reclined on his side. "Come lie beside me," he said.

She sat, slipped off her shoes, and stretched out facing him. They were only inches apart. Her heart pounded as he leaned forward, smiling, and inched toward her.

But she had no patience. She wanted to kiss him. Now.

Sliding her fingers into his thick hair, she pulled him close. She pressed her mouth against his.

Their first few kisses were gentle and slow, and he seemed to be restraining himself, letting her take the lead. When she finally kissed him more deeply, he growled softly and pulled her closer. His kisses grew more demanding, and she opened her mouth, yielding to him. He tasted wonderful—wicked and heavenly all at the same time. All other thoughts vanished for she knew not how long, until he abruptly drew away.

"I want to see all of you," he said, his voice rough.

"Yes," she whispered. "I want you to."

He reached down, pausing as his fingers brushed the hem of her skirt. "If you want me to stop," he said, "at any moment, just say so—"

"I will. But right now, I want you to undress me." She grasped her skirt in both hands and dragged it up, baring her stockinged legs to her knees.

So he would have no doubt that she meant it.

Smiling, he did as she wished. First, he rolled down her silk stockings, tugged them off, and tossed them aside. Then he found the drawstring of her dress and loosened it until he could slide the garment off, leaving her in only her stays and chemise. She tried to pull off his cravat, but he pushed her hands away.

"No," he said gently. "Right now, only you."

She longed to see all of him too, but if he wished to undress her first, so be it. Shivering with anticipation, she helped him to remove her stays and chemise until she lay naked on the bed.

"Will you unpin your hair?" he said hoarsely.

She quickly pulled out the dozen pins Reed had arranged so carefully that morning, and she dropped them onto the floor. Then she unwound the bun and let her hair fall free.

He reached out and slowly combed his fingers through her hair. "You are so beautiful," he whispered, his voice hitching. He kissed her again, starting with her mouth, then her neck, and finally her breasts. "Let me know what you like."

The confident way he kissed and touched her suggested that, unlike her, he had pleased lovers before. He kept glancing up at her, asking in heated whispers what she liked best, and watching what made her gasp loudest and clutch his head more tightly. Then he did those delicious, wicked things again and again.

She did not want him to ever stop. At the same time, she grew increasingly desperate for him to move lower. At last, he did, caressing her stomach, the curve of her hips, and her legs. Through the haze of sensation and longing, she recalled her intention to comfort him, to focus on his pleasure. Then his hand was between her thighs, and any coherent thought was gone.

Again, he asked what felt best. Soon he was caressing her in the way that made her the most breathless, until she felt an exquisite pressure building, more intense than any she'd known before. She fought to slow down the sensation, so she might touch him more before she was completely lost. But when she reached for him, her fingers brushing against his trousers, he gently pushed away her hand.

"No," he rasped, his other hand never leaving her. "Right now, only you." He leaned closer, his mouth soft against her cheek as he whispered, "I want to see how beautiful you look as I pleasure you."

His words sent her over the edge, and she called out his name as she fell apart.

As her breathing slowly returned to normal, she kept her eyes closed, savoring the gradually ebbing pleasure that washed through her. She could feel the heat of him beside her. When she opened her eyes, he lay propped up on one elbow, smiling down at her.

"Now you," she whispered, raising a hand to stroke his rough cheek. She wanted to give him such pleasure in return. Wanted to pull off his shirt and trousers, see his magnificent body, and caress his bare skin. She longed to discover him, to touch him as he liked best as he had done for her.

He smiled. "If you insist."

She would start with his boots, she decided. Except when she began to pull off the first one, the boot would not budge.

He shifted forward to help, but she gently pushed him away.

"I can do it," she said.

He shrugged and lay back, still grinning.

Grasping the boot more tightly, she yanked fiercely, dragging the boot with him still in it halfway off the bed.

He started laughing.

"Shh," she said, trying not to laugh too, and failing. "What if someone hears you?"

Slowly, he let himself slide the rest of the way off the bed and onto the floor. She stepped toward him, and he grasped her hands and pulled her down on top of him. The carpet tickled her bare shins and feet. His warm breath on her face sent shivers through her.

He pulled her close, drawing her into an achingly deep kiss that lasted she knew not how long. Then he shifted away—barely.

"I'll get the boots," he whispered. "You get everything else."

She moved off him. He quickly sat up, yanked off his boots, and tossed them aside. Then he lay back down on the carpet, pulling her on top of him once again.

She frowned. "The bed—"

"Is too far away," he murmured. "And too noisy." And he kissed her again. And he kept kissing her.

She immediately decided he was correct. The bed was far away, and it had creaked, though she'd only half-noticed, distracted as she'd been by other matters.

"Now you," she said, breaking off the kiss.

His eyes were half-shut as he nodded.

She loosened his cravat first, and soon his clothing lay scattered around them on the rug.

She sat up and simply stared at him for a moment, admiring his masculine beauty. Then she slowly began to explore his body as he had hers. She kissed and caressed his neck and his broad chest with a dusting of dark hair. His wide shoulders and strong arms. His muscled legs. All the while, she watched to see his reactions to her hands and mouth, to savor the desire evident in his heavy-lidded eyes, his parted lips, and the way his breath caught as she touched him.

At last, she trailed her fingertips across his taut

stomach, brushing against the thicker, darker hair leading downward to that most male part of him.

"No." He stopped her hand. "Forgive me," he added more gently. He entwined his hand with hers, drew her hand to his lips, and kissed her fingers. "One more touch and I'll likely be undone." His breathing was heavy, his face flushed.

She had some idea of what he meant, but she had no idea what she should do about it.

"Tell me…what you want," she said softly.

He groaned, and then he was silent for a moment. "I want…to feel you against me," he finally said, still clasping her hand. With his other hand, he traced a finger down her stomach and then made a circle low on her belly.

She smiled, understanding. "Yes."

He pulled her on top of him and slowly settled her into place. His strong hands held her hips, shifting her so he remained too high to fully compromise her, but he still pressed against her where her pleasure was the most intense. The heat and the feel of him was exquisite.

Holding her close with one hand, he began to caress her with his other hand. Then he started to move, and suddenly she understood. How easy it would be to abandon all reason. How it was that so many people made such foolish choices so often.

How desperately she wanted to be utterly reckless. To know what it was to be one with him completely.

He must feel the same desperate temptation. How easy it would be for him to give in right now. To shift just enough and to push inside her.

But she knew he would not.

Do you trust me, Cecelia?

Yes. Completely.

She leaned down and kissed him hard as he moved against her. Gasping, she found her pleasure building, faster than the first time.

He whispered breathless, wicked words of encouragement until once again, she was awash with pleasure. A moment later, he followed her, whispering her name as he found his release.

Joy filled her knowing that she had brought him such pleasure in return. They kissed, deeply, gently, and when she finally drew away, he looked tired but profoundly content. For the moment at least, he seemed to have forgotten everything else. She slid off him and onto her side, smiling.

He leaned toward her and kissed her tenderly. Then, shifting away, he drew a handkerchief from his coat and quickly cleaned up the evidence of their scandalous behavior. When he was done, he lay beside her again, facing her.

He began to caress her undone hair, his brown eyes soft with satisfaction. She leaned into his hand as he touched her. Would this be the only time they could be so close? She did not want to break the peaceful silence, but she had to know.

"Will Grey try to find you?" she asked quietly.

"I believe so." His smile faded and his hand stilled on her hair. "But I will do my best to keep him from succeeding."

"But he will not give up easily?"

"No." He drew his hand away.

"What…kind of man is he? Is he like the stories say?"

He shrugged. "Yes and no." He did not seem to wish to elaborate.

"Did you know when you first joined the ship that he was a free trader?"

He shook his head. "Not at first. Though it became clear soon enough." He paused. "I was surprised, foolish as it sounds. I had thought him so different from the thieves I knew in London. But it did not take long for me to adjust, to decide what he did was not only acceptable, but clever." He sighed. "He did not need to steal or smuggle to survive. He chose to. But his argument for why duties were unjust was persuasive."

His gaze drifted to a spot beyond her. "Isn't that how many people seem to lose their way?" he said. "One small justification after another, until they are far from the person they once were, or the way they'd imagined they would be." Shifting away from her, he folded his hands behind his head, looked up at the ceiling, and fell silent.

Was he only speaking of Grey, or of himself too? If he believed that he had once lost his way as he described, he'd certainly found a path back to an honorable life. Until it had all fallen apart, anyway. It was so unfair that he must lose all he'd worked so hard for.

His brow furrowed. "I should prepare to leave."

"Where will you go?"

He did not look at her. "Scotland, perhaps."

"Not overseas?" she said.

"No. I may have to leave Westbury, but there are places I can hide without having to go so far from all I know." He paused, still staring at the ceiling. "Not long after I returned from the war, I vowed that nothing would compel me to ever leave English shores again."

His tone was decisive. Like a heavy gate clanging shut.

Disappointment washed over her—which was foolish. It was not as if he would run off with her and travel. What a preposterous thought, for so many reasons.

To run off with him would mean giving up everything else. Her reputation. Her family and friends. Her dream of making a match that would please both herself and her family. She would not only damage her family's standing with such a reckless act, but she would likely never be able to return to her life in England.

Much as she longed to travel, she eventually wanted to return home to England. She would not give up that future for any man, even a man as wonderful as him.

And she suspected James would never allow her to act so rashly, anyway. A life spent in hiding? It was unthinkable to her.

"And what will you do now?" he murmured, still not looking at her. "Search for a new suitor?" His tone was even and his expression unreadable.

"I…suppose I must." Though she had no interest in contemplating that right now. "Once my aunt returns in a few weeks, it will be much more difficult to choose my own…path." She had almost said husband, but she couldn't bring herself to say that in front of him.

He smiled sadly and turned his head to look at her. "No matter how determined your aunt may be, so are you. Like the lady you met on the ship with the lioness walking stick, the lady whom you so admired." He paused and added softly, "You also deserve a gentleman who will support your dreams."

Her heart seemed to twist in her chest at his words. *I wish you could be that gentleman,* she almost blurted. But she wisely kept silent.

How she longed to have his shrewd dark eyes look upon her so warmly every day. To hear his deep voice filled with affection. And desire. To have him smile at her, make her laugh, kiss her, touch her—every day of her life.

Her breath caught. This wasn't only passion. Wasn't only infatuation. She truly did wish for every day with him.

She loved him.

Some combination of shock and realization must have shone on her face because his smile faded.

"What is it?" he asked.

She shook her head. "It's…nothing." She couldn't tell him. Should not tell him. To do so could make everything even worse and add yet another burden for him in an already overwhelming situation. And the stark reality was that if he did not run, he might have no future at all. "It's just…that I will worry about you." She leaned closer, reached out, and caressed his shoulder. "You must…hide somewhere you'll be safe."

He stiffened and pulled away from her touch.

She wished she hadn't broken the spell by reminding him that he must go.

"My grandmother could return soon," he said, his voice cool. "We really should get dressed." He rolled away from her and got to his feet.

Reluctantly, she nodded.

He would have to tell his grandmother about Grey finding him. Mrs. Stewart would be heartbroken. And what would it mean for his grandmother's future? No wonder he looked so grave.

Without seeming to look at her, he helped her stand. They dressed in silence. She watched in wonder as his handsome body disappeared beneath his clothes. She had seen all of him, touched him, known him almost completely and now she must behave, at least in front of others, as if their intimacy had never happened.

She must behave as if she did not love him.

When he helped her with her stays—with suspicious skill—his gentle touch once again sent shivers through her. After she was fully dressed and her hair pinned up once again, she helped him straighten his cravat. He stood stiffly, not meeting her gaze.

Carefully, she looked him over, searching for any signs of dishevelment, and then brushed a long blond hair from the back of his coat. She looked for more excuses to remain close to him, even as she felt the happiness, the deep connection they had just shared, slipping away.

She wasn't ready to let him go. To return to a reality where she would have to hide her feelings for him. Even worse, to a future where she would likely never see him again.

She slid her arms around him and rested her head

against his chest. But he did not truly return her embrace, only held her lightly, standing silently. She sensed that she should not speak, that to do so might only make everything worse, but the words flooded out anyway.

"Perhaps…" She shifted back enough to look up at his face. "Perhaps I might visit you sometime, in Scotland?"

He jerked away, forcing her to drop her hands as he moved out of reach. He clasped his hands behind his back and stood quietly, his eyes narrowed.

"You would sneak away to visit me…in hiding?" His voice was rough. "I doubt very much that your husband would approve."

"That is not what I meant."

"Then what did you mean, exactly? You would visit me only before you married?" He closed his eyes and took a deep breath. When he opened his eyes, his expression had softened. "Forgive me," he said. "Of course I am aware that even under the best of circumstances, I am hardly a suitable match for you. But despite what we have just done, I am not completely without honor—"

"I am sorry," she said. "I should not have said that. I have offended you—"

"You have reminded me of reality," he said, his eyes narrowing again and his tone cool. "Lady Cecelia."

Her throat tightened and she struggled to hold back tears.

"I thank you for…your comfort," he added, only slightly less harshly, "but we should not deceive ourselves that we have any future. In fact, it is the very last thing I should want."

The very last thing? Did he truly mean that or was he saying it only because she had hurt him? Or perhaps, now that his passion had cooled, he was thinking again of how this tragedy was, in a way, her fault? But asking him felt impossible. She felt as if she could barely breathe, let alone speak.

He looked away and cleared his throat. "I'll make sure the stables are empty," he said, his tone horribly ordinary. "Wait a while before you return to the house."

She managed to nod.

As if he could not get away from her quickly enough, he spun around, crossed the room, and undid the lock. Without hesitating and without glancing back, he left her.

As his steps faded, she turned slowly, debating whether to sit on the bed or a chair. She instead dropped to the rug, the gown she had just carefully straightened and smoothed crumpling beneath her.

She leaned forward and pressed her hands against the carpet where they had been intimate, as if to recapture the joy. His harsh words repeated in her mind.

I thank you for your comfort, but we should not deceive ourselves that we have any future. In fact, it is the very last thing I should want.

She had offended him with her impulsive words about visiting him and carrying on a dishonorable relationship. Insulted his honor and angered him when she should have been doing all she could to ease his distress.

She again recalled his grandmother's accusation, that she was toying with him. Loath as she was to admit it, perhaps his grandmother had been correct. But it wasn't like that now.

She loved him.

But her words had been thoughtless. Much like her actions, which had drawn him into disaster in the first place when her behavior had destroyed his peaceful life.

You put us all in danger. How desperately she wished she could go back to that night and decide against eloping. If only she could undo all the harm she had caused.

She allowed herself to cry quietly for a few minutes. When she'd felt she'd indulged enough, she sat up, breathing deeply to stop the tears. She should not wallow in self-pity. To focus on her role in this was only more self-indulgence, only more of the selfishness that had already caused so much harm.

After all that James had been through and all he had done for others, he deserved that peaceful life for which he'd worked so hard. If she had any chance to help him become free from his past, she would do so—whatever the cost.

CHAPTER EIGHTEEN

JAMES STUMBLED DOWN THE STAIRS. He had to get away from Cecelia. Now.

After confirming the stables were still empty, he strode outside.

For a brief, wonderful time, he'd been lost completely in her. He'd been intimate with a few other women—also beautiful, passionate women—but none had come close to affecting him as Cecelia did. For a few heavenly moments, he'd even forgotten that his life was about to fall apart. That was how profound an effect she had on him.

He strode away from the manor until he reached the path leading to the river. Then he walked even faster, until he was almost running.

She had not left.

That was what his mind kept returning to. That despite knowing the truth of his past, she had not left. Not only had she stood by him, she had drawn him even closer, offering him not only words of compassion but the comfort of her body. Amid the ruin of his life, she'd given him a few precious moments of joy.

His entire world had shifted during that time, into something better and more beautiful than he'd believed possible. That wonderful illusion had lasted until she'd spoken those simple words: *You must hide somewhere you'll be safe.*

Her tone and expression had conveyed only concern, no judgement, but those words had been like a knife to his gut. Reminding him that he must, yet again, run from his past. Hide.

Then she'd twisted the knife. *Perhaps I might visit you sometime.*

The idea of her stealing away from her life to spend time with a criminal, a fugitive, and the suggestion they might engage in such a dishonorable relationship made him feel…ill. So he'd lashed out at her. But the deeper truth was that another, perhaps even stronger cause of his anger remained unspoken.

His steps slowed and he drew deep breaths, letting the realization slowly settle over him.

She hadn't only reminded him of the painful truth that he was not worthy of an honorable relationship, that he was not of high enough status to marry her. She had reminded him of what he was about to do, once again—hide.

And she was someone who did not run. Who did not hide.

Even knowing he had been on the *Fortune*, and what he had done, and the danger he now faced, against all good sense, she had not run from him.

His first impulse had been to dismiss her refusal to leave as recklessness, impulsiveness, and perhaps a love of excitement. But as she told him she wasn't leaving, despite her determined gaze, the trembling in her voice and hands gave away her fear.

She was brave. Unlike him.

Since that fateful day on the ocean when he'd fled the *Fortune*, he'd been a coward. Perhaps he'd found some semblance of courage at times, such as when the desperation of war forced it upon him, but he had always chosen to run from his past. Ever since he'd suspected Grey might be alive, he'd certainly never summoned the true courage needed for what he should do—avenge Nate and all those wronged by Grey.

When the news had first spread that the *Fortune* had sunk, James had no reason to doubt Grey's death. Perhaps he would never be free of his past, but he'd believed Grey was at least gone from the earth. But all that had changed just over two years ago when, during a visit to Plymouth, he'd recognized a man from the *Fortune*, a man who had been one of Grey's loyal companions and who was also supposed to have been lost at sea. James had made some discreet inquiries and learned that the man frequently traveled between two English ports where Grey had kin, as well as a few foreign ports. James had begun to wonder if Grey was still alive as well and perhaps hiding out near one of the seaports the man frequented.

The idea that Grey might still be alive and living free gnawed at him. Yet James did nothing. He'd not wanted to stir up the past and risk upending his peaceful life.

Hidden away on his estate living in comfort, he knew how fortunate he was, and yet true contentment eluded him. He'd assuaged his guilt by helping sailors and their families, whether by hiring them or contributing to charities such as the orphanage. Still, he'd been restless, but just as he avoided London and romantic attachments, he'd resisted anything that might threaten his illusion of peace—any choice that called for real valor.

That night long ago, he'd caused so much death and misery, and then he'd fled. And now once again he would run and hide.

He reached the spot where he had fished with Cecelia not long ago. Dropping to the ground, he sat and dug his fingers into the soil. He breathed in the scent of freshly disturbed earth.

How like a fairy tale that time fishing with her seemed now, that he had enjoyed such a day, blissfully unaware of how his life was about to fall apart.

What would become of him, anyway, after he left Westbury? Would he spend his years in some small

Scottish village, living a lie under another false name, a failure at what truly mattered? He would certainly never regain even the façade of peace he'd had here at Westbury. No, he would be miserable, and surely die full of regret for all he failed to do.

He stared at the river until, slowly but steadily, his anguish retreated. In its place grew a sudden clarity and calmness.

Perhaps now there was only one choice—but it was not to hide.

Rising, he brushed the dirt from his hands. Then he turned back toward the manor, his strides growing longer and more determined.

This time, he would not run. This time, he would finally face his past.

As Cecelia climbed the stairs to her room, she heard a carriage arriving. Soon after, Mrs. Stewart's voice carried up from the entryway.

The poor woman was facing shock and heartbreak. Would she go with James? If not, she would be separated from her grandson all over again.

Guilt twisted Cecelia's stomach. She had caused so much misery.

Moments later, Reed entered Cecelia's room. When she caught sight of Cecelia's hair, Reed stopped short.

"What on earth?" Reed said. "Was it that windy today, milady?" When Cecelia didn't answer, Reed's eyes widened before she quickly hid her surprise. "Would you like my help?" Reed's voice held no judgment, only sympathy.

"Yes," Cecelia said. "Thank you."

Cecelia asked her to create a somewhat complicated hair style, one that would give James more time to break the terrible news to his grandmother.

"Are we still leaving soon?" Reed said as she began arranging Cecelia's hair.

"Soon," Cecelia said. "But not…yet." She should speak with Mrs. Stewart, painful as that would be, and discuss how she might help her and James. Was Mrs. Stewart even her real name, or had she too taken on a false identity?

After a few moments, a knock sounded on the door, and Alfred entered.

"Milady," the footman said, "a messenger just informed us that Lord Wareton is on his way here and should arrive today."

"Thank you, Alfred," Cecelia said.

He left, closing the door behind him.

Adrian was finally on his way here. How would he react to the news? He would undoubtedly be shocked about James's past. But Adrian would do his best to help his friend, of that she was certain.

She must conceal her feelings for James, however, and hide any hint of the attraction between them. There were few things that could make Adrian turn against a friend, but if Adrian suspected anything scandalous had happened between them, it could jeopardize his willingness to help James.

After more than an hour had passed, she finally descended the stairs and entered the drawing room.

James was not there. Mrs. Stewart sat at one end of the sofa clutching a handkerchief in one hand, her eyes red. Her cap was crooked and her usually pristine fichu was wrinkled and partly untucked, her cross tangled in it. Standing beside her, with Urchin sleeping at her feet, was Mrs. Thornton, with a comforting hand resting on Mrs. Stewart's shoulder.

Mrs. Stewart lifted her gaze to Cecelia and narrowed her eyes.

"Where is Mr. Wright?" Cecelia asked.

A brief silence followed.

"He's gone," Mrs. Thornton said quietly.

"So quickly?" Cecelia said. Her heart sank. Could he not have delayed a short time more to say goodbye to her? Unless he had wanted to avoid seeing her.

"He feared this day would come," Mrs. Thornton said, "and he always kept his affairs in order just in case. There was little he needed to do, nothing that others could not do for him." She paused. "He has even seen to it that we are all provided for, no matter what happens."

Of course he had.

"He has gone north?" Cecelia said.

A sob escaped Mrs. Stewart. Mrs. Thornton silently shook her head.

"What?" Cecelia said. "Where, then?"

"I tried to persuade him," Mrs. Thornton said, "but he's determined."

"Determined to do what?" Cecelia asked.

"He is sending information to the authorities," Mrs. Thornton said, "explaining that he believes Grey may still be alive and where he might be. I tried to persuade him to do only that and then flee to Scotland. But he is on his way to London, determined to face whatever awaits him."

"H-He is not running?" Cecelia stammered. Her legs suddenly felt weak, and she moved to the nearest chair and clutched the back for support. A confusing mix of emotions washed through her—shock, fear for his safety, and admiration that he would be so brave. And why had he changed his mind about going to Scotland?

"He went alone?" Cecelia asked.

When Mrs. Stewart didn't answer, the housekeeper said, "Mr. Long insisted on going with him."

Mrs. Stewart shook off Mrs. Thornton's hand and she pushed to her feet. "His life is ruined," Mrs. Stewart said, glaring at Cecelia. "All thanks to you. He was living in peace until he went to London searching for you."

Cecelia felt the ache in her chest grow. "Yes," she said. She glanced at Mrs. Thornton. The housekeeper frowned, seemingly torn between sympathy and anger, but she remained silent.

"It is my fault," Cecelia said, meeting Mrs. Stewart's gaze. Cecelia certainly could not blame the woman for her anger, and she finally understood why his grandmother was so protective of him. But her acknowledgment only seemed to make Mrs. Stewart more furious.

"I should never have allowed you to stay so long," Mrs. Stewart said raggedly. "Once again, I failed him." Once again? "I should have—"

The sound of a carriage approaching interrupted her. Cecelia moved to a front window. A large coach pulled by two sets of familiar matched grays stopped before the house.

"It's my brother," Cecelia said, turning to Mrs. Stewart and Mrs. Thornton. "Come to take me home."

"Good," Mrs. Stewart said.

A moment later, Adrian stepped into the drawing room. Cecelia hurried forward and clasped his hands.

He smiled, seeming happy to see her, but also tired, with faint circles under his hazel eyes. He looked down at her searchingly. "You are well, I trust?" he asked gently.

She nodded. "How is the countess?"

He sighed. "Fine. Tired, and longing for her confinement to be over, of course, but fine."

Cecelia released his hands and turned to the others. She hastily made introductions. Adrian's expression grew somber as he seemed to note Mrs. Stewart's red eyes and the dismal mood overall.

Mrs. Stewart did not glare at Adrian quite as fiercely as she did at Cecelia, however, and she invited him to sit. He settled himself beside Cecelia on the settee that faced Mrs. Stewart.

"Did you see Mr. Wright on the road?" Cecelia asked him.

"No." He frowned. "Wright's not here?"

Cecelia quickly related all—well, almost all—that had happened and what they knew of Mr. Wright's plans. Adrian listened intently, surprise and worry alternating in his expression.

When she was done conveying everything he needed to know, he sighed and leaned back on the sofa.

"I suspected Wright had a past," he said, "but I never imagined anything like this. What authorities in London is he planning on contacting?"

Cecelia looked to Mrs. Stewart.

"I do not have names," Mrs. Stewart said.

"I might be able to help him," Adrian said. "I must attempt to catch him as soon as possible." He turned to Cecelia.

She knew his expression all too well. "You are *not* sending me home," she said quickly.

He frowned.

"Because I wish to help as well," she added.

"Absolutely not. It is too dangerous." He shook his head. "You must distance yourself from all of this."

She straightened, clasping her hands in her lap. "Distance myself? No."

Adrian stared back at her and tapped his fingers against the settee, a habit of his when he was thinking intently. Then he leaned forward until he was practically looming over her.

"You wanted to travel," he said, "and now it seems the best course, after all. I shall provide funds to send you and Reed on your way, along with the proper additional servants and chaperone. We can discuss where might be a suitable destination—"

"So *now* you wish for me to travel?" Scowling, she rose

and faced him. Perhaps she would loom over him for a change.

Her hands began to shake. What was she doing, speaking this way to him? She almost sat down again.

No, she would not back down from this. It was too important.

Clearly startled, Adrian also got to his feet, forcing her to look up at him again. "The danger from remaining here is greater than that of traveling," he said. "I can arrange for—"

"No." She tried to make her tone as commanding as his. Her voice wavered only slightly. "I do still want to travel. But not yet."

When he did not answer right away, she glanced at the others. Mrs. Stewart had stopped glaring at her and now sat silently, watching them intently.

Cecelia could finally travel without even having to marry, not only with Adrian's support, but at his insistence. It was exactly what she had wanted for so long. But she could not summon even a spark of happiness. The idea of leaving right now, with so much at stake and especially with James's future at risk, was unthinkable.

And it wasn't only about James. She looked to Mrs. Thornton, with Urchin at her feet, and thought of the endless heartbreak she suffered from her son's death. And she was only one of many mothers and families who forever carried anguish in their hearts because of Captain Grey. Nothing would bring their loved ones back, but if Grey were brought to justice, perhaps all those souls could find some small amount of peace.

And Cecelia could help. She should help. She had not spent nearly enough time thinking of others. She should be more compassionate, more thoughtful. More like James.

When had she ever had a chance to help accomplish something so meaningful, to make such a difference in the world? And she could potentially help in ways that even Adrian could not. As a woman, she had social capital and connections different from his, and she had her skills of persuasion.

Skills she must first use on her brother.

"I am not going anywhere." She tilted up her chin as she held Adrian's gaze. "We owe it to everyone hurt by Grey to see him brought to justice. And we owe it to Mr. Wright to help him as well. Both of us."

"No," he said, scowling. "Not both of us. Not for a situation this dangerous."

"It is my fault that Mr. Wright's life was upended," she said, "so I am staying and helping."

Still frowning, Adrian stared at her silently. He obviously continued to view her as someone in need of protection rather than someone useful.

She curled her hands into fists. "Mr. Wright deserves all the assistance he can get, and I am far more capable than you give me credit for."

"Capable? Of what? Running off and courting scandal?" But Adrian looked immediately regretful.

"I admit that I have made mistakes," she said. "Many mistakes. But I am also capable of changing, and of fighting for what is right." And she *was* capable of standing up to her brother. She looked Adrian in the eye. "I fought off a robber in the London streets."

His brows shot up. "You did what? How?"

"I hit him with my bag."

He stared at her as if he didn't believe her.

"It is true, my lord," Mrs. Thornton said. "Her lady's maid told us all about it." The housekeeper bent down, scooped up Urchin, and stepped closer to Adrian. "And that's not all. She put herself in danger by jumping into a river to rescue my Urchin from drowning."

"You rescued this dog?" Adrian said, glancing between Mrs. Thornton and Cecelia. "From a river?"

"Well, I attempted to," Cecelia said. "Then Mr. Wright had to rescue both of us."

Adrian glanced at the dog again and then back at Cecelia. He seemed speechless. Finally, he found his voice again. "How…did I not know of any of this until now?"

Cecelia shrugged. "I did not feel the need to put it in a letter."

He looked at her as if she'd sprouted a second head.

"She's really quite formidable, my lord," Mrs. Thornton said, "if you'll forgive my intrusion. And Mr. Wright certainly could use as much help as possible."

Mrs. Thornton thought she was *formidable*? Satisfaction surged through Cecelia. Especially coming from Mrs. Thornton, that was quite the compliment.

Mrs. Stewart rose. She gave Cecelia a long, hard look and then turned to face Adrian.

"I must agree, Lord Wareton," Mrs. Stewart said. "Lady Cecelia stayed here even after James was attacked by Grey's men, even after knowing the danger, despite James's efforts to send her away. She was frightened, rightfully so, but she stood by him."

Cecelia was stunned. Not only that Mrs. Stewart described her in such terms, but that she knew about her reaction to the news.

Mrs. Stewart met her gaze. "James told me," she said.

When Cecelia looked back at Adrian, he was frowning, but in contemplation now rather than anger. He seemed to be considering that they might be correct about her.

"How will you help?" Adrian said. "What can you do that I cannot?"

"I can gain support from others," Cecelia said. "As his past becomes known, as it inevitably will, I can help present Mr. Wright's story as it should be told. Sympathetically. By highlighting the strength of his character and all he has done for others."

Adrian stared at her with his mouth set in a thin line. Then his expression softened. "Very well," he murmured.

Cecelia tried not to grin. "I'll prepare to leave at once."

Mrs. Stewart stepped closer. "Please allow me to go with you."

"Yes, of course," Cecelia said, "and you must stay at the town house with us."

Mrs. Stewart nodded. "Thank you."

Cecelia paused and said to her, "You must tell us how you wish to be presented in all this."

Mrs. Stewart straightened. "What do you mean?"

"Your name, for one," Cecelia said gently. If James lived under a false name, then it was entirely likely she did as well.

"Mrs. Stewart is fine for now," she said stiffly. As if suddenly aware of her disheveled appearance, she began adjusting her fichu and straightening her cross. "The truth will come out soon enough, but in the meantime, only helping James matters."

Cecelia nodded.

"Pardon me, Lady Cecelia," Mrs. Thornton said, "but I also want to go to London. Mr. Wright's done so much for me, and, well, Grey killed my son."

"Yes," Cecelia said to Adrian, "she has the right, more than anyone." She nodded at Mrs. Thornton. "Of course you should come with us."

"And Urchin too," Mrs. Thornton said. It wasn't a question.

"Certainly," Cecelia said. "He is most welcome too." And her aunt wouldn't even be there to complain about the presence of a dog.

Adrian looked at Cecelia. "Anyone else?" he said. But his tone was soft now, his gaze warm.

"No," Cecelia said, "no one else. However, it will take us some time to gather all our things and travel to London."

She took his hand. "You should leave right away, and ride ahead to catch up with Mr. Wright."

Adrian nodded. "You have grown wise," he said softly. He gently squeezed her hand before letting go.

His words filled her with joy and fueled an even greater determination to help James.

"Take one of James's horses, Lord Wareton," Mrs. Stewart said as Adrian turned to leave. "The groom will tell you which is best."

Cecelia said goodbye to him and then hurried upstairs to prepare to leave.

She and Reed began to gather her belongings, but Reed paused as she was packing up Cecelia's bonnets.

"I do not believe this one can be saved," Reed said, holding out the white bonnet Cecelia had worn yesterday. "I tried to get the stains out and reshape it, but…" Reed shook her head.

Cecelia took the hat from her, smoothing the ribbon that encircled the base of the brim. The fabric still smelled of the river water and the grassy bank. The scent evoked memories of James and their wet, scandalous embrace. Yet even that was nothing compared to the intimacies they had shared earlier today—

She should not be dwelling on such thoughts. James was on his way to London at this very moment, on his way to immense danger. Part of her wanted to chase after him and convince him to turn around, to run to Scotland as he'd first planned and not risk his life. Another part of her was in awe at his bravery.

She'd never felt such a mixture of joy and anguish over any man before. In the past, she'd believed herself to be in love a few times, but nothing came close to how she felt about James.

And yet, she must conceal her feelings. She could only treasure the memories, only cherish the fact that she had known what it was to be in his arms. Perhaps, in time, it might become easier. It had to. For no matter what her foolish heart might long for, they had no future.

She thought again of her suggestion that she might visit him in Scotland and of the pain she'd caused him. Her chest tightened with shame.

"Milady, did you hear me?" Reed's soft voice interrupted her thoughts.

"No, forgive me. What did you ask?"

"I asked if I should bother packing the bonnet?" Reed's brow was furrowed.

Cecelia sighed and lifted the hat to her face again. "I fear you are correct, and it is hopeless." She breathed in the scent of the grassy riverbank, savoring the memories of James. "I wish to keep it anyway."

CHAPTER NINETEEN

TWO DAYS AFTER LEAVING WESTBURY, James strode through the London streets, squinting in the hazy afternoon sun as he headed for the tavern known as the Black Bell. As he turned a corner, the wind suddenly carried the scent of the Thames, and he knew he was nearing the wharves.

And nearing whatever fate had in store for him.

Every few steps, his mind shifted from thoughts of Cecelia to fears about Grey and back to Cecelia. Over the past two days, he'd spent at least as much time thinking of her as he had worrying about Grey.

Never would he regret his time with her. He knew she wouldn't permit their indiscretion or any affection she might have for him to keep her from the future she wanted and deserved. Her suggestion about visiting him in Scotland had angered him, but it had also reminded him that when it came to her future, she was, above all else, pragmatic. She had no illusions about their different social standing.

Her words had hurt his ego and his sense of honor, but she was only expressing the truth of the world and their positions in it. And perhaps his offended honor should hardly matter given that he was in no position to ever be her—or any woman's—husband. To focus on impossibilities was pointless.

He must take consolation in the fact that he'd been fortunate to have even that brief time with her. Until his last breath, he would treasure those memories.

His greatest regret at the moment was that his mind kept returning to her when Grey should be his sole focus.

When they'd arrived in the city, James had sent Long to deliver messages, insisting that afterward Long should keep his distance for his own safety. The letters would inform the authorities of James's suspicions about Grey and his possible whereabouts, so that no matter what happened to James, Grey would hopefully face justice.

James thought it unlikely that Grey would harm those close to him. Grey almost certainly wanted revenge on him, but him alone. Grey had always fancied himself a gentleman sea captain and a man of honor, and that seemed to still be the case. Even so, the farther away others were from James, the better. That was why he'd insisted, despite their protests, that his grandmother and Mrs. Thornton remain in Westbury.

Saying goodbye to them had been so painful.

Mrs. Thornton had sobbed, reminding him of the first time he'd met her. She knew more about his past than anyone other than his grandmother. Her son, Nate, had been his one true friend at sea. Telling her the truth of how her son had died had been one of the most difficult things James had ever done.

At first, James had not planned to seek her out. But after thinking about what Nate would have wanted, he had brought Urchin to her. James had told her the truth because she deserved to know how her son died.

James had expected to face her anger when he told her that he'd been unable to save her son and that he'd fled like a coward. She'd broken down and cried for a long time, clutching the dog. But when she had composed herself, she'd shown only gratitude.

He told her that he was joining the army. She had asked that he visit her when he returned. So he did. And when he bought his estate, he offered her the job of housekeeper. She had been as good a housekeeper as a friend. Like Mr. Long and many whom he employed, she was a better friend than James likely deserved.

Saying goodbye to his grandmother had proved even more difficult. He'd wanted to tell her so many things, including how grateful he was for all she'd done for him. For seeking him out, for leaving her old life behind to be with him, for caring for him so deeply, even insisting he take money from her to buy the estate because in the end, her wealth would be his anyway when she died.

She was his only family, and he owed her everything. Yet all he could bring himself to do was to embrace her and tell her that he loved her.

He kept telling himself that he would see her again, even though he knew the chances were small. At least he would meet his fate having finally confronted his past and having tried to do what was right.

Perhaps Grey's men were already waiting for him at the Black Bell, or perhaps they wouldn't appear until tomorrow. But he had no doubt they would inevitably appear. And better to face them and Grey soon than to spend every waking moment in hiding, living in constant fear of when they might track him down.

As to what Grey had planned for him, James could only guess. Grey surely wanted him dead, but he must want something else from him first, even if it was just to be the one to kill him.

When James was only a few streets away from the tavern, a man approaching seemed to recognize him and walk purposely toward him. The old dread hit him before he realized that he no longer had to fear recognition. The tall man's face was in shadow under his hat, but he looked very familiar. It took James a few seconds to realize who it was, as the gentleman was dressed in more ordinary clothes than usual.

It was Wareton.

A rush of happiness swiftly turned to fear for his

friend. He had to get rid of Wareton quickly. It was bad enough that Lady Cecelia had become mixed up in this, and he would not have Wareton embroiled in it as well. His friend must have learned something about what had happened or he wouldn't be here.

As Wareton stopped before him, James said, "You should not have come."

"I can help," Wareton said.

Of course he wanted to help. Likely even knowing about his past wouldn't shake his friend's loyalty. But if he knew about Cecelia—

James forced that thought away. First things first.

James suggested they go to a coffee house a few streets away to speak, and Wareton agreed. As they headed toward the river, they turned down a lane that was surprisingly empty.

Rapid footfalls sounded behind James. He started to turn and something heavy crashed against the back of his skull. Staggering, he tried to stay upright. He smelled the coppery scent of blood and he heard Wareton curse. Out of the corner of his eye, James glimpsed Wareton struggling with a man.

Then shadows clouded his vision. Someone—no, two men—grabbed him, one by each arm. Then he tumbled into blackness.

"Lord Wareton will find James, I am certain of it," Mrs. Stewart said, rising from her seat in the drawing room of Adrian's town house. She seemed to force a weary smile. "Now, if you will forgive me, I will rest before dinner."

"Of course," Cecelia said.

As Mrs. Stewart retreated upstairs, Cecelia turned back to the desk where a stack of messages, all promoting James's good character and heroics, sat waiting to be sent to various influential people.

If word was not already spreading about James and his past, it would very soon. Such matters never remained secret for long. And when the time was right, she was prepared to send the letters and to fight for the future that James deserved.

She had never written so much in such a short time. When she lifted her pen to begin a new message, her fingers still ached too much to write smoothly. She would have to take a longer break.

She rose and strolled to the window that looked out on the quiet London street. She and Mrs. Stewart had arrived in the city earlier in the day, along with Reed and Mrs. Thornton. Cecelia had immediately learned from the butler that Adrian had gone out shortly before their arrival, probably to search for James.

James occupied her thoughts almost constantly. It seemed impossible that only a few weeks ago, she did not even know him. Every day, her regard and love for him grew.

Whenever she thought of the peril he was facing, she could not bear to dwell on it for long. She tried to focus on helping him, and on the slim hope that somehow he would survive and all would turn out well.

Hopefully Adrian would return soon with news, perhaps even with James.

When she finally heard the front door open, her heart lifted. She rushed to the hall, but instead of Adrian, her brother Edmund and her aunt stood in the entryway. Lady Carlton was already barking orders at the startled butler.

As her aunt paused for breath, she caught sight of Cecelia standing in the doorway to the drawing room.

"What are you doing here?" Cecelia said, not bothering to hide her shock and disappointment.

Her aunt narrowed her eyes. "I received some alarming news about you, so I was forced to return early."

Edmund met Cecelia's gaze, his expression grave with sympathy.

"You should not have changed your plans," Cecelia said, looking back at her aunt. "I am fine."

"Fine?" Lady Carlton scowled. "From what I have learned, you are quite the opposite of *fine*." She tugged off her gloves. "Now, we shall go into the sitting room, and you will tell me exactly what has transpired in my absence."

Lady Carlton marched into the room and lowered herself onto the largest settee, perching on the edge like a hawk ready to swoop.

"Sit." Her aunt pointed to the nearest chair.

Her heart now racing, Cecelia slunk to the chair and dropped into it. Edmund took the seat beside Cecelia, but their aunt ignored him, her steady glare fixed on Cecelia.

Cecelia's throat tightened and her hands felt clammy. Why did her aunt always make her feel like a tiny child caught stealing biscuits? No matter how many times she told herself she would not be intimidated, that she was an adult now and would stand up to her aunt, her courage always failed her.

But she had finally challenged Adrian, and perhaps she could now defy her fearsome aunt as well. Yet her stomach churned at the thought, far more than when confronting Adrian.

"I have heard some very disturbing talk about you," her aunt began. "First, that you took a sudden trip to the country to stay with a friend of Adrian's and his grandmother." She sniffed. "From what I understand, they hardly seem suitable people for such an extended visit. I can only wonder what mischief prompted such a strange event."

Lady Carlton stared at her in silence for several long seconds.

"You will tell me why you went on this peculiar trip," her aunt finally said. "This instant. And do not try to conceal the truth. I shall learn it eventually, and it will be all the worse for you if you lie."

That, unfortunately, was likely true.

"So, tell me," Lady Carlton said, leaning forward. "What did you do?"

Cecelia forced herself to meet her aunt's icy gaze. "I… tried to elope." She hated how timid she sounded.

"Good heavens," Lady Carlton said. "I knew it. With whom? No, wait, let me guess. William Trent?"

Slowly, Cecelia nodded.

"Ugh. How dare he! The blackguard."

"What stopped you from eloping?" Edmund asked.

"Mr. Wright, Adrian's friend, found me," Cecelia said. As always, Edmund's gaze was the opposite of her aunt's—kind and without judgment. "Adrian asked him for assistance in recovering me, and that is how I came to visit him and his grandmother."

"And Mrs. Clarke did not try to stop you?" her aunt asked.

"No, in fact, Mrs. Clarke was happy to accompany me to London—and then ran off herself."

Her aunt gasped. "That ungrateful wretch. After all the kindness I showed her."

Cecelia and Edmund exchanged looks.

"How was your visit?" Edmund said to Cecelia.

"It does not matter how the visit was," their aunt said. "At least the attempted elopement seems to have been hidden. Thank goodness, or she would have to marry William Trent. Imagine, with a father in trade." Lady Carlton gave a small shudder. "Still, it seems you found even more trouble to involve yourself in." She narrowed her eyes at Cecelia once again.

Cecelia's nausea grew. What did her aunt mean?

"What were you thinking," her aunt continued,

"flirting so publicly with a man so unsuitable? He is even less worthy of you than William Trent."

Cecelia took a deep breath. "If you mean Mr. Wright—"

"I heard you danced with him repeatedly at a ball," her aunt said. "To spend several weeks at his estate and show him such attention, you must realize that you have invited speculation."

Cecelia shook her head. "We danced more than once only because Mr. Wright was kindly trying to help me recover from…my disappointment with Mr. Trent, after he ended our understanding."

"He ended it?" Edmund said, his eyes wide. "Why?"

"We…were not as compatible as we first believed," she said. "No one outside our families seems aware of it, and we are still on good terms."

"Who cares as to why?" their aunt said, barely glancing at Edmund. "Just so long as it has ended and ended without scandal. However," Lady Carlton continued, "we still must deal with the speculation about Mr. Wright. Although in truth, this Mr. Wright seems to have so little to recommend himself that he should not even be considered a potential match for you."

"Aunt," Edmund said, frowning, "Mr. Wright is Adrian's friend. He saved his life, and by recovering Cecelia and having her at his estate, he has done our family another great service."

One that has cost him so dearly, Cecelia added silently.

Her aunt sniffed. "But the gentleman—is he a gentleman?—is of no rank or fortune, or even connections other than Adrian, correct?"

"He is a gentleman, and his estate is lovely," Cecelia said. "Well managed and—"

"A very modest estate, from what I hear," her aunt said. "And I can't imagine the society is any better."

No one there was as ill-mannered as you, Cecelia thought, wishing she had the courage to say it aloud. Instead, she said quietly, "Aunt, you should know that Mr. Wright's grandmother, Mrs. Stewart, is here, right now, as our guest." And hopefully not overhearing this conversation.

"What?" her aunt said. "Why is she here?"

Just then, someone pounded on the front door. Cecelia could hear the butler rush to answer, and a moment later, footfalls sounded in the hall.

The butler stepped inside the drawing room. "A Mr. Long is here, and he says it's an urgent matter."

Long hurried past the butler and into the center of the room. Long was breathing hard, as if he'd been running.

He stopped short as he glanced at them all. "Forgive me," Long said, focusing on Cecelia, "but I didn't know where else to go. I hoped you'd be here."

Lady Carlton frowned at Long. "Who is this person?"

"This is Long, Mr. Wright's butler," Cecelia said quickly, rising. "Where is Mr. Wright?" she asked him.

"He's gone," Long said. "I'd been following him, even though he asked me to stay away from him after we reached London. But I had to keep an eye on him, you know." Long shook his head. "In the street, he met up with a man who I believe was Lord Wareton, but I lost them when they got close to the wharves."

"Lost them?" Edmund said.

"They went around a corner," Long said, "and when I followed, only a moment later, they were just gone."

"Gone?" Cecelia said. "Where?"

"I searched all around," Long said, his voice cracking. "I finally figured out what happened, by talking to some people who saw."

"Saw what?" Edmund said.

"They were attacked and dragged off by four men. To a ship. Once I had finally pieced it together, I ran back to the wharves, but it was too late. The ship had already sailed." Long blinked as if fighting tears. "I think Grey's men have taken them."

Dread washed over Cecelia. Her hands began to tremble. Her legs felt weak.

"What in heavens is going on?" Lady Carlton said.

"A-Adrian has been kidnapped," Cecelia managed.

"What?" her aunt said.

"Why?" Edmund asked.

The fear in his expression made Cecelia even more frightened. She took a deep breath, trying to slow her racing pulse. She would be no help to Adrian or James if she did not—somehow—remain calm. "Because Mr. Wright," Cecelia said, "once sailed with Captain Grey."

Edmund's eyes were wide. "Wait…Adrian's friend is…a pirate?"

"A pirate? Really?" Lady Carlton looked deeply offended.

"H-He sailed with Grey before he turned pirate," Cecelia said quickly. "Mr. Wright was never a pirate."

"So," Edmund said, "he was a smuggler, but not a pirate? Well that's—"

"Hardly much better," their aunt said.

Cecelia took another deep breath and said, "Mr. Wright was present for the *Sentinel*."

For once, both Edmund and her aunt seemed at a loss for words.

"But he had no part in harming His Majesty's sailors," Cecelia added. "And Mr. Wright fled Grey's ship because of what happened that day. He has made amends and has lived an honorable life ever since."

There was a long silence.

"Am I to understand," her aunt said, her voice like ice, "that you have been courting scandal with a man soon to be revealed as a former criminal? And an associate of one of the most despised men in England?"

Cecelia stiffened. What could she say? Her aunt wasn't wrong. But at the moment, none of that mattered.

"Adrian is in danger," Cecelia said, meeting her aunt's gaze. "That should be our focus now."

Edmund's expression darkened. "Indeed." He stepped close to Cecelia. "Tell me everything."

With help from Long, she told Edmund everything—almost—while they listened silently. Even her aunt didn't interrupt her too often.

"We have to find that ship," Edmund said when Cecelia had finished.

"Do you know what the ship looks like?" Cecelia asked Long.

"I believe so," Long said. "But there are many similar crafts on the river. It will not be easy to locate. And the River Police have so few boats—"

"We must enlist the Royal Navy," her aunt said.

"Yes," Cecelia said, "but even that might not be enough."

Her aunt scowled. "What could be better than the Royal Navy searching for Adrian?"

Cecelia rose and began pacing before the sofa. "The Royal Navy *and* a fleet of private ships."

Edmund's eyes widened. "You mean merchant vessels?"

Cecelia nodded. "Precisely. The Trent family's shipping company has dozens of vessels here in the city, and many more nearby."

"The Trent family?" Her aunt wrinkled her nose in distaste. "You are suggesting that we ask them for help?"

"Every ship searching for them is another chance at saving them," Cecelia said. Unless they were already—No. They *would* be saved. If she thought too much about any other outcome, she would collapse into tears.

Edmund nodded. "She's quite right."

"Yes, but why should they help us," Lady Carlton said, "especially now that William has ended your understanding?"

"They will help us," Cecelia said, her tone much more confident than she felt. "I will convince them."

CHAPTER TWENTY

JAMES SLOWLY WOKE. WHEREVER HE was, it was pitch black. He was lying face down on a wooden floor, that much he could tell. And the smell—a familiar mix of smoke and brackish water—suggested he wasn't far from the Thames.

The back of his skull throbbed. He reached to where he'd been hit, and he felt matted blood in his hair. Even a slight touch sent pain shooting across the back of his head. Nausea churned his stomach.

"Wareton," he said softly. When there was no answer, he spoke louder, "Wareton!" He paused and called out his name again. Still, nothing.

Where was his friend? James prayed he was unharmed. If Wareton hadn't been dressed so plainly, no one would have likely dared to attack him. But Wareton was not who Grey's men were after, so if he had been injured, hopefully he'd been left in the street and then had been helped quickly.

With any luck, Wareton was already back at his town house, and if he needed it, under the care of a physician and his sister. Cecelia—

No, he would not think about her.

James managed to raise his head. His hat was gone, but he still wore his clothes and boots. He didn't seem to be restrained in any way.

Suddenly the floor beneath him shifted. Was he dizzy? No—the room really was moving.

He was on a ship, and a wave had just rocked the vessel.

A ship. Bloody hell.

The floor settled, the gentle roll fading away. His nausea abruptly grew much worse, and he felt lightheaded. As his heart began to race, he took several slow breaths.

He must focus.

He was on a vessel, but someplace calm, perhaps anchored. Maybe he was even still in London. He had no way of knowing exactly how long he'd been unconscious.

Likely he was in a hold of some sort. Trying to ignore his pain and nausea, he listened intently. He made out footfalls above, then shouts, and then creaking. The noises were all familiar, the sounds of a vessel preparing to sail. Then the ship suddenly shifted, this time not stopping again, but continuing to move.

Why, of all places, did he have to end up on a ship? If they'd kept him in the city, he might have a fair chance of rescue or escape, but on a vessel… He was well and truly trapped.

His pulse sped up again, and his head throbbed even more painfully. His stomach churned. A wave of dizziness and exhaustion washed over him, and his head dropped to the floor. He struggled to stay conscious.

And failed.

Not long after the arrival of Lady Carlton and Edmund, Cecelia donned her most elegant carriage dress and her most ostentatious hat, one that her aunt had chosen for her and which Cecelia had refused to wear until now. Such trappings mattered greatly to Mr. Alistair Trent, William's father, and she must convince him to help them.

She knew she had chosen her outfit well when she descended the stairs and her aunt looked her up and down, frowning. Lady Carlton seemed unable to summon a critical comment, a truly rare event.

"You should adjust your fichu," her aunt finally managed.

Moments later, they were in the carriage, traveling at a brisk pace toward Alistair Trent's town house. The unusually spacious London home was located in one of the grandest neighborhoods. After her aunt handed the butler her card, they did not have to wait long. The man quickly returned and ushered them into a large, opulent drawing room. Only Alistair Trent was present, standing ready to greet them.

"Lady Carlton," he said, "Lady Cecelia, what a delightful surprise." Making no mention of the unusual hour of their visit, Mr. Trent ordered the butler to bring tea and motioned them toward a very expensive mahogany sofa.

As Cecelia and her aunt sat, Mr. Trent remained standing. His square face and curly ebony hair resembled William's, but where William's demeanor was gentle and full of good humor, Alistair's was sharp and intimidating. Beneath prominent, bushy brows, his dark eyes seemed to take in every detail of Cecelia's appearance, and her aunt's as well. He seemed pleased with what he saw.

"Unfortunately, I am the only one home at present," Mr. Trent said as he finally sat across from them. "If we knew you were planning to call, William would have made certain to be here."

Her aunt glanced around the room with a disapproving frown. Cecelia suspected Lady Carlton was judging the furnishings and artwork, expensive as they clearly were, as vulgar compared to that of their own residences.

Cecelia smiled. "We actually came to call upon you."

Mr. Trent's eyes widened. "Indeed?" He shifted forward, smiling at both Cecelia and her aunt. His smile made him seem only slightly less ferocious. "I am surprised. Although most pleasantly surprised, I assure you."

Focusing on Cecelia, he added, "William told me of your correspondence. I wish that matters had turned out differently." His hard stare made it clear, however, that he had not changed his mind about William and her not traveling.

Before she could respond, the butler entered and served them tea. After he left, Cecelia took a deep breath. "Mr. Trent, we have come to ask for your help in an…unusual matter. An unusual and urgent matter."

"Oh?" His expression brightened. She knew he enjoyed having others, especially those of higher social status, indebted to him. "And what matter is that?"

"My eldest brother," Cecelia said, "Lord Wareton, along with a friend, has been abducted."

Mr. Trent had been about to take a sip of tea, but quickly returned the cup to the table. "Abducted?" he said. "Where? By whom?"

"Here in town," Cecelia said. "We believe they have been taken aboard a ship, possibly bound for the open ocean. The River Police and the Royal Navy will be searching for them, but we hoped that you might also aid in the search."

Mr. Trent's brows drew together. "You want me to send ships to search for Lord Wareton?"

"That is our hope," Cecelia said. She glanced at her aunt, wishing she would say something pleasant to help convince Mr. Trent, but Lady Carlton remained silent.

"Do you know who has taken his lordship?" he asked Cecelia.

She nodded. "We believe it is the work of Captain Grey."

Mr. Trent's eyes widened. "*The* Captain Grey?"

Again, Cecelia nodded.

"He's not dead?"

"Apparently not," Cecelia said.

Mr. Trent leaned back and stared at her in silence, as if deciding whether she was a lunatic.

"I apologize if my request has shocked you," Cecelia said. "But would you be willing to help us?"

Mr. Trent did not answer, but his frown faded.

"Tell me," he said at last, his gaze unwavering, "why his lordship has been abducted by Captain Grey."

"We believe it is because of his friend, James Wright," Cecelia said, "and Mr. Wright's connection to Grey. My brother happened to be with Mr. Wright in the city when they were both abducted."

"Lord Wareton hardly knows him," her aunt said. "More acquaintances, really."

"Grey or Wright?" Mr. Trent asked with a smirk.

Her aunt tilted her head higher and gave him a scowl that would have cowed most men. Mr. Trent only laughed.

Then Mr. Trent's smile faded. He looked to Cecelia. "This is the same Mr. Wright whose estate you visited when your plans with William were changed?" He glanced at her aunt. "A mere acquaintance?"

"She was visiting Mr. Wright's grandmother," her aunt said.

"Of course," Mr. Trent said. He watched Cecelia carefully. "And what is Mr. Wright's connection to Captain Grey?"

Cecelia hesitated. Naturally, she had no wish to tell him. She had no wish to tell anyone. But she also knew gossip was likely already spreading and there was no containing it now. So she must ensure that James's story was told correctly.

"Mr. Wright sailed with Grey," Cecelia said. "Almost a decade ago."

"He sailed. With Grey." Mr. Trent shook his head, as if disbelieving.

"Yes," Cecelia said. "However, Mr. Wright did not sail with him after the incident with the *Sentinel* and he had no hand in harming the sailors. Furthermore, afterward,

Mr. Wright joined the army and was honored for saving English lives on the battlefield."

"Yes, well, admirable indeed," Mr. Trent said. "However, no matter how respectable Mr. Wright might seem to be now, his past is notorious. And any connection to Captain Grey or his crew, even for a man of Lord Wareton's consequence, is…unfortunate."

Her aunt tilted her head higher. "When Lord Wareton is rescued, he will make it quite clear that his connection with Mr. Wright is only that of having served together in the army. He had no knowledge of Mr. Wright's past, naturally."

Mr. Trent drew his brows together and looked to Cecelia.

"Lord Wareton did not know of Mr. Wright's past," Cecelia said, "I am certain, until a few days ago, when I learned as well." She straightened. "However, Mr. Wright is his good friend, and my brother will stand by him, of that I am also certain."

Her aunt sighed. "Really, Cecelia, must you be quite so—"

"Honest?" Mr. Trent said, smiling.

Her aunt glanced at him out of the corner of her eye and said nothing, as if replying was beneath her.

"Mr. Trent has a right to know the full truth of the situation we are asking him to become involved with," Cecelia said. Thank heavens Mr. Trent seemed amused rather than offended by her aunt's snobbery. "And what you would be involved with," Cecelia continued, meeting Mr. Trent's gaze, "is the chance to not only save the life of the Earl of Wareton, but also save the life of an exceptional, heroic gentleman who is soon to be the toast of England."

Her aunt's eyes widened, and she blurted, "The toast of England?"

"Yes," Cecelia said, leaning forward, her gaze on Mr.

Trent, "for not only was James Wright a hero in the war against France, but he has secretly been aiding sailors in His Majesty's Navy, as well as their families."

"He has?" her aunt and Mr. Trent said in unison.

Cecelia nodded. "The staff at his estate are almost entirely relatives of navy sailors. The butler, the housekeeper, footman, maid…I believe even the gardener."

Mr. Trent stared at her intently, but he still frowned.

"Furthermore," Cecelia said, "Mr. Wright is a benefactor of an orphanage for the children of sailors."

"An orphanage?" Her aunt sniffed, as if this was a point of dubious merit.

"Yes," Cecelia said, "and the only reason he was at sea was because he was orphaned as a child. He ended up on the streets and was forced to fend for himself." She would leave out the thieving part—no need for that much honesty. "And he joined Grey's ship not knowing that Grey was a smuggler, and he sailed with Grey only for a brief time, and again, never after the incident with the *Sentinel*." True enough, if missing a few details.

"This is extraordinary," Mr. Trent said.

"Indeed," Cecelia said. "And when Mr. Wright's full story is known, the hardships he suffered, his deep compassion for others, and the great lengths he has gone to make amends for his association with Grey…"

Her aunt was staring at her, holding her teacup frozen in midair and her eyes as wide as Cecelia had ever seen.

"He shall not only be forgiven," Cecelia continued, "Mr. Wright will be celebrated as a hero." She paused and smiled, leaning toward Mr. Trent. "And you, Mr. Alistair Trent, will be celebrated as the gentleman who commanded his fleet of ships to rescue him and the Earl of Wareton."

Still smiling, she shifted back, waiting for Mr. Trent's reaction.

After a moment of silence, he slowly returned her

smile. "Lady Cecelia," he said softly, "I knew you were clever, indeed, but you have…exceeded my expectations. I am very impressed."

She let out a long breath. Thank heavens she had convinced him. But before she could reply, footsteps sounded in the hallway. William strode in and stopped abruptly as his gaze fell on Cecelia.

"Lady Cecelia," William said, immediately smiling. "Lady Carlton. An unexpected delight." As always, he looked handsome, his dark curls carefully arranged, his gaze warm and kind.

And yet, looking at him, she felt…mild fondness, nothing more. The true happiness she once felt upon seeing him was gone.

"Indeed, it is a delight," Mr. Trent said. "And good you are home, William. Lady Cecelia and Lady Carlton have asked for our help."

Mr. Trent quickly explained the situation to William, who said little, though he was wide-eyed at the details of Mr. Wright's life.

"And Lady Cecelia has been so forthright about the situation," Mr. Trent added, turning to look at her. "I cannot tell you how much I appreciate that. Honesty is important to me, very important." His gaze never leaving Cecelia, Mr. Trent paused before adding, "How truly fortunate you are, William, to have gained the favor of Lady Cecelia. Rarely does such beauty and cleverness reside together. She is an incomparable treasure, and one you must not let slip away."

"I agree," William said quickly. He smiled at his father, not at her.

"Of course," Mr. Trent said to Cecelia, "I shall do all in my power to help rescue Lord Wareton from this peril. I could hardly refuse, especially when it is a request from my future daughter-in-law."

My future daughter-in-law.

Cecelia's throat tightened. She looked to William, who was now gazing hopefully at her.

"If that is acceptable to you," William said gently.

"You presume a great deal," her aunt said, glaring at Mr. Trent. "To my knowledge, you have never even spoken to Lord Wareton about the matter."

Mr. Trent leaned forward in his chair, steepling his fingers. "I shall be glad to speak to Lord Wareton about it once I have sent my fleet to rescue him." He held her aunt's gaze.

Her aunt opened her mouth, paused, and then shut it again.

Few things would make her aunt hold her tongue, but thankfully the chance to save Adrian was one of them.

Mr. Trent looked to Cecelia. When she did not answer right away, he said, "Lady Cecelia, perhaps I was too hasty when I told William I did not approve of you traveling."

William's eyes widened. "Really?"

"I believe we may come to an agreement on the matter," Mr. Trent said, keeping his steely gaze on Cecelia, "once you are married."

She clutched her hands together to stop their trembling. He would allow them to travel? Then she would gain exactly what she had long wished for, assuming Mr. Trent kept his word.

"I keep my promises, Lady Cecelia," Mr. Trent said. "And I expect others to do the same."

She swallowed against a lump in her throat. She did not doubt him.

She shifted her gaze to William. Beyond the physical resemblance, he was little like his father. William was a gentle and kind man, and she did like him. And an alliance between their families would be highly advantageous, she was certain. But evidently William's agreeable nature meant that he would easily bow to whatever his father wanted.

As she glanced at her aunt and back to Mr. Trent, her stomach churned at the thought of many more years spent under another domineering person's control. However, agreeing to marry William could make the difference in saving Adrian and James. Mr. Trent could also be a powerful ally in promoting James as a hero.

And now it seemed she would gain what she had most wanted—her dream of traveling—and possibly save her brother's and James's lives. How could she refuse?

But even as she told herself this, her chest tightened. Memories flashed in her mind. James's smile. His laughter. His deep voice. His sharp wit and delightful conversation. How it felt to kiss him and be held by him—

How pointless. After all, even if James were rescued, and even if he were free from his past, they still had no future together. But James could perhaps still have a future, and maybe a life free of deception. She wanted that for him, so dearly.

She focused on William. He was decent, handsome, and pleasant company. An excellent husband by many estimations. Not long ago, she had desired to marry him, and likely she could feel content about it again eventually.

She forced herself to smile at William, and she nodded. Looking relieved, William glanced at his father, who inclined his head. Then William stepped forward and took her hand.

He smiled warmly and held her fingers gently. But she felt no comfort from his touch, only a hollowness. Tears threatened, but she pushed them away.

She must be prudent. This was the right choice. This was precisely what ladies like her were raised to do: to marry strategically, whether for power, wealth, status, or other gains.

And in this case, perhaps even save lives.

CHAPTER TWENTY-ONE

JAMES REGAINED CONSCIOUSNESS, ONCE AGAIN in complete darkness, his head throbbing only slightly less than before. As he remembered where he was, his chest tightened and his breath came faster. The lightheadedness returned, making the thought of even lifting his head unbearable.

But gradually the pressure in his chest eased and his breathing slowed. His mind cleared somewhat, and though his nausea wasn't gone completely, he no longer felt in danger of casting up his accounts.

He must focus and learn as much as possible about his situation.

The ship was moving swiftly now, but smoothly—the water calm enough that they might still be on the Thames. He strained to make out any sounds, but at present the walls seemed to muffle all outside noise.

He pushed to his knees and began crawling to take the measure of his surroundings. Before he got very far, he bumped into something—a leg. A leg with a boot that felt like the ones Wareton had been wearing. James cursed. He'd hoped his friend had been spared. His heart racing, he found an arm—which thankfully felt quite warm and alive—and he shook it.

He heard a shuddering breath and shook him harder. Finally, he heard a groan.

"Wareton, can you hear me?" James said quietly. "We're in a ship's hold, I think."

More groaning followed and then a curse that was distinctly Wareton.

"Are you hurt badly?" James asked.

"I've felt better," Wareton muttered. "Although I suppose it could be worse."

"How?" James said.

"Well, they wanted to keep us alive it seems."

True, although James wasn't certain for how long. But at least he still had a chance of saving his friend.

"Are you injured?" Wareton asked.

"My head," James said. "Hurts like hell."

"Mine too."

James could hear Wareton getting to his feet, but after a second his friend cursed again and apparently collapsed onto the floor with a loud thud.

"Are you all right?" James asked.

"Not yet ready to stand, it seems." Wareton sounded weak.

"Quiet," James whispered. "Listen."

Footfalls came from above and grew closer, sounding like two men. A dim sliver of light appeared several feet away. As the light grew brighter, James could discern the faint outline of a door.

He slowly rose. He could stand fully, but barely—he lifted his hands and bumped into wooden beams only a few inches above his head. When he felt around further, his fingers brushed against pegs for hanging storage bags. As far as he could reach, the pegs were empty, but they confirmed that he was in a ship's hold.

In the growing light seeping through the door, he could now make out Wareton's form. His friend was sitting but slouched forward, looking as if he could barely hold himself upright, let alone fight anyone.

The door creaked and swung open. James stepped back, the brightness of a lantern blinding him. Before his eyes could adjust, he heard someone slide something into the hold. The door slammed shut and the bolt scraped back into place.

James stumbled toward the door. "We need help," he called. "Come back!"

The footfalls paused, but only for a second, and then continued to fade along with the light.

James dropped to the floor, feeling around for whatever had been left, until finally his fingers brushed against a jug. He leaned close and sniffed it.

"Water," he said in Wareton's direction. "I'll bring it to you."

After they both drank, Wareton said, "Perhaps you could tell me what the hell is going on."

"You shouldn't have come looking for me," James said.

"And miss all this?" Wareton sounded slightly better. After a brief silence, he added, "Besides, it seems if I hadn't asked you to help recover Cecelia, we would not be here."

"This is no one's fault but mine," James said quickly.

Previously, anytime James had avoided questions about his past, Wareton had never pressed him. James had felt guilty for keeping secrets from his friend, but he'd told himself Wareton was better off not knowing. But now it seemed the time had come for James to finally tell him.

"I assume that you've learned something of my past already?" James asked.

"Cecelia told me what you shared with her," Wareton said. "But what she could not tell me is what Grey wants with you now."

"Most likely, he wants revenge for my betraying him."

"But why give you three days?"

"It is exactly like Grey to do something like that," James said. "To allow time for me to make arrangements for those who depend on me, to believe himself still a man of honor."

Wareton snorted.

"He always fancied himself a gentleman sea captain," James said. He briefly told Wareton of his time sailing with Grey, how it was an exciting adventure and Grey was an admired captain, until that fateful day.

James hesitated. He'd seen no point in telling Cecelia more details about what had happened with Grey, not wishing to distress her further, but informing Wareton now made sense. His friend might have to face Grey, so it was best he knew the type of man Grey was.

"Grey had seen his ship boarded before," James said, "and had lost some men to the press gangs, but he always managed to evade being caught smuggling. He had the cover of his legitimate trade and when necessary, he used his charm and generous bribes to avoid trouble." James paused. "But that night he seemed intent on hiding from the press gang, and it wasn't hard for him to talk most of the crew into it."

"Understandable," Wareton said.

"Yes," James said. "But hiding did not sit well with my friend Nate. He believed in the right of the navy to press men, and he believed we'd be caught eventually and be worse off for trying to evade them. So he stole up on deck, intending to light a lantern to give us away, though I did not know that at the time. I followed him to see what he was up to." He paused, clenching his fists at the memory. "Grey had followed Nate too, and he slit Nate's throat."

"Dear God," Wareton muttered.

"Grey didn't know I was there in the dark. When I realized he'd killed Nate, I was so furious, I didn't think past revenge. So I lit the lantern." He took a deep breath. "Grey smashed the light and went after me with his knife. He got me in the back, but I jumped overboard. By then, the *Sentinel* was heading toward us, and there was no chance of outrunning them."

James lowered his voice. "I wanted Gray to suffer for killing Nate. I never thought beyond that. But even if I had, I'd never have imagined he'd resist if he were caught, and certainly not kill sailors and talk enough of the crew into it as well."

After a brief silence, Wareton said, "I never understood why he did it. Why not just yield to the press gang? Why not just try to bribe his way out of trouble as he apparently had before? I always felt there must be more to the tale."

"There was," James said. "Though I didn't make sense of it all until later. Earlier that day, when he looked through his spyglass at the commander of the *Sentinel*, that's when Grey became so determined to hide. I believe he recognized the commander and knew the man already suspected he was a smuggler and that he couldn't be bribed."

"And Grey would have faced a death sentence," Wareton said.

"Yes. So Grey probably blames me for everything that happened that night, and for him becoming a fugitive and a pirate." James paused. "I'm sorry you are caught up in all this. But perhaps if he still fancies himself a man of honor, he can be convinced to free you."

"Perhaps," Wareton said quietly. "But I'll not—"

"If you have a chance to leave without me," James said, "promise me you will take it." He knew it went against everything they'd been through in the past to even think of leaving one another in danger, but this was different. He had to convince his friend. "Your wife, and soon your child, they need you. And Ce—the rest of your family needs you as well."

Wareton was silent a moment. "Wright," he finally said, his voice weaker, "is there anything else I should know?"

"About Grey?" James said.

"Not about *Grey*." Weary as he sounded, Wareton's

tone had an edge to it. Did he suspect that something had happened between him and Cecelia?

Likely Cecelia would not have revealed anything, not intentionally. Guilt filled him for not confessing. But it was Cecelia's place to tell her brother or not. And telling him now would not likely help their situation.

"No," James lied, "there is nothing else."

Nothing except the fact that he spent nearly every waking moment thinking of Cecelia. That he could hardly draw a breath without her image filling his mind.

Not long ago, he'd believed that all he wanted was to live quietly on his estate, leaving his past and all its heartache behind him. Sometimes he had even convinced himself that he was content. Until Cecelia had entered his life and set off a chain of events that had changed everything.

Now his peaceful existence was not only gone, but his life was likely almost over. Only now he finally understood that even before Grey's men had arrived, his life had already been in too many ways, not only dull, but empty.

From the first moment he'd set eyes on Cecelia, his thoughts had increasingly centered on her. First, on her beauty, but then her personality, and the joy of her company—everything that she was—had captivated him. And shone a light on the hollowness of his life.

Until he met her, he'd never felt so alive. Never recognized how much braver he wanted to be.

With a sudden unshakeable certainty, he realized how enormous his lie to his friend really was. It had taken being trapped in darkness in a ship's hold likely hours from death for him to finally admit to the truth.

He wasn't merely hiding an indiscretion. He wasn't merely infatuated with Cecelia.

He was in profoundly, deeply, in love with her.

CHAPTER TWENTY-TWO

JAMES PASSED WHAT SEEMED LIKE an eternity in the dark, his mind swirling with thoughts of Cecelia. Finally, he heard muted sounds of activity on deck. Someone was shouting, and the ship was slowing. He had no clear sense of how much time had passed since they'd been brought onboard. Perhaps only four hours, or as many as eight.

"Wareton," James said, "are you awake?"

"Yes." Wareton still sounded weak.

James sat up. "I think we're tying up to another ship."

Soon after, he heard men descending toward the hold. This time, it sounded like three—no, four people.

James stood and took deep breaths to prepare himself. As dim light slowly filtered in, he backed away from the door. Wareton was struggling to sit up.

The scrape of the bolt was followed by the creak of the door opening. Light spilled in, and three men crowded into the small hold. The first was a bald, heavy man who had to turn sideways to enter. The second man, who was holding a lantern, was short and wiry, with a pock-marked face. James didn't recognize either of them. But the third was the hulking, red-haired man who had attacked him on his estate, the same man he'd seen in the tavern that first night when he went to London to find Cecelia.

After they stepped through the doorway, the short man hung the lantern on a nearby hook, and the three men moved to the side to reveal a fourth man behind them.

The man was of average height, with a weathered face

and plain black hat. His clothes were nondescript, and he could have been anywhere between forty and sixty. His graying black hair hung loose, cut just below his chin. At first glance, he was a man so unremarkable as to be easily forgettable, which James had no doubt was intentional.

But when the man stepped closer, the uncommon evenness of his features became notable—the square, strong jaw, straight nose, and thick brows above intelligent blue eyes. His was a face that put people at ease, an appealing face that was easy to trust.

Then the man smiled, and the effect was magnified.

"Mr. Wright now, is it?" the man said in a refined, smooth voice that had plagued James's nightmares for years.

Captain Grey.

The red-haired man lunged forward and grabbed James, gripping him by both arms. As Grey eased closer, his gaze moved briefly to Wareton before settling on James.

When he had last seen Grey, James had been fifteen, and like most of the crew, he'd been in awe of the sea captain. He'd quickly been taken in by Grey's charm, and soon became fiercely loyal to him—until that terrible night had revealed the man's true character.

"When one of my men said he spotted you," Grey said, "I thought he must be mistaken. He'd seen you on the streets back before you joined my crew, and a few weeks ago in London, he swore he'd seen a gentleman who looked like that street boy. So I had to look into it, just to be sure." Grey smiled. "How fortunate that I did."

"Not the word I'd use," James said.

Grey's smile vanished. "You betrayed me and my crew, and you do not deserve the life you've had since."

James's gut twisted at the truth in those words.

"You and Nate plotted against me," Grey said. "And now I learn you've lived free all this time, while I've been forced to hide."

"I never plotted against you," James said. "And I would never have lit that lantern had you not killed Nate."

Grey shifted on his feet. "I don't believe you."

Rather than a decade past, everything somehow felt as if it were only weeks ago. James vividly recalled the coppery scent of Nate's blood as he died. The awful thud of his body falling to the deck. His own raw shock and rage.

For the months that James had sailed with him, Grey had filled a void for many of the fatherless crew, him and Nate included. Afterward, James couldn't comprehend how a man he had so admired could ruthlessly kill one of his own crew, and one of his seeming favorites at that, whom he'd affectionately called "son" and "my boy."

"Nate and you planned to give us away," Grey said. "You both might have been passed over by the press gang for being too young, so what did you care? But you would have condemned others to years of misery."

"So instead," James said, "you condemned them all to being outlaws."

Grey's eyes narrowed. "They chose to do what was necessary to avoid a worse fate. Once you'd given us away, that was the only way to keep our freedom."

Not a day had passed since then without James regretting lighting that lantern. How he wished that he had attacked Grey instead. Or even done nothing at all.

"You chose to resist," James said, "you chose to kill those men."

"I had no choice."

"You always had a choice."

Grey's eyes narrowed even further.

"You knew it wouldn't end with just some of the crew impressed," James said. "You knew you were also about to be arrested for smuggling. That commander, you knew him and knew he couldn't be bribed. Knew he had to be killed or you'd never be free again."

Grey's scowl told him that he was correct. "If we hadn't resisted," Grey said, "we all would have been charged with smuggling."

"Perhaps. But you'd be the one most likely to hang for it."

"You're wrong." Grey's gaze was icy. "And how pathetic that you've dragged a friend into your mess." Grey focused on Wareton.

"Your men dragged him into this," James said.

Wareton tilted up his head to meet Grey's stare.

"Too well-groomed to not be a gentleman," Grey said. "And those boots are expensive. At least you've improved your choice of friends." Grey looked back at James. "Certainly he's an improvement from a wretch like Nate."

At the mention of Nate, James felt a fresh stab of fury. The red-haired man seemed to sense it, and he tightened his grip.

"A wretch?" James said. "Nate was one of your favorites."

"Not really," Grey said with a shrug. "Never trusted him."

And Grey had likely convinced himself that was true. How else to justify what he'd done than to vilify the boy he'd killed? And by now, he'd apparently made James out to be far worse. Arguing with Grey about any of this was surely pointless, but perhaps Wareton might still be saved.

"Let him go, at least," James said, nodding at Wareton. "You've no quarrel with him."

"I can't do that," Grey said.

"Of course you can." James's pulse began to race. "And if you don't free him, you'll be hunted like never before. He's no ordinary gentleman." Perhaps it was a gamble, but he saw no disadvantage at this point. "He's an earl."

Grey's gaze snapped to Wareton. His eyes narrowed, as if he was trying to determine if James was lying.

The bald man and the short man exchanged uneasy glances, clearly unnerved about having a noble as their prisoner.

"If the authorities are looking for you," James said when Grey met his gaze again, "holding him can only make them search harder."

The short man and the bald man again exchanged looks, their expressions suggesting that they agreed.

Grey shook his head. "Thanks to you, now it's known I'm alive. And I'm wanted for smuggling and piracy. Nothing can make me worse off." Grey paused, looking him and Wareton over.

"Bind them," Grey said to the red-haired man, "and gag them, too. Don't want them making noise when you move Mr. *Wright* to my ship."

If Grey was worried about noise, they must be close to land—James's gut tightened. Grey hadn't said move *them* to his ship.

The men grabbed James and began tying his hands.

"I've plans for you," Grey said quietly. "A quick death is far too good."

James couldn't think about that right now. He had to find a way to save his friend.

Soon he and Wareton were both gagged, and their hands tied behind their backs. At Grey's instruction, the short man snuffed out the lantern. Then the men dragged James and Wareton out of the hold and up onto the deck.

It was nighttime, with a bright moon partly obscured by clouds. A few lights twinkled far across the water, indicating land was close by. That, the calmness of the water, and the brackish scent suggested they were nearing the mouth of the Thames but not yet out on the open sea.

The vessel they were on was a two-mast schooner. A smaller ship, a single mast sloop, which must be the one Grey arrived in, was tied to the stern of the vessel.

Grey stopped mid-ship, turned, and watched as his men dragged James and Wareton to a halt before him. The red-haired giant kept a tight grip on James, and the other two men held on to Wareton, half-supporting him. He still looked weak.

Grey drew a knife from his belt and eyed Wareton.

James tried to pull away from the man holding him, but the giant only held him tighter.

James would not watch Grey kill another friend. Grey would have to kill him first.

As Grey stepped toward Wareton, James abruptly twisted and then kicked the man holding him. Hard. The giant groaned and his grip loosened.

James wrenched free. He lunged at Grey and knocked him to the ground. The knife flew from Grey's hand and slid across the deck, clattering onto the stairway below.

Cursing, Grey stumbled to his feet. The red-haired man grabbed James again, and Grey called for one of the others to help.

While the two men held James, Grey stepped close. He punched James in the stomach. James faltered, but stayed on his feet. Then Grey kicked him between the legs. James crumpled and the men released him, letting him fall to the deck.

Grey moved closer and got in two more painful kicks, one to James's back, and one to the side of his head, before James managed to roll away. His gag seemed to be loosening slightly, but his hands were bound as tightly as ever.

Laughing, Grey followed James as he rolled. He kicked him yet again, in the chest this time.

"Pathetic," Grey said. "You've no chance. But if you want a beating, I'll oblige."

James swung out a leg, trying to knock Grey down, but Grey easily dodged it. Grey kicked him again, landing another blow to his gut, and James gasped from the pain.

Still he kept moving, rolling away from Grey once more. Every moment he kept Grey busy was a moment Wareton was still alive.

Grey came after him, ready to strike him again, but then he abruptly stopped. The moon had come out from behind the clouds. Grey and his men and Wareton were all looking silently at something off the starboard side of the ship.

Despite his gut being on fire with pain, James managed to sit up. His head throbbed worse than ever. He struggled to stay upright even as the deck seemed to spin around him.

"A big ship and well-armed, I think," the bald man said.

"We've no chance," the pock-marked man said.

Grey cursed.

Wareton seemed to find his strength, straightening until he was standing on his own. Wareton said something through his gag, something James couldn't make out.

The two men holding Wareton looked at each other, then back at Wareton. The bald man nodded. Then the short man began pulling Wareton aft, away from Grey. The bald man kept alongside them and was untying Wareton's gag. James thought he heard the man say something that included "my lord" to Wareton.

"Cowards!" Grey spat at them. He looked as if he might lunge at them, but the red-haired man stopped him with a hand to his shoulder.

"There's a second ship," the man said to Grey. "A navy ship is headed this way too. We're done."

James let himself fall back to the deck and rolled onto his side. He lay still, grinning now despite all the pain. Every breath was agony, but he didn't care. He couldn't see any approaching ship, but he could hear shouts carrying across the water. In a few moments, it would be over.

His friend was safe. And Grey would finally be caught.

"Hell if I'll let you live again," Grey muttered, stepping close to James. "Help me," Grey said to the red-haired man. "We have time. They won't be able to see to port."

Grey and the man grabbed James and dragged him to the side of the ship opposite the approaching vessel. They hauled him up onto the rail.

"Heavy bloody bastard," Grey muttered.

James thought he heard a shout from far away, maybe Wareton's voice. He tried to roll back onto the deck, but they were too strong.

They heaved him off the ship. He plunged into the cold water. Before he sank, he glimpsed the bright moon. Then he was underwater and struggling to keep his mouth tightly closed around the gag.

He kicked hard and tried to surface, but his clothes and his boots were like weights, dragging him down. He writhed and fought against his binds. They loosened slightly. But not enough.

The faint light above vanished. The water was completely black.

Dizziness hit him. He struggled to stay conscious and fought to keep kicking. But soon enough, his last bit of energy was gone. His legs went slack.

At least his friend would live. And Grey would finally face justice.

The water grew even colder. The pressure on his ears and the need to draw breath grew almost unbearable. Within seconds he would have to succumb and inhale the deadly water.

All he could control now were his final thoughts. He closed his eyes and let Cecelia's image fill his mind. And he let his love for her fill his heart.

CHAPTER TWENTY-THREE

JAMES WOKE TO THE SCENT of the ocean and the distant squawking of gulls. When he opened his eyes, he was in a vaguely familiar and sparsely furnished bed-chamber. On the right side, two open windows framed a distant gray sea. The only other person in the room was his grandmother, slumped in a nearby chair with her eyes closed and an open book in her lap.

"Grandmother," he said hoarsely. He began to cough.

His grandmother jolted upright, tossed the book aside, and stumbled to her feet.

"James? Oh, thank heavens." She moved to the bedside. "You know who I am?"

He nodded.

"Oh, my dear boy." She clutched his arm. "How do you feel?"

"Like hell," he said, his coughing over, but his voice still rough.

For some reason, this made her laugh. Sniffling, she wiped away tears. She had dark circles under her eyes. A silver curl had fallen from her cap and drooped against her forehead. She took a moment to compose herself, and then leaned closer.

"The physician examined you a few hours ago," she said, "and he thought you'd regain your senses soon. Your fever finally broke last night."

"Where am I?"

"An inn, near where you were brought ashore. When

word reached us that you'd been rescued, I rushed here as quickly as I could."

He frowned. "How long have I been here?"

"Over a week. The first few days you hardly moved… We weren't certain if you'd ever wake up. Then you seemed to improve, but became ill."

Vague memories returned of half-waking in the room, and of someone trying to get him to drink water, or sip broth.

He started to sit up, and abruptly realized how weak he felt. Then he recalled something of what had happened.

He had been on a ship. His friend had been in danger.

"Wareton?" he asked. He attempted to sit up again, but his grandmother gently pushed him back.

"You shouldn't try to get up yet. Lord Wareton is fine," she said. "He…well, you wouldn't remember of course, but he rescued you."

"From what?"

"Drowning."

Drowning? It took a few seconds for his mind to clear.

"What of Grey?" he asked.

"In prison. Marshalsea."

"Thank God."

"Yes." She smiled. "And also, thanks to you." She paused to straighten the bedclothes. "Lord Wareton was here for a few days, but then he went home to be with the countess. He was reluctant to leave you, but he feared that she would come here if he didn't go to her, and in her delicate condition, well…" She sighed. "I assured him that it was the correct decision and that you would agree. He hired the best physician here to care for you, and an excellent nurse, who's taking a rest at the moment. As soon as she returns, I'll send a message to Lord Wareton to let him know that you're better."

She moved to a nearby table, poured a drink of water, and returned with the cup. "Here, you must be thirsty."

She put the cup into his hand and smiled as he took a few sips. "Are you hungry?" she asked.

"No." He was, in fact, but he still didn't feel like eating yet. "Did…anyone else accompany you here?" he said, trying to keep his tone even.

Sadness flashed across her face, as if she knew the real reason he was asking. Of course she knew.

"No one else," she said quietly. "Long and Mrs. Thornton wanted to, but we decided it best that they remain in town to…well, I'll explain more about that later, after you've had more rest."

She took the cup and arranged the pillows behind him so he could sit up straighter.

He felt exhausted, but at least at the moment, not sleepy.

"Tell me now," he said.

"Very well." She moved the chair closer to the bed and sat down. "Mrs. Thornton came to London with me, the day after you left Westbury. Ever since we learned you'd been abducted, she and Long have been working to gain support for you from the families of sailors, both navy and merchant sailors. People involved in the orphanage are also speaking out for you, and many others, including Lord Wareton, his family, and their allies. They are all trying to sway public opinion in your favor."

"They are all trying to help me?" he said.

She nodded, her eyes shining. "I can see that you don't believe me, but it is true." She leaned forward and clutched his hand. "Your story has spread and gained you allies. Apparently, even at least one member of the Admiralty."

A member of the Admiralty was defending him, rather than wanting him imprisoned?

"Thanks to my friends," he said, still half-disbelieving.

"No. Not all thanks to your friends. You owe them a great deal, true, but it is just as much your own doing."

"I do not think so."

"Yes. Your story, all you have been through, your good deeds, and now, you helping to bring Grey to justice, all of it has touched people's hearts." Her voice cracked as she added, "I have received dozens of messages of support, including from members of the aristocracy. Even one from a duchess. You have earned the admiration of some powerful people."

He stayed silent, trying to understand.

"However," she said, "even though many people are arguing in your favor, others still feel strongly that anyone who sailed with Grey must be brought to justice."

He nodded. He'd always expected as much. What he hadn't expected was anyone supporting him.

"I believe," she said, "that it would be best if you avoid undue attention for a while." She patted his arm. "We should pick a quiet location, perhaps somewhere in Scotland where no one knows us, to stay until matters are sorted out."

She wanted him to run off to Scotland after everything that had happened?

"We'll go as soon as the physician says you're well enough." She gently squeezed his hand and then began straightening the counterpane around him. "Getting far away from everything is surely the best course," she said, as if to reassure herself, repeatedly smoothing the quilt without meeting his gaze. "No matter what the authorities decide in the end, you'll likely be safe outside of England."

Safe. How he hated that word.

"Now," she said briskly, "where shall we go? I can begin to make inquiries—"

"No."

She frowned. "No, I shouldn't make inquiries yet?"

"No. I'm not going away."

Her shoulders slumped. "James, please, for your safety—"

"No. I'd rather face it all here in England."

She opened her mouth and closed it again. "Very well," she murmured.

He reached out and touched her arm. "If it brings you pain or more cause to worry, I'm sorry, but I cannot run any longer."

She took his hand and squeezed it. "I do understand," she said, her voice breaking.

"At least," he said quietly, "I no longer must pretend. And I have…my name back."

She nodded, looking even more despondent.

"What is it?" he asked.

She briefly met his gaze and looked away.

"Grandmother." His tone conveyed he'd not be put off.

She looked him in the eye again. "I am just exhausted, that's all."

Of course, she must be. But she continued to fidget with the edge of the counterpane. There was something she wasn't telling him.

"Well," she murmured, "there is something else you should know."

"What?"

She released the counterpane and folded her hands in her lap. "Lady Cecelia…convinced Alistair Trent to send ships to search for you and Lord Wareton. It was one of his ships that first spotted you."

So Cecelia had been behind their rescue? He was not surprised.

"And you should also know," she said, "that it all came about because…because she is once again engaged to William Trent." She fell silent.

"I see," he managed, fighting to keep his voice even.

A vise seemed to be crushing his heart.

His grandmother looked at him as if she knew exactly how he felt.

"So Wareton gave the match his blessing?" he blurted.

"Seeing as how Mr. Trent sent a fleet of ships to search for him, perhaps that changed Lord Wareton's opinion."

"Yes," he muttered. "Of course." It made complete sense for Wareton to approve the match with everything that had happened. "Mr. Trent," he added, "he has agreed to let her travel?"

She nodded. "He apparently changed his mind."

So Cecelia would not have to give up her dream. She would get all that she wanted after all. But the idea of her married to Trent…made James feel ill.

"When are they to be married?" he asked.

His grandmother leaned back in her chair. "I am not certain. Nothing has been announced publicly, as they are still negotiating the details. I believe the announcement might be planned for the week after next, at the Duke of Dulverton's ball."

Then in two weeks, Cecelia would be celebrating her engagement to William Trent.

He felt as if he could barely breathe.

"James," his grandmother said, looking even more grave, "there is another matter I must share with you… something I must confess before you hear it from someone else."

"Confess?" What on earth could she be talking about?

She looked down at her lap. "Now that your real name is known, it's only a matter of time before someone learns my identity as well, and my story spreads." She lifted her gaze to meet his, twisting her fingers in the counterpane. "You see…I lied to you. About something so terribly important." She spoke in a rush. "I know it was wrong, but when I finally found you again, I was so afraid you would want nothing to do with me if I told the truth, and I wanted to be with you so terribly much."

She glanced away and cleared her throat. "The fact is," she said, her voice barely above a whisper, "your father was angry about my moving to Scotland not because he disapproved of my marriage, but because…I was never married."

"What?"

"I went to Scotland," she said, speaking quickly again, "to be with a man who was already married, quite unhappily, mind you, but married nonetheless."

His grandmother, who was always so concerned with propriety, had been someone's mistress?

"I-I cannot believe it," he stammered.

"That is why your father arranged for you to go to his cousin. Because I was not fit to be your caretaker."

He did not know what to say.

"And that was why I did not fight for you when I learned he had died." Her voice slowed. "I feared such a situation would hurt your future and that you'd be better off with a respectable relative, even one you did not know." She paused, shaking her head. "But then when you ran off, I realized I'd made a terrible mistake, to have put myself in a position where I could not care for you."

"That…is not your fault." He was too stunned to say much else.

She sighed. "I loved him, and he loved me, but it was still wrong. And if I had made different choices and been there for you, then you would likely never have run away, and never had all these terrible things happen to you."

Surprised as he was by her confession, he felt no anger, only confusion. "Grandmother, I chose to run away. You had no control over that. It was not your fault."

"Isn't it?" she said. "Perhaps not in my head, but in my heart, it is."

"Not in mine," he said quickly.

She shook her head again. "And all this time I have let you believe that I made a sacrifice by changing my name and cutting ties with my old life to be with you." Her voice quavered. "But in fact, it was a relief to leave the shame behind and pretend to be respectable again."

She paused to take a handkerchief from her pocket and wipe her eyes.

"But I am so sorry," she said. "I hope someday you can forgive me."

He leaned forward and gently took her free hand. Her skin felt paper-thin. Her eyes were bloodshot, and the lines around them seemed deeper than ever. Eyes that had always looked upon him with love.

"You have been here for me," he said quietly, "these past few years. That is all that matters."

She sniffled, clutching his hand tightly. "Thank you for saying that." She gave his hand a squeeze and then let go. "But it does matter. What if my story comes out and lessens support for you? We both know how fragile such things can be, and your fate is still uncertain. I…I should distance myself from you. If I go away, there will be less risk of my scandal harming—"

"No."

She looked at him doubtfully.

"If there is hope I might survive a past as a member of Captain Grey's crew," he said, "surely I can survive a notorious grandmother." He smiled. "You are my only family, and I'll not lose you again."

She laughed and, still sniffling, she nodded.

And he meant it. Except perhaps she no longer had to be his only family. He had his real name back. That meant he could *marry*.

His chest suddenly felt horribly, wonderfully tight.

He wanted to be with Cecelia. He wanted to share everything with her—a home, a bed, his name, children. All the precious dreams that had long been lost to him came rushing back with her at the center.

As if a beautiful noblewoman who could have her pick of gentlemen of rank and fortune would ever choose a gentleman of modest means like himself—even if he were a man without a past.

But the way she had kissed him, the way she'd been with him, and the way she had looked at him…

"What are you thinking, James?" His grandmother's soft voice broke into his thoughts.

"Ridiculous ideas," he muttered.

"About Lady Cecelia," she said. It wasn't a question. She knew. She'd known he loved her before he'd even realized it himself, he could see that now.

"Yes."

"They are not ridiculous," she said.

He shook his head. "I am hardly worthy of her."

She frowned. "You are worthy. You deserve every happiness, especially after all you have been through."

"I am not so certain."

She let out a sigh. "Because of the *Sentinel*?"

"That is one reason, yes."

She narrowed her eyes. Then her eyes widened, and she leaned closer. "You always say what happened with the *Sentinel* is your fault," she said in a rush, "because had you not given away the location, none of what followed would have ever happened. Even though you did not kill anyone. Even though you had no idea what would follow."

He hesitated before answering. "Yes."

"So, it follows that it is also my fault for what happened after your father died and I could not take care of you."

"No. You did not know he would die before you. And, well, none of that matters now, anyway. It was long ago. You have been here for me these past few years, and that is what is important."

"Then," she said, "what you did nearly a decade ago is not as important as how you have behaved recently."

He frowned. "It's different."

"Is it, truly?" She raised one eyebrow.

"It's not the same."

She shook her handkerchief at him. "Yes, it is. You

have helped to catch Grey, and according to what Lord Wareton told me, you saved your friend's life. What more could you have done to make up for any past failings? You absolutely deserve every happiness.

"And as for Lady Cecelia," she said, "I did not think highly of her at first, and of course, I was furious with her when you were forced to leave Westbury." She paused. "But over these past weeks, she has shown herself to be a woman of strength, character, and compassion. She did so much to not only try to rescue you and Lord Wareton, but to share your story. She has written dozens of letters, and she has spoken with many influential people on your behalf."

"She has?"

His grandmother nodded. "I believe she is trying to make amends for her role in exposing your past. And I believe she might possibly be worthy of you after all. Possibly. But you are most certainly worthy of her."

"She is sister to an earl," he said.

"So? You are dear friends with that earl, and you are a gentleman. And now—to some, at least—you are a hero."

A hero? Ridiculous. And even if he were… He shook his head. "She could have anyone, even a duke—"

"Dukes are overrated." His grandmother waved one hand. "I believe she would be bored with some stuffy noble. And I know she would be exceedingly fortunate to have you."

Of course, his grandmother would say as much. But the reality was that it was unlikely Cecelia would ever marry him, no matter what her feelings were. Even if by some miracle he remained a free man, he was hardly her most prudent choice. Although the way they had been together, it was impossible not to have some small hope…

"Did she…send a letter?"

His grandmother shook her head.

Not a promising sign. And yet, despite all the reasons any future for them was unlikely, one difference now made his foolish hope burn brighter. Cecelia had no idea what he truly wanted. Likely she had no idea he loved her. And she certainly had no idea what new dreams she had made possible and how profoundly he had changed in these past weeks.

Telling her would likely change nothing, but he had to try. At least now he *could* try. But there was one crucial matter he must resolve first.

"I must go to London," he said.

His grandmother frowned. "You could write to her—"

"No. A letter will not do. I must go to town."

"Appearing in town when so much is uncertain might be seen as too bold." His grandmother's voice was thick with fear. "You might lose what goodwill you've gained and anger those already set against you even further. And many of those who want to see you punished are in London now. Returning home quietly to Westbury would surely be the safer course of action."

"No." He would go where Cecelia was. He was done hiding on his estate.

"You…you must at least recover first."

"I will go to London as soon as possible. And I want to return by water."

Her eyes widened. "I should think the very last thing you would wish is to set foot on a boat again. If you are determined to go, you should travel by carriage."

"No." He shook his head. "It must be by ship."

Cecelia rushed up the town house stairs. She wanted to slam shut the door to her room in her haste, but she forced herself to close it quietly so as to not draw her aunt's attention.

The door creaked as she leaned against it, the wood cool

on her back through her thin muslin gown. With shaking hands, she broke the seal and unfolded the message from Mrs. Stewart. The crisp paper smelled of the ocean and contained only three lines:

James is expected to fully recover. I have sent word to Lord Wareton, but I also wanted you to know as soon as possible. We are grateful for all you are doing on his behalf.

Cecelia slid to the floor. She clutched the letter to her chest. Her hands felt wet, and she realized it was from tears. She placed the message aside and wiped her eyes.

He would recover. He would live.

The silent tears turned to sobs. She dragged herself away from the door and fell onto her bed.

She cried for some time with her face pressed into the bedclothes to muffle the sound. Eventually, her sobs faded into hiccups. She sat up, opened the drawer in the table nearest to her bed, and yanked out a bonnet—the crumpled, grass-stained bonnet she'd worn that wonderful day at the river.

She fell back into the bed and held the bonnet close, breathing in the now barely perceptible scent of the riverbank.

James was still in danger of imprisonment—perhaps worse—but he would not die right now. There was even a chance, tenuous as it was, that he could remain free. That he might return to Westbury and be able to enjoy the peaceful life he dreamed of.

And be able to marry.

Her sobs returned.

He would live. And she did not want a life without him.

What had he said when they were last together?

I thank you for your comfort, but we should not deceive ourselves that we have any future. In fact, it is the very last thing I should want.

Had he spoken those cold words only because she'd

hurt him? He might not have truly meant them. Or perhaps that was only what she hoped was true.

He had not sent word to her himself. Of course, he might not be in any condition to communicate yet. Perhaps in time—

Footfalls sounded in the hall. She quickly sat up, wiped her eyes, and began to straighten her hair.

The door swung open. Her aunt, resplendent in a canary yellow gown, marched into the room.

"I heard you received a mess—" Lady Carlton's gaze swept over Cecelia. "Is he dead?"

"No! No. He is…expected to fully recover."

"Hmm. That complicates matters." Her aunt frowned at Cecelia's disheveled hair and gown. "Apparently even more than I feared." Her aunt was silent for a moment. "However," she said, "in the end, even you would not be so foolish. Even if he is spared execution, imprisonment is still quite likely, and infamy is a certainty." She sniffed. "And no matter what, he would never be a worthy husband for you. He has no title, only a modest fortune, and few connections."

"He is a hero," Cecelia said.

Her aunt shrugged. "To some. To others, no matter his fate, he will always be a criminal."

"Without him, Grey would've remained free! He gave up his own freedom to—"

"Please." Lady Carlton waved a hand. "Spare me recounting his heroics. It does not signify to us."

"It does to me."

Her aunt's shoulders stiffened. Her scowl returned, and she stepped closer to the bed. "If so, then you have even more reason to forget any foolish ideas you might be entertaining. As you are no doubt aware, Mr. Trent has great influence over certain members of the Admiralty, the same two that have not yet decided what should be done about Mr. Wyatt."

Cecelia rose and clutched her hands together. "And what is Mr. Trent's opinion?"

"He is withholding judgment—for now."

"Why?"

"Humph. I think you well know the answer. You have made him a promise, and you best show no signs of breaking it. If the certainty of harm to our family isn't enough to persuade you, it could very well cost Mr. Wyatt his life. That is, if he is not doomed already."

She spoke of him being doomed so lightly, as if she were commenting on the weather.

Lady Carlton tilted her head back and looked down her nose at Cecelia. "So have a cry if you must. Then pull yourself together and get on with what you must do. Which is to convince Mr. Trent—and everyone—that you are content to marry William. He is your future, not Mr. Wyatt."

Cecelia opened her mouth to argue. But, as always, her throat constricted and her heart pounded. She wordlessly watched her aunt stride from the room.

Yet again, she had failed to challenge her aunt. But this time, her heart ached with far more than regret over her cowardice.

This time, it was also from the realization that her aunt was right.

CHAPTER TWENTY-FOUR

Two weeks later

CECELIA FORCED A SMILE AND pretended to give her undivided attention to the conversation around her, all the while surreptitiously watching the entrance to the ballroom. If James actually appeared this evening, she must show no more than mild affection for him.

To reveal her true feelings could ruin everything.

As much as she was accustomed to hiding her emotions and playing her expected role, however, tonight was already proving to be unusually challenging. Ever since this afternoon when she'd heard the rumor that James was in London, after a brief moment of intense joy, she'd felt nauseous with anxiety.

As to why—if the gossip was even true—he might come to London and to this particular assembly hall, she reasoned it was to see Adrian. After all, James had sent no word to her, so she refused to torture herself by reading any more into the rumor.

And even though she longed to see him, she still desperately hoped the talk was not true. Over the past two weeks, he had gained far more public support, but many still called for his punishment. The Admiralty had yet to come to an agreement on his fate, and Mr. Trent remained frustratingly indecisive on the matter.

If James dared to appear here, he would be taking a terrible risk.

"What do you think, Lady Cecelia?" Mr. Trent asked from her left. "Do you believe the talk is true and he'll appear?" His tone was pleasant enough, but, as always, his dark eyes searched for any sign of weakness. Or rebellion.

She knew better than to pretend that she didn't know to whom he referred.

"I have no idea," she said with a tone and smile that she hoped conveyed she was not especially concerned either way.

"Coming to London at all seems unwise," he said, "when so many here wish to see him arrested. And to show his face here in particular, when there are such strong opinions about him, seems especially foolish. Hardly seems the behavior of a contrite man."

"Perhaps," Cecelia said. "But perhaps to some he seems more guilty if he hides?"

Mr. Trent's bushy brows drew closer together. "And do you not find it odd that he is said to have traveled here by boat?" His stare suggested she might know the reason and was hiding it from him.

"I do not know what to make of that detail," she said, quite truthfully. "Perhaps…he has injuries that would make a journey by carriage uncomfortable?"

On Cecelia's right, her aunt sighed deeply, flapped her ornate fan one last time, and snapped it closed.

"Frankly," Lady Carlton said, "I am weary of all this talk of Mr. Wyatt. He hardly seems worthy of such a fuss."

"He did help to capture one of the most wanted men in England," Cecelia said.

"And almost got your brother killed," her aunt answered.

Out of the corner of her eye, Cecelia could see that William, who stood a short distance beyond his father, was conversing with a group of women. One lady in particular, Mary Mercer, had captured most of his attention. Miss Mercer had arrived in town last week and had been quite helpful in spreading tales of James's bravery and good deeds. Cecelia had been most grateful and so had carefully ignored Miss Mercer's increasingly bold flirtations with William.

As William laughed with Miss Mercer now, Cecelia once again pretended not to notice. In the past she had found William's flirtations annoying and even experienced twinges of jealousy. But these last few days, she'd only felt irritated because his flirting required her to adjust her behavior to appear to not notice, not because she wanted William's attention. And although William was unfailingly agreeable, he did not attempt to be alone with her as he had in the past. Her novelty had clearly faded. Rather than disappointment, she felt only relief that he did not attempt any intimacies.

Glancing around the ballroom, she noted how many other couples were similarly engaged in managing their indifference to one another. A few pairs seemed deeply attached but overall, practical tolerance was more common. Such unions based on affirming status and power were matches that her aunt always held up as ideal, and the sort of practical alliance Cecelia had decided upon. Like many well-born women before her, this would be her future: a sensible marriage in which she would play a carefully scripted role. But a marriage in which, despite all her privileges, she would likely be unable to control her own destiny.

She was about to trade one gilded cage for another.

Her stomach twisted. She reminded herself that she had done what was necessary to help save her brother and James. Certainly, she would never regret that. And the alliance would undoubtedly benefit her family. Now she would even be able to travel, as she always longed to.

Yet somehow even that thought held little joy.

Because of James, of course.

Over the past two weeks, she'd thought of him constantly. She had spent hours every day promoting his good deeds and advocating for forgiveness of his past.

She'd endlessly worried about what his future might hold. And before she fell asleep each evening, she'd allowed herself to become lost in memories of their time together in Westbury.

She'd also written him three different letters—and immediately afterward, she'd wisely tossed each one into the fire.

She had disrupted his life so much already, and she dared not make matters even worse for him now.

He had never professed to love her, anyway. The last time they were together, he'd stated that he wanted no future with her. And she had no reason to believe his wishes had changed. Much as she'd obsessively checked the post every day, he had not sent her a letter or communicated in any way. Painful as his silence was, surely it was for the best.

At that moment, the conversation around her stopped. Everyone turned toward the entrance of the ballroom.

James had stepped into the crowded room, wearing an outfit worthy of a hero. His stunning ebony coat, trousers, and matching waistcoat trimmed with silvery gray were perfectly fitted to his muscular form and complemented by an exquisitely knotted gray-and-black striped cravat. His gorgeous, thick hair was barely disheveled. He looked as aristocratic as any nobleman in attendance.

His grandmother stood beside him, dressed in a gown of pale blue, her usual heavy cross replaced by a string of snowy pearls. James seemed to be searching the ballroom for someone. He met her gaze and flashed her a grin.

Heat washed over her, and her breath caught. Her aunt was suddenly at her side.

"Do not be so obvious," her aunt hissed, digging her fingers into her arm. "You cannot risk—" Lady Carlton abruptly released her arm as Alistair Trent stepped closer to them.

"Mr. Wyatt cleans up well," Mr. Trent said. "Do you

agree, Lady Cecelia? He hardly looks as I would have expected."

"Quite well," Cecelia said, keeping her tone light, with no hint, she hoped, of her yearning to rush to James.

The ballroom had quieted with all attention focused on the new arrivals. As word spread about who they were, reactions varied greatly. Some people were frowning. Others, many of whom Cecelia had spoken to about James over the past days, looked upon him with evident admiration. And many more were obviously excited at the potential drama his arrival would ignite.

But no one stepped toward James and his grandmother. The ballroom fell into an awkward hush of whispered conversation.

Then the crowd slowly parted not far from where the newcomers stood. The Duchess Dulverton glided up to them, smiling warmly at James and his grandmother. Several other high-ranking noblewomen followed close behind her.

As the duchess welcomed them, some disapproving glances in the crowd softened. Cecelia let out a long breath. She had spoken to the duchess about James and had been counting on her support. Few dared cross the duchess directly, so James and his grandmother would at least be generally tolerated this evening. And many others followed the duchess's lead and would no doubt now be welcoming.

Thanks to the duchess's welcome, his impressive appearance, and word spreading of his story these past weeks, some here now seemed even ready to celebrate him as a hero. As they should, Cecelia thought with a mixture of pride and heartache.

James had not looked her way since that first glance. The duchess eventually moved on, and he was swarmed by a crowd of people wishing introductions that included many young ladies.

Would he find his future bride tonight among the many young women intrigued by him? Now that he was free to marry, he would likely fall in love, devoting himself to one fortunate woman.

A stab of jealousy pierced Cecelia to the core.

She clutched her hands together to conceal her trembling fingers. Forcing her gaze back to her aunt, she struggled to keep her expression serene. Her aunt narrowed her eyes at her as if she could read her thoughts.

"What do you say, Lady Carlton?" Mr. Trent asked. "Mr. Wyatt looks as if he'll fit right in with the grandest here, does he not? More gentleman than free trader tonight."

"He's passable," her aunt said with a sniff, glancing from James to Mr. Trent and bestowing equal amounts of vague disapproval on them both. "However, it requires more than expensive clothes to make a true gentleman." She tilted up her head and gazed down her nose at Mr. Trent.

Mr. Trent laughed. "But true gentlemen are rarely as interesting, are they not?" He paused, still smiling. "By the way, where is Moreland this evening?"

Her aunt glowered. "*Lord* Moreland is not feeling well."

As her aunt glared at him, Mr. Trent's smile seemed to only grow. But he glanced at James and his grin faded. "Well, mark my words, Mr. Wyatt's dark past will only make him even more intriguing to the ladies." He turned to Cecelia. "Do you agree, Lady Cecelia?" His brow furrowed as he glanced at her trembling hands.

"To some, certainly," she managed.

Mr. Trent stepped closer. "It appears that Mr. Wyatt is a hero now to many, and perhaps rightfully so. But his future is still far from certain, and it is so easy to fall from favor."

Her throat went dry. She forced her hands to her sides, willing her fingers to steady, and she met his gaze.

"Indeed," she said calmly, "but you have the power to

secure his future. If only he was fortunate enough to gain your support."

He nodded, smiling at the acknowledgment of his power, as she knew he would.

"See that Mr. Wyatt understands your future is truly settled," he said, "and he shall have my support."

Almost as soon as he stepped into the ballroom, James spotted Cecelia through the crowd. She was impossible to miss—a vision in a pale pink gown, her upswept golden hair shining in the light of the many candelabras.

He thought he caught her gaze and he smiled. She gave no sign that she saw him, however, and she quickly looked away.

She stood near William Trent, but not too close; her attention seemed fixed on the elder Mr. Trent. While she smiled at whatever his father said, William flirted with a group of young ladies that included someone James recognized: Mary Mercer.

James had no doubt that Cecelia was aware of William's distracted attention, but she skillfully pretended ignorance. And so she might pretend for years to come. His gut twisted at the idea of her married to a man who, while not the worst gentleman by any estimation, was still in no way worthy of her. Nor likely to ever be worthy. He pushed aside the thought that he was even less worthy than Trent.

He wanted to rush through the crowd and go to her immediately. But he was risking so much simply being here. To have any chance of success, he must be patient and behave properly.

When he dragged his gaze from Cecelia, it seemed as if the entire ballroom had turned to look at him and his grandmother. He suddenly felt intensely self-conscious. His new clothes were far more expensive than any he'd owned before. His grandmother had insisted that it was necessary for him to dress elegantly to gain acceptance tonight. He must look like one of them—a gentleman rather than a smuggler.

For what seemed like the longest few seconds of his life, no one stepped forward to greet them.

Would he be condemned for appearing here, rather than hiding at home to await his fate? Perhaps he was about to lose everything. But he would not go quietly—not without first declaring himself to Cecelia.

Then the crowd parted, and a group of ladies approached, led by one especially regal lady wearing a fortune in jewels. The murmurs of those nearby told him she was Duchess Dulverton.

She glided to a stop before him. As the duchess proceeded to greet him and his grandmother warmly, he saw the fear in his grandmother's expression ease into only nervousness.

Soon they were drawn into a whirlwind of introductions. When James finally had a chance to look for Cecelia again, she was still speaking with Mr. Trent. But now she held herself stiffly and despite her smile, he knew her well enough to recognize that she was only pretending to be happy.

Behind him, a familiar voice broke through the noise. "Wright!"

James turned to greet Wareton.

"I should call you Wyatt now, I suppose," Wareton said, grinning and clasping his hand. He drew James away from the crowd.

"You look well," James said. A faint bruise at one temple was the only sign of what Wareton had endured a fortnight ago.

"As do you," Wareton said.

"How is the countess?"

"Enormous. Ill-tempered. Impatient to be done with

her confinement." Wareton sighed. "She sent me to London for a few days. Thank heavens."

"Thank you for rescuing me," James said softly. "Thank you for everything. I cannot—"

"Stop." Wareton shook his head. "None of that. It's not needed, especially with all we've been through."

James held his friend's gaze for a moment and then nodded. He only hoped their friendship would survive what he was about to do.

"You are taking a big gamble coming here," Wareton said quietly. "You must know this."

"Yes. But I had to."

"Why? What could be so important as to risk—" Wareton frowned. A small group seemed ready to approach them, but Wareton scared them off with a glower. He drew James farther away from the others to an empty spot in the ballroom.

"What makes you risk so much?" Wareton said quietly.

James hesitated. "You…may not like my answer."

Wareton stared at him silently. "You might be correct," Wareton finally said. "If you are here to speak with Cecelia."

"You knew?"

"Of course I know," Wareton muttered. "You are not as good as hiding it as you think."

"I know I am in no position—"

"An understatement," Wareton said.

James nodded. "I also know I am unworthy—"

"No."

James nodded again.

"No," Wareton repeated. Scowling, he added quietly, "The idea that you might somehow not be worthy in my eyes is…preposterous. And frankly, offensive."

Wareton did not believe him unworthy of his sister? Other than Cecelia herself, no one else's opinion mattered as much. James tried not to grin like a fool.

Wareton sighed. "But let's be realistic. Your position is… precarious. The details have already been settled and Mr. Trent is expected to make an announcement tonight." He paused. "Most importantly, my sister seems…set on the path she has chosen. So you are likely too late."

After everything that had happened, after so many years of being unable to even contemplate marriage, he would not leave without speaking to her, hopeless as it might be.

"Then I must speak with her now," James said.

"Very well." Wareton's expression was somber. "I'll help you by keeping my aunt at bay so you may speak with Cecelia, but beyond that, I shall not interfere."

James nodded. "Thank you."

A moment later, James followed several paces behind as Wareton approached Alistair Trent and a regal, middle-aged woman. The lady was strikingly beautiful and looked remarkably like Cecelia. She had to be the infamous aunt, Lady Carlton. Wareton quickly drew his aunt and Mr. Trent into conversation, shifting to divert their attention from Cecelia. Cecelia then stepped back, as if she were about to go elsewhere.

James swiftly approached her. "Lady Cecelia," he called out.

She stopped and turned to face him. "Mr.…. Wyatt." Her voice was cool, and she did not smile.

She was even more beautiful than he remembered. Every day since he'd left Westbury, he'd dreamed of seeing her again, often doubting that he ever would. He'd imagined knowing her soft gaze again. Tasting the fullness of her mouth once more. Touching her soft skin as he had that heavenly afternoon. He wanted to pull her close and kiss her until they both could barely breathe.

Somehow, he remained composed. He knew those nearby were watching them closely. Out of the corner of his eye, he could tell Mr. Trent and her aunt were staring at them.

"It is a pleasure to see you again," he said, sounding remarkably normal.

"I am…so pleased you are recovered." Her voice had softened, just a bit.

"If you will permit me," he murmured, "I wish to speak with you in private."

She paused, glancing toward her aunt and Mr. Trent. Her shoulders stiffened and when she looked back at him, her gaze was focused somewhere beyond him.

"That would be unwise," she said.

The aunt was alternately scowling at Wareton and then at Cecelia, clearly wishing to interfere, but being held in conversation. She did not seem like a woman who would be kept from her purpose for long. James likely had precious little time.

"Then permit me a dance," he said quickly. If he could not get Cecelia truly alone, at least a dance might allow them some private conversation.

She hesitated, but then she nodded.

He took her hand, and they walked toward the other couples. Were her fingers trembling in his? Or was it his own hand that was shaking?

She turned to face him, her posture stiff, and she avoided his gaze. As the music began, she remained just as reserved.

Fortunately, it was a simple reel that he was familiar with. As they danced, the harsh words he'd spoken when they were last together flooded his mind.

We should not deceive ourselves that we have any future. In fact, it is the very last thing I should want.

She had no idea of his true feelings. Nor was he certain of hers. And no matter what, perhaps there was little hope of her changing her mind about marrying Trent. Chances were far greater that he was about to make a fool of himself. But he had to tell her.

At last, it was their turn to wait to the side while other

couples danced, and no one stood close enough to overhear a quiet conversation.

"I understand," he said, "that it is in great part thanks to you that I was rescued, that I am not locked up in prison, and that I have been welcomed by so many."

She finally met his gaze. "You deserve the life you've always dreamed of," she said, her voice not quite steady. "If I had a part in making that possible, it is only right after all the trouble I caused."

"You have done so much more than you realize." He stepped nearer. "It is because of your courage that I found my own, and I decided not to run from Grey."

Her eyes widened. "What?"

"Because of you," he whispered, "I realized that I could no longer hide from my past. I want you to know that if not for you, Grey would still be free. His victims would remain unavenged. And I would not have my life back."

She gazed up at him with a wrinkle in her brow, as if she didn't quite believe him.

"In fact, thanks to you," he whispered, "I now have everything I ever dreamed of." Leaning closer, he breathed in the delicious scent of her lavender soap. "Well, almost everything."

When he shifted back to look into her eyes, they were wide with shock. But she did not move away. Or glance away. Were those tears in her eyes?

Hope sent his pulse racing. He shifted nearer again, leaning so close that his mouth nearly brushed against her upswept hair.

"I am finally free to speak the truth," he whispered. "Allow me the chance to prove that I might make you happy, Cecelia. I love you."

CHAPTER TWENTY-FIVE

H E LOVED HER.
How wonderful. No, how terrible.

As soon as he'd stepped close, he'd filled her senses. He looked so handsome that she'd had to struggle not to reach out to him, not to bare her heart to the whole assembly.

She mustn't reveal her true feelings. But as he stepped back to a respectable distance, still holding her gaze, she couldn't look away. How she'd missed his shrewd brown eyes and deep voice. His disheveled hair. The scent of him. The way his presence made her feel…alive and full of wonderful possibilities.

She had feared he would die. Feared that she would never see him again. But he was here, recovered from his ordeal, alive and well, and breathtakingly handsome.

And he had come here tonight because he loved her.

His declaration was exactly what her heart longed for. But if she accepted him, she would make an enemy of one of the most powerful men in England. Her family would surely be harmed. And the future that was now within James's grasp could be ripped from him. He could lose his freedom and possibly even his life.

She could not do that.

Fighting to remain calm, she tried to appear as if they were chatting about the food, the weather, or the temperature of the ballroom.

"I must marry him," she said quietly.

He stared down at her solemnly. "I know my wealth is

nothing compared to his, and I have no title to offer. I am not even sure what my future holds. But," he added, "I love you, and I promise that if I keep my freedom, I will ensure you have the freedom you desire too."

Her breath hitched. She opened her mouth to answer when movement behind him caught her attention. Her aunt clearly wanted to approach her, but Adrian was blocking her way.

Likely Lady Carlton would not be kept back for long. From beside her aunt, Mr. Trent also glowered at her and James.

Cecelia took a deep breath and made herself look directly at James. "I am marrying William," she whispered.

"You truly wish to?" he murmured. The hope that lingered in his voice was achingly hard to resist.

"I am sorry," she said, forcing out the lie, "but, yes, I do wish to marry him."

He held her gaze, and she witnessed the hope in his eyes die. His expression turned grim. He glanced away, and then it was time for them to rejoin the dance.

She somehow kept her composure as she moved mindlessly through the steps. All the while, her heart felt like a stone. When she finally dared to glance at James, he would not meet her gaze. His brow was furrowed, his eyes downcast.

Nonsensically, she wished he would see through her lie. Refuse to accept it. Fight for her. Which of course would ruin everything. To ensure James gained the future he deserved, she must marry William.

The dance was ending. When the music stopped, James immediately released her and clasped his hands behind his back. His face was like a mask.

"I have your final word on the matter?" he asked coolly.

Out of the corner of her eye, she could tell that Mr. Trent was still staring at her.

"Yes," she said quickly.

"You are too brave and determined," he said softly, "to let anyone else choose your future." He finally met her gaze, his dark eyes shining. "So I must accept this is what you want. I did not truly expect you would choose a man like me as your husband," he added quietly. "But I could not live with myself if I did not ask." He inclined his head and said in a hollow voice, "I wish you every happiness, Lady Cecelia."

Then he turned away, leaving her standing there with her heart pounding.

As she watched him disappear into the crowd, she knew people were staring at her. She knew that she was standing frozen, likely looking anything but composed.

She had just ruthlessly broken his heart. And her own. But she had no choice.

You are too brave and determined to let anyone else choose your future…

If only she truly was the strong woman that he believed her to be. But even if she were, there was simply no way for them to be together. Not without bringing ruin to their lives.

Her stomach churned. Her head began to ache.

She could claim illness, retreat from the evening, and hide alone in her sorrow. But that might make everything even worse. She must return to her aunt and Mr. Trent. She must make clear she had done what she'd promised and now Mr. Trent must keep his word. James's future must be protected, even if she would have no part in his life.

When she spotted her aunt and Mr. Trent, she headed in their direction. They were facing away from her as she approached, their attention focused on watching William dance with Mary Mercer.

"He is paying far too much attention to her," her aunt said sharply.

"He's being polite." Mr. Trent said. He leaned closer

to her aunt. "Besides, it is always good to be open to other options, just in case. And the Mercers are also an excellent family held in high regard."

Usually, when Mr. Trent said something to offend her aunt, her aunt would scowl at him and shift away. This comment, however, apparently proved so offensive that her aunt turned toward him, subjecting him to the full force of her displeasure. Her aunt leaned close to him and began to whisper heatedly about how superior their family was to the Mercers.

Cecelia froze. Hope sent her heart racing.

Perhaps there was a way out, after all.

After William left, Cecelia remained alone in the small sitting room, her pulse slowly returning to normal. She had been to this assembly hall several times before, and she'd known this room at the end of a side hallway was unlikely to be occupied. No one had seemed to notice when she and William had slipped into the room, or when he left.

She stood near the cold hearth, her arms drawn around herself. Speaking to William had been awkward, but next she must face her aunt. It was like enduring a pinprick of discomfort before facing the guillotine.

She began pacing, then stopped. Uncrossing her arms, she realized her hands were shaking. She clutched them together to still them.

Could she truly do this? Perhaps she was mad for even considering it.

Rapid footfalls echoed in the hall. The door swung open, and her aunt marched into the room. Adrian and Edmund followed her, both looking wary. William had said he would inform Lady Carlton that Cecelia wished to speak with her. Her aunt apparently suspected what she was up to, and she had brought reinforcements. Edmund stepped into the room last, and he quietly pulled the door shut behind him.

Her aunt strode up to her, clutching her closed fan in her right hand like a dagger.

"William Trent said you needed to speak with me," Lady Carlton said. "I am almost certain that I know why. But please inform me, and your brothers, that my suspicions are wrong."

Her aunt might often seem to read her mind, but in this case, even her aunt surely wouldn't expect everything.

"You are probably not wrong." Cecelia glanced at them all, her heart pounding. She took a deep breath, looked her aunt in the eye, and said, "I am not marrying William Trent."

Her brothers exchanged glances. They did not look surprised or angry, only concerned. Thank heavens.

"I knew it!" Her aunt gave her an especially venomous scowl, one she reserved for only the most outrageous situations. "Are you mad? You cannot change your mind after all his father has done for us. For heaven's sake, he saved Adrian's life."

"I am well aware of what he has done for us," Cecelia said.

Her aunt jabbed the fan in her direction. "You will recall that I was against this alliance from the start, but now that it has gone this far, there is no turning back."

As Cecelia met her aunt's icy glare, her throat tightened. She opened her mouth to respond, but no words came out. Her heart raced, and she froze. Just as she always did.

Her aunt stepped even closer, so near that Cecelia could smell her face powder.

"You *will* marry William Trent," her aunt said. "And we shall announce it this evening, and while it may not be the most illustrious match, at least your future will finally be settled."

No. For once, stand up to her.

Cecelia swallowed against her constricted throat. She took a deep breath. Then she straightened, tilted her head back, and looked down her nose at her aunt, just as her aunt had done to her countless times.

"No," Cecelia said, her voice quavering. "I will not marry him."

Her aunt's eyes widened. "No?"

"No." This time, her voice was smoother. "I spoke with him, and he understands. He agrees with me."

Her aunt scowled. "Of course he agrees with you. He agrees with everyone. What matters is what his father wants. And he wants William to marry you."

Cecelia fought the urge to back down. "I will not marry him."

Her aunt blinked several times and then spun toward Adrian. "Tell her. Tell her she must marry him."

Adrian shook his head. "No."

Her aunt's mouth dropped open.

"I am done telling her what to do," Adrian added, crossing his arms.

Edmund let out a bark of laughter. Lady Carlton glared at him.

Cecelia felt a rush of love and gratitude for her brothers. This time, they were truly on her side.

Her aunt briefly closed her eyes, tightening her grip on her fan until the sandalwood yielded with a loud snap. Then she slowly turned back to face Cecelia.

"Rather than make a match to strengthen our family," her aunt said, her voice tight, "you will break your promise and make an enemy of one of the most powerful men in England?" Her aunt's voice actually held a tremor of fear. "That would be beyond foolish."

"So, you admit that you respect Alistair Trent?" Cecelia asked, grasping her hands together to still their trembling. "You admit that he is formidable and worthy of your respect?"

Her aunt scowled. "I would not go that far."

"Well," Cecelia said, "perhaps you will learn to."

"What do you mean?"

"Because…" The fear that had overwhelmed her when facing her aunt for all these years once again flared. Her pulse sped up, her throat tightened, and she felt as if she couldn't speak. But she forced herself to push through it. "Because…we will keep the alliance between our families. But I am not marrying William. You are marrying Alistair Trent."

Her aunt went utterly still. She stared wide-eyed at Cecelia.

Adrian muttered what might have been a curse. Edmund cursed loudly and clearly. Then he laughed, and he seemed to have difficulty stopping.

Her aunt's face was flushed and was becoming a darker shade of red by the second. "What nonsense!" she hissed, finally finding her voice. "Even if such a match was to be considered…I am engaged to Lord Moreland."

Cecelia shrugged. "So break the engagement."

Her aunt shook her broken fan at her. "Toss over a viscount for… for…that beetle-browed, arrogant upstart who barely knows proper manners?"

"That 'arrogant upstart' is one of the richest men in England," Cecelia said. "Even wealthier than the viscount. And even more influential."

"That's true," Edmund said with a smile.

Her aunt sniffed.

"And he's far more interesting," Cecelia added.

"Also true," Adrian said. His shock seemed to have faded and he now looked thoughtful.

"Humph." Her aunt tilted her head higher, not meeting anyone's gaze. "*He* certainly thinks so."

"I think you do too," Cecelia said in a rush.

She thought back to the many times Mr. Trent had leaned close to her aunt when speaking to her. In the past, Lady Carlton had shifted away, appearing deeply offended and contemptuous. But just moments ago in the ballroom, she hadn't moved away. Her former genuine contempt had faded. She'd shifted closer to him, almost scandalously close, and it wasn't only anger that shone in her face.

"In fact," Cecelia added, "I know you find him interesting." And she now also recognized that it bothered her aunt—intensely.

Abruptly, Lady Carlton's head drooped and her shoulders slumped. Cecelia had never seen her look so uncertain. Shock filled Cecelia, and something she rarely experienced before: empathy for her aunt. Lady Carlton constantly strove to control everyone around her, and she usually succeeded. But Alistair Trent would be a challenge unlike anything she had dealt with before.

If Cecelia could persuade her.

"Think, aunt," Cecelia added in a gentler tone. "With your knowledge and refinement, you could polish him as no one else could. You could transform all his…potential into a true gentleman." She paused and then spoke more quickly, "You have surely heard the rumors that he may be knighted soon. With you at his side, a knighthood would become a certainty."

Her aunt was frowning, but for once, in doubt rather than disapproval. She was even fidgeting, which she never did, by tugging nervously at the lace on her crumpled fan.

Edmund and Adrian watched them both silently. Edmund was smiling. Adrian's brow was furrowed.

"William believes his father would be quite agreeable to the idea," Cecelia said, focusing on her aunt. "He told me that recently his father has spoken of having been a widower long enough and of wishing to remarry. Unless," Cecelia added, "you believe Mr. Trent would be too difficult for you to manage?"

Her aunt scowled. "Humph. He is no match for me." But there was a touch of doubt in her voice.

"Or perhaps you fear he wouldn't agree to the match?" Cecelia said.

That did it.

Straightening, her aunt peered down her nose at her, any hint of uncertainty gone. "Of course he'd agree. He'd be exceedingly fortunate to have me. I have no doubt that if he believed he had any chance at all, he'd ask me at the first opportunity."

Her aunt was quite likely correct on that count.

"Then, you will do it?" Cecelia asked.

Still frowning, her aunt tapped her fan against her palm. "If this madness is all so you can be with that…that pirate, you are being ridiculous. Hero or not, and impressive as he may look this evening, he is far less worthy than William Trent. He is certainly nowhere near your equal."

"I do not agree." Cecelia sighed. "And for the last time, he was never a pirate. He was a free trader."

"Oh, and that's infinitely better," her aunt snapped.

"Yes, he was a smuggler," Cecelia said, her voice rising, "when he was very young. He knew great hardship, survived terrible events, fought for king and country, and he has done so much for others, including our own family, and now he only wants a peaceful life. He deserves it as much as anyone could," Cecelia added. "Any woman would be most fortunate to have him as a husband."

And most especially her. Never before had she loved and admired a man as she did him, and likely she never would again.

But he did not know.

I did not truly expect you would choose a man like me as your husband.

He had spoken those horrid words without any anger, judgment, or self-pity, only with the calm recognition of how things were. And she had said nothing. Just as she'd not contradicted him those last moments together in Westbury.

I am aware that even under the best of circumstances, I am hardly a suitable match for you.

"Oh hell," she blurted. "I have been an utter fool."

Her brothers and her aunt all stared at her wide-eyed.

She focused on her aunt. "Will you do it?" She held her aunt's gaze, refusing to look away.

The anger in Lady Carlton's expression faded, replaced by a look Cecelia knew equally well: cold calculation.

"Adrian," her aunt said, turning away from her, "please come with me while I speak with Mr. Trent."

Adrian raised an eyebrow, but he nodded.

Cecelia let out a long breath as they marched from the room. Edmund stared at the empty doorway for a few seconds before turning back to her.

"That was…unbelievable," he said, grinning. "I always knew you would stand up to her one day, but the way you turned the tables on her… It was utterly brilliant."

Perhaps it was, but she was too filled with excitement and worry to revel in it.

"Now," she said, "I must speak with James."

Edmund's smile faded. "I am afraid you've missed your chance. He's gone."

"Gone? Did he say where he was staying in town?" She'd not wait another day to speak with him. If she had to court scandal by following him to his lodgings, she would.

"I believe he's not staying," Edmund said.

"He is returning to Westbury? Tonight?"

Edmund shook his head. "No, he said he was headed to the docks. Back to the ship he arrived on."

CHAPTER TWENTY-SIX

JAMES STARED OUT THE OPEN window of the carriage without truly seeing the city around him. His mind was still on the ball they had just left—until he recognized a familiar street.

He ordered the driver to halt the coach.

"Why have we stopped?" his grandmother asked from the seat across from him. She lifted the curtain on her side to peer out. Her eyes widened.

"Oh, James," she whispered, looking as if she were about to cry. Then she scowled and yanked the curtain across the window. "I am sorry, but she has only proven that she does not deserve you. You should not torture yourself."

His grandmother spoke as if he had any control over the matter. As if he could stop thinking of Cecelia, stop recalling her soft touch and her warmth in his arms when they'd danced not long ago.

As if he could stop thinking about the sadness in her voice when she'd crushed all his hopes. *Yes, I do wish to marry him.*

He was utterly heartbroken, but he'd not hide from his sorrow. He was done running from things.

The ache in his chest grew even worse as he gazed at the spot where he'd first met her. The lanterns outside the carriage cast enough dim light for him to see that the street looked much the same as it had that evening.

But so much had changed in the weeks since. Most of all, he had changed.

A short distance away, the ship they'd arrived on was docked, not set to sail again for several days. They'd left their belongings there when they'd headed to the ball earlier, and the captain had been glad to accept payment for the safekeeping of their bags.

"I know you are probably not ready to hear it," his grandmother said, "but whenever you are ready, you will have no trouble finding a wife. Someone who will recognize how fortunate she is to have your affection. A woman who will love you as you deserve. Not someone who toys with a gentleman's affections and—"

"You are right. I am not ready to hear this." He knew she meant well, but right now her words were not helpful.

His grandmother opened her mouth, but then, thankfully, closed it again.

After a moment, she spoke much more gently. "I know it is nothing to your pain, but I too am…disappointed."

He did appreciate that. And he understood that she was angry and hurt on his behalf.

"But is it wise to stop here for long?" she said.

Perhaps she was correct. He was about to knock on the roof to signal the driver to move on when the sound of a swiftly approaching carriage stopped him.

He leaned out the window to see a well-appointed coach halt barely a dozen paces from them. Before a footman from that carriage could even step down, the door swung open. A woman slipped out and rushed toward him.

James opened his coach door and stepped onto the street. Behind him, his grandmother said something, but his focus was on the woman hurrying toward him.

"James!"

It really was her.

Cecelia stopped just before she would've run into him. He reached out to steady her, and she clasped his hands.

"I knew it had to be you," she blurted, entwining her

fingers with his. "Who else would stop here?" Her smile was wide and joyful.

The promise in her eyes made him want to sweep her up in his arms and kiss her soundly. And he might have done so, except her brother Edmund had followed her out of the carriage and now stood several paces behind her.

"You were chasing after me?" James said to her. Surely, she could have only one reason to do so.

"Yes. You were right about me," she said in her beautiful voice. "I *will* choose my own future. And I want to be with you. I love you, James."

"I love you," Cecelia repeated as James stared down at her. His handsome dark eyes were wide and what she saw in them made her heart race faster. She clasped his hands even more tightly.

"I thought I had to marry William Trent," she said in a rush, "but I found a way out, a way that protects my family, and you."

He raised one eyebrow.

"My aunt is marrying Alistair Trent."

Both his brows shot up. "Whose idea was that?"

"Mine." She could not help but smile. "But that is not as important as what I must tell you now…" She took a deep breath. "I have behaved selfishly, foolishly, and disrupted your life terribly. In spite of all of this, somehow, you still love me. I am sorry for everything, and most especially, I am sorry if I ever let you believe you were unworthy. The truth is…you are the most wonderful man I have ever known. I wish to be with you, no matter what your future will be."

His gaze softened. "Cecelia," he whispered. He seemed about to step closer when someone cleared their throat.

"Perhaps," Edmund said from over her shoulder, "you might speak further in his coach."

James released her hand, but kept near to her, his gaze never leaving her.

"That would be wise," Mrs. Stewart said, moving to stand behind James. She was smiling. "And perhaps we might all go to Lord Wareton's town house?"

"Would you care to join me, Mrs. Stewart?" Edmund asked.

"I should be delighted," Mrs. Stewart answered, as if the entire situation were quite ordinary. She stepped around James and walked to the other carriage beside Edmund.

When Cecelia looked back at James, his stare made her breath hitch.

Silently, he helped her into his coach and then climbed in after her. The footman promptly closed the door.

They were alone.

Cecelia slid onto one seat, and James settled across from her. He leaned forward, his knees brushing hers as the carriage began moving. The light from the hanging lantern was soft on his handsome face. The way he was looking at her had her struggling to recall what she wanted to say.

"I…believe I can secure Mr. Trent's support for you," she managed, "which in turn could very well convince the Admiralty to finally decide in your favor. And with so much public opinion behind you, I believe your chances of remaining free are good." She leaned forward and took his hands. "But no matter what happens, I shall stand by you. I shall keep fighting for you."

He was silent for a moment and his expression turned serious.

"But what of your plans to travel?" he asked softly.

She shook her head. "That is not important. Not as important as you."

"No."

"No?" What exactly did he mean?

He released her hands, and she drew them back into her lap. Shifting, he slid one hand into his coat pocket and pulled something out. With his other hand, he reached out and took her hand, turning it palm up.

He pressed a solid circular object into her hand. A beautiful gold brooch about an inch in size looked up at her. A lioness.

"I thought a brooch would suit you far better than a cane," he said.

A chill passed through her. He had remembered how deeply she admired the amazing woman on the ship, the woman who traveled with her husband and had a cane with a lioness handle.

"You must not give up your dreams," he said.

"But I...it is not as important as—"

"It is important. To me as well."

"Oh. I see." But she did not see. What was he saying?

He rose and moved across the coach to sit beside her. "The reason I came to London," he said, turning toward her, "without writing to you was because...first I had to know I could support your dreams."

He reached out and took the brooch from her hand.

"May I?" he asked.

She nodded.

He gently fastened the brooch to the bodice of her gown. His fingers brushed against her breast as he did so. She blushed, her breath coming faster.

"My dearest Cecelia," he said, "you should travel all that you desire. And assuming you wish it, of course, I will be with you."

For a moment, the only sounds were the rattle of the carriage and the clop of the horses' hooves.

"I...do not understand," she said. "You told me that you've had enough adventure to last a lifetime. That you never wanted to leave England again."

"I did. And that was true once. But it's not true now."

She frowned. Was he only saying this, or did he genuinely mean it?

"I never wanted to leave England because I couldn't," he said. "Or I believed that I couldn't."

"Because you feared recognition?"

"No," he said. "Well, that is why I avoided London, but…you see, when I was returning from the war on a ship, I was afflicted with…terrors. They only stopped when I reached land."

Terrors?

He sighed. "A few months later, I tried again to board a boat and I could not do it. I felt so ill that I was sure I was dying, but I soon realized I was paralyzed with fear. I tried twice more and couldn't even go near the dock." He paused. "I was certain that I would never set foot on a ship again."

She stared at him, letting this revelation sink in. He had said he'd never travel because he was afraid to be on a ship?

Well, she certainly knew what it was like to be immobilized with fear, even though her situation was nothing compared to all that he had endured. And with everything that he had suffered through—being orphaned, living on the streets, sailing with Captain Grey, and then war—it was hardly surprising he was so afflicted.

"These last years I was living quietly and hiding," he said, "because I had to. I wasn't free. Now, at last, I am."

He moved closer, until his leg brushed against her skirt. Her heart raced faster.

"I'm not just free to live under my own name again," he said, "or free to enjoy London again, but free to leave England. Having been forced onto a ship, I learned that I could endure it." He paused. "That is why I returned to London by water. Before I spoke with you, I had to be sure I could do so again."

Oh heavens.

"But there is one matter I must make clear," he said. "I do not wish to marry you. Not immediately. First, my future must be settled."

"No. No matter what your future is, I—"

The carriage hit a bump, knocking him against her. Wonderfully, he didn't shift back. He was so close. So warm. And he smelled so good…

"It's not only that," he murmured. "It's also that I wish to court you properly, here in London. I want to take you to the theater, shops, museums, gardens…" His voice grew even softer. "I wish to enjoy everything that I've been missing, with you. Then, after a proper courtship, if you'll have me, we can marry and sail off to wherever you desire. For as long as you desire."

She was speechless.

He not only loved her, but he offered her freedom too. And she knew, as she always had, that she trusted him. Completely.

Caught between laughter and tears, she flung herself onto his lap. He slid his arms around her and held her close as she gazed up into his gorgeous face.

How had she ever thought him grim? He'd endured so much and through it all, he'd become a man of profound compassion, goodness, and honor. A man she loved deeply and whom, she realized now, she began to love the first day she met him.

I could gaze at his face and his smile forever.

The truth of that was so clear now. But as he looked down at her, his expression was solemn again.

"So, will you allow me to court you properly?" he asked.

"Yes," she said. "And I might marry you as well. But only under one—no, two—no, three conditions."

He raised an eyebrow. "And they are?"

"One, when we return to England after traveling, we live at least part of the year in London."

He nodded. "Agreed."

"Two," she said, "we use a large portion of my inheritance to help sailors and their families."

Again, he nodded. "Whatever you wish." He drew her even more tightly against his broad chest. "And three?" he whispered.

She reached up, slid her fingers into his thick hair, and pulled him closer. Gently she pressed her mouth to his in a lingering kiss. Still holding him, she shifted away— barely.

"Three," she whispered, "you kiss me back. Always."

He smiled. "If you insist."

And so he did.

EPILOGUE

Six months later

CECELIA LEANED AGAINST THE RAILING of the ship and gazed down at her family gathered on the dock. Beside her, James shifted closer and slid a warm arm around her waist.

The haze that typically blanketed London had been driven away by unusually strong winds at daybreak, winds that had settled into a gentle breeze that now fluttered the sails and rigging above them. The weather could not be more perfect for sailing away on an adventure.

"Will this ship never leave?" Cecelia muttered, keeping a smile on her face for the benefit of her family below.

"As soon as we are out of sight of them," James whispered, "I am taking you to our cabin."

"I shall race you there," Cecelia replied. In the hectic weeks leading up to their wedding this morning, they'd enjoyed barely any time alone.

From beneath an overly feathered hat, her aunt peered up at her. At her aunt's side, the recently knighted Sir Alistair Trent nudged her aunt with his elbow, whispered something, and waggled his bushy eyebrows. Her aunt frowned as if offended, but at the same time she shifted nearer to her husband. Sir Alistair drew his wife even closer in what not long ago her aunt would have considered a truly scandalous display of affection for midday at a London dock.

James laughed. "Lady Carl—I mean, Lady Lucretia seems…content."

Lady Lucretia. Her aunt had married Sir Alistair over three months ago, but Cecelia had yet to grow accustomed to hearing that name. Perhaps she never would.

Her aunt did look content, however.

James's grandmother stood beside Sir Alistair and Lady Lucretia. She eyed the affectionate couple warily and took a step away. After the excitement had died down over James being pardoned by the Admiralty, his grandmother had chosen to remain Mrs. Stewart in defiance of the gossip that swirled around her.

A few paces from Mrs. Stewart, Adrian stood with his wife, Anna. Next to them, Edmund swayed gently as he cuddled his new nephew. Edmund had returned from his previously delayed travels only a fortnight ago. He alternated between making ridiculous faces and cooing at the baby.

"Edmund!" Cecelia shouted.

Edmund tore his gaze from his nephew and looked up at her.

"You're next!" Cecilia said.

Edmund laughed and shook his head. "Never!" He shifted the baby to his other side and proceeded to waggle his head at his nephew like a fool.

Cecelia looked back at James and sighed. "Edmund adores children. He would be such a good father. When we return, I must see about helping him to find—" She paused. "Why are you looking at me like that?"

"Your bonnet," James said. "I just realized…is it the same one as that day by the river? That wonderful, scandalous day?"

She smiled and twirled one bonnet ribbon around a finger. "Yes." She warmed from her face all the way to her toes.

"Is this the first time you've worn it since?"

"Yes. It seemed right to wear it now, when we

might finally—finally—abandon all restraint and be... completely reckless."

James groaned. He leaned down and scooped her up into his arms.

"My dearest, shockingly outspoken wife," he whispered against her hat, "I must have you in nothing but that bonnet. Right now."

"James!" She laughed and glanced down at the dock. Everyone was smiling at them, save for Lady Lucretia, who was scowling, although perhaps a touch less than usual.

"We've waited this long," Cecelia murmured. "You cannot wait a few more minutes, until we sail?"

He sighed. "Of course. If that is your wish."

"I wish..." She gazed up at his handsome face and into his beautiful dark eyes. "I wish...for you to carry me to the cabin. This instant."

And so he did.

About the Author

Elizabeth Rue is an editor and writer. She lives in Massachusetts with her husband, two children, and two cats. Her debut, *Undone by the Earl*, has won multiple awards for historical romance. *Undone by a Lady* is her second published novel. Elizabeth loves to hear from readers, and she can be reached through her website at ElizabethRue.com.